Swaying

Swaying

Lucinda Blanchard

Cover created by Daniel Gustar and Fran Heath

For Oliver, James and Sophie,
all of whom I love equally,
regardless of gender.

1

The sperm charge about, zigzagging and bumping into one another. The picture is magnified, each cell the size of a baked bean but with a thin tail attached, flicking erratically. I switch off the television, my jaw tight. Designer Baby! As if choosing the gender is designing them. It's not as if you are determining their appearance - blonde hair, blue eyes, no garish birth marks, straight white teeth, small ears that don't protrude like a trophy cup. Not one of the women mentioned looks, intelligence or personality - they were just hoping for a he or a she.

I pace into the kitchen, my hands supporting my bulging belly. Why is the stupid biased debate bothering me anyway? Making people who have a preference out to be selfish and ungrateful! Should they be ashamed of their hopes? The whole thing was ridiculous. But why do I feel uncomfortable? Is the reason I didn't want to find out the sex of my baby because I can't face up to my own disappointment? Of course not. I'm not like those people on the TV programme.

I walk back to the lounge, suddenly annoyed at myself for being so impulsive in switching it off. I turn it back on and sit myself down, completely engrossed. Am I having a girl?

'Ready?' Ian says, startling me.

I search for the remote, then give up and struggle off the sofa to the telly, pressing the middle button, turning the screen black. I hope he didn't hear any of the discussion. He looks confused. I grab my handbag and follow him out to the car, grateful that he didn't ask any questions.

'A walk, you said?' He flicks his hair off his face, probably annoyed at its length in this heat.

'A firm stride. I've tried eating pineapple and hot curry.'

'But you're not overdue?'

'I know, but the midwife suggested it to help the baby along the way.'

Ian starts the engine and manoeuvres out from the parked cars in our street. He smirks. 'So what other ways are there to induce the baby?'

I playfully smack his thigh. 'We tried that last night. It didn't work.'

He laughs, then turns the radio up.

We arrive at the chine and start the three-mile ramble. Maybe this was a bad idea – what if something happens and we're in the middle of nowhere? We walk on, taking in the beautiful Isle of Wight scenery. My mind strays back to the debate.

'Look, a seat,' I say, pointing at a bench-shaped rock camouflaged with moss and overgrown fern.

'It's a wishing seat,' Ian says lifting up some foliage to reveal the hidden engraving.

'My turn first.' I sit myself down and squeeze my eyes shut, ignoring the damp feeling on my bottom. What's my wish? It hits me straight away of course. Breakfast television said it all. I want a daughter.

'Say cheese, Char.'

I open my eyes, guilt pinning me down into the seat. I force a smile as he takes my photo. I can't tell him how I feel. I know it's wrong. Surely all that matters is this baby is healthy. But I want a girl. Why have I never realised this before? Maybe I have and I'm only just admitting it?

'Come on, angel. We'd better make a dash for it before it rains.'

I hadn't noticed the dark clouds. I struggle off the rock still repeating my wish over and over in my head. What's wrong with me?

The sky is oppressive. I feel sticky and my swollen ankles throb. I look at my legs - they are the same thickness from the knees down. Ian says I look wonderful. I don't feel it. I feel rotten. Well, I didn't, until this morning. I'm wearing my dad's shorts since I can't fit into any of my own and a huge white maternity T-shirt. Ian's shorts are all surfing boardies and would swamp me; at least Dad's only go to just above my knees. I smile at my husband as he pulls me up the cliff path. 'So do you think it will be a girl or a boy?' I ask. Why am I saying this? I don't want him to catch on to my true feelings.

'Probably a girl - I can imagine a miniature you. You'll have your own little dolly to dress up.'

Relief spreads through me, I hope he's right. I twist a strand of my strawberry blonde hair around my fingers; I'm making it damp with the sweat from my hands so I flick it behind my back. It's so long and thick since I became pregnant. I need to stop damaging it with my anxious twisting.

'Maybe we should have found out at the twenty week scan?' I so wish I had now.

'I thought you wanted a surprise?'

'Yes I do; I'm just being impatient.'

'Not long to wait now. Only a couple of weeks until we meet our prince or princess.'

Please let it be a princess. Princess. Princess. Princess.

The next two weeks pass slowly. I've finished work, and I miss my colleagues already. I'm a dental nurse for a small practice, with just one dentist and a receptionist. A new girl, Chloe, started as a trainee nurse a few months ago. When I go back we are going to job share – that's the plan, anyway. Chloe is only twenty, seven years younger than me, and has flawless skin. She's very competent. I'm momentarily worried that everything will change so much in the time I'm off, I won't be needed. I've worked for Bridge Road Dental Surgery for just over nine years and know the job inside out. Most of the time I know what instruments and materials the dentist, Marie, wants and needs before even she does, which is why I think we make a great team. I hope that Chloe gets on well with Marie, but not too well. I do want a job to come back to...

Ian saunters into the bedroom, having just brushed his teeth. Lying in bed, I glance at the clock; eight a.m. No more early starts for me for a while – until the baby's here.

'So it's Verity-May if it's a girl. What if it's a boy?' he asks.

'I'm not sure. What do you like?'

Ian runs his hands through his sun bleached, shoulder-length hair, deep in thought. 'I don't know either. Thomas?'

There are so many girl names that we both like, but we really fell in love with Verity-May. Boy names we are stuck on. Is that an omen? Do we know deep down that we won't need them?

'Yes, maybe Thomas, or Joseph?'

'I don't like Joseph, I wouldn't like it being shortened to Joe,' he says, zipping up his work overalls.

'Okay, how about Luke?' I suggest.

'Yes, that's not bad.'

Maybe we won't have to think of a boy's name anyway.

'I'll call you if the baby's on its way.'

He kisses me goodbye then jogs down the stairs to leave for work at the garage. Ian loves his job as a mechanic; tinkering with cars is his passion - that and surfing.

'Have fun,' I call out. I feel a small twinge just as I hear the front door close. It's probably nothing.

Right, I must get organised. Ouch, I ignore the nudge

and grab myself some breakfast. Cornflakes, that'll do. Forcing down a couple of spoons, retching in between, I give up and scoop it away in the bin. A pain shoots through me, I stop and exhale. It won't happen today - only a small number of women give birth on their due date. It'll be another few days, maybe a week. I slowly climb the stairs to the bathroom to get a towel ready for the leisure centre.

There's a knock at the door, then Rose lets herself in. 'Hi Char, how you feeling?'

'Fat,' I reply as I add the towel to my bag.

'So are we still on for swimming?'

'Yes, I'm all set.' Bending down to pick up the swimming bag I feel another niggle, stronger than the others I've had. A firm tightening sensation. I screw my eyes up and stay motionless. Teeth clenched.

'You okay?' Rose asks, coming over to me and resting her hand on my back.

'I'm sure it's nothing.' I straighten up, taking a deep breath.

'Could be one of those Braxton Hicks thingies we read about the other night.'

'Hang on, Rose, there's another.' I bend over, with my hands on my knees for half a minute. 'Right, I'm fine now.'

Rose looks concerned. I glide my arm over my sweaty forehead; it slides with ease. Pain assaults me and I can't stop myself from crying out. After the agony subsides it's not long before I'm in that position again.

Rose looks up from her watch, 'That's every three

minutes now, Char. That's really quick. Are these your first pains?'

'I have had some strange prodding aches for a few hours, on and off. They didn't hurt much, so I didn't think it was worth mentioning it to Ian.'

'Forget swimming. We're going to the hospital. Where's the bag you packed?'

'On the landing!' The twinges are really starting to become painful. Not out of control, but it's happening. Now!

During the car journey I rummage around in my handbag for my mobile. I phone Ian. After four rings, I start to panic. Why isn't he answering?

'Hi angel.'

'I think the baby's coming.'

'What? You were fine an hour ago!' He sounds shocked.

'Well, I'm not fine now. Meet me at St Mary's. Rose is driving. Must go, I want to phone Mum too.'

I find her on my contacts list and hit dial.

'Mum, it's happening. I'm on the way to the hospital.'

'Is Ian with you? Are you okay?'

'I've phoned him.' My voice shakes. 'He's going to meet me there - Rose is with me. She's driving.'

'What's up?' she asks.

'I'm scared.'

'It will be fine, darling. I've done it three times. If I can do it, anyone can. Do you want me to come too?'

'Thanks, but Ian's on his way. I'll call you when I've had her... or him.'

'Good luck, darling.'

When I hang up, I have tears in my eyes. Maybe I should have asked her to come too? I'm terrified. What if something goes wrong? 'I can't do this, Rose. It's too painful.'

'I don't know what to say; this is a bit different from horses. Oh, you'll be all right, Char. Nearly there.'

She doesn't sound confident. And kids are definitely not her thing, that's for sure. She owns a riding stable and is used to horses giving birth to foals. That's as far as her experience will ever go. She drops me at the maternity entrance and goes to park the car.

I wait anxiously. Hurry up Rose, I don't like being on my own in this state.

She comes back struggling with my bag over her shoulder. About time - this is so painful!

'Jesus! Char, what have you packed?'

'All essentials, Ro... Aaargh.'

With great effort, we make our way to the reception desk. I'm in agony. I have to stop every minute, I can't walk when I'm having a contraction. A midwife introduces herself but I don't take any of it in.

'You need to be in the labour room. I can tell by the way you're walking.' Why is she smiling? 'Have you got your notes?'

I look at Rose. 'I think they're in the bag. In the middle bit. No, the side bit.'

Rose unzips the side pocket. 'They're here,' she hands them over with a relieved expression.

The labour ward has light pink walls - maybe that's a

sign? It's practical looking but not very inviting. I do feel a bit calmer, now that I'm in the delivery room.

'Change in to your nightie and lie on the bed,' the midwife says.

Rose sorts out the TENS machine I bought, and sticks the pads to my lower and upper back. It's supposed to take my mind off the labour pain but I can only faintly feel the electric shocks it produces. Maybe I should turn it up. I fiddle with the dial. A strong tremor runs through my back so I quickly turn it down again.

'Will you stay with me, Rose? Everything's happening so fast. I don't think Ian's going to make it in time.'

'Of course I will, Char.'

Rose and I have been best friends since primary school. Besides Ian and my mum, I can't think of anyone else I'd rather have with me.

I gasp in shock as the worst contraction yet claws from deep inside. 'I need an epidural!'

'No time,' the midwife says. 'Your baby is coming now. Gas and air - you can have that.'

What? No drugs? They can't do that, can they? I place the plastic tube in my mouth and greedily breathe it in as fast as I can. Wow, I like this.

'Aaargh!' A sharp tightening pain surges through my tummy.

'Keep on with the gas.'

I do as I'm told. 'Where's Ian? I need him now!'

'He'll be here,' Rose reassures me. 'He's on his way. Shall I go and fetch us a cup of tea or something? You can have tea, can't you?'

'Tea? I don't want tea? I need to push!' I shout.

'Already?' Rose looks over to the midwife.

'Push at your next contraction, Charlotte. You can do this.'

I can't do this. I can't do this.

Another abdominal spasm rips through my body. Agony. I bite down on the tube and push.

'That was great. Now do that again at the next contraction. Push right into your bottom.'

Here it goes again; the next surge pulsates through me. Oh my God! I'm horrified at the strange feeling I have.

'I need the toilet,' I say, my eyes darting to Rose.

'The baby's head is pushing down on your bowel,' the midwife explains. 'If you go it doesn't matter, lots of ladies have accidents.'

I don't want to poo, not in front of Rose. Or Ian. Where is he?

'Where the hell is Ian?' I say when the pain has subsided. He can't miss it, he just can't!

'You're doing really well, Charlotte,' the midwife says.

Her face blurs. I feel light-headed with the gas but it definitely helps, unlike the stupid TENS machine, which doesn't seem to be doing much except irritate me! 'Aaargh!' The noise coming out of my throat is a strange guttural sound. Animal, rather than human. If I wasn't in so much pain, I'd be embarrassed.

Ian charges through the door. Thank God he's here.

'Ian.' Tears roll down my face. 'It's too difficult, I can't do it anymore.'

'Yes you can, angel,' he says. Why does his usually

tanned skin now look ashen? 'Aaargh!'

'Oh, Char, are you okay?' he says.

'NO I'M NOT OKAY!'

I feel a huge warm gush. Have I wet myself?

'You're doing really well, Charlotte,' the midwife says to me again. 'There goes your waters.'

A good forty minutes later, and still no baby. After each agonising contraction, I wonder if my baby will ever come. When I'm not in pain, I'm worn out, resting. It's so strange that you can go from being in crippling pain to being fine the next moment. The only problem is the next contraction is coming. I bite down on the tube in readiness and start sucking at the gas. That strange sound escapes my throat. Where does this noise come from?

'Why isn't the baby coming out?' Rose asks the midwife. 'You said it was about to happen over an hour ago.' Rose, always the one with the sensible questions.

Ian's hair is stuck to his face - he looks as though he might pass out.

I'm also dripping with sweat, but then again, I am doing the biggest workout of my life. If someone said to me that they'd make it all disappear and I can try again at a later date, I honestly think I would say yes. If I were climbing a mountain I'd give up, turn round and walk back down. But this I can't stop - I have to endure the pain, and it's just too much. Biting down, that noise rings around the room again. I'm past caring now. I try staring at one spot on the wall. A grubby mark on the pink paint, it fuzzes and blurs. I feel an alteration of consciousness. I'm so tired.

'I think your baby's stuck, Charlotte. Nothing to panic about, try pushing on one more contraction, then we'll need help.'

'Help?' Rose asks.

'Yes,' the midwife replies. 'Forceps.'

Ian's expression makes me anxious, hitting me hard like a slap, forcing my abstract world to come into focus. I know my goal. I have to push.

I strain with every ounce of energy I have. I don't want forceps. You have to come out, baby, you have to!

'That's it, well done,' the midwife says. I feel a stinging pain and I clamp down, pushing with all the force I can muster. I feel as though I am tearing in half. It stings so much.

'The head is out. Feel it if you like, baby has lots of hair.' I do this and smile. My daughter has hair. I'm exhausted, but it's nearly over.

'Now, on the next contraction push out the shoulders.' A couple of minutes later, I feel the next one beginning to rumble. A slippery sensation travels through my belly. I hear slurping noises; everyone is holding their breath, including me. My stomach feels empty. Then nothing, I don't hear anything. Why isn't she crying? Not long after that thought, I hear the piercing but pleasing sound of my baby wailing. Relief rolls through me.

'It's a boy,' Ian says.

My breath catches, then my son is passed to me. He's a strange shade of purple and has white and red goo on him. He has fair hair and I can't believe he's mine. But I feel empty, not just in my stomach physically, but mentally. I wanted a girl. Is there something wrong with me?

'I've got a son,' Ian says, full of enthusiasm. He got what he wanted then. I look down at the baby in my arms – my baby. The baby I've longed for and carried for nine months within me. I do love him, don't I? I must do, even if he's not what I wanted. But I'm so exhausted, I don't feel anything. This is so new to me. How would I know?

'Would you like to cut the cord?' the midwife asks Ian. I can't really see what's happening. Other than tired, I don't know how I feel. Exhausted. Vulnerable. Joyous maybe. You are supposed to be joyous when you have a baby, so I must be then. Sweaty - I definitely feel unclean.

'Congratulations,' Rose says.

I am given an injection for the afterbirth to follow on quickly, which it does.

'So is it Luke?' Ian asks.

'Luke is a lovely name,' Rose agrees. So Luke it is.

I feed my son. It feels weird. I wince as he suckles. Taking deep breaths, I try to relax. After a few minutes I become used to the new sensation, as he latches on more comfortably. Looking down at his tiny features, I feel love. I do love him, he's beautiful.

The midwife cleans Luke up, puts a nappy on him and swaddles him up in a blanket. He's put in a perspex cot next to me while she stitches the tear he caused. I quickly grab the gas as the local anaesthetic is injected, but after that it's pretty much painless, just pulling sensations.

'All done. Good as new,' she says.

I think I might cry. Is it tears of joy? I'm tired and confused. Disappointed, maybe. But I can't be, he's perfect, he's mine, and it's not his fault that he's a boy.

'Do you feel up to having a shower?' the midwife asks.

Rose leaves, mumbling something about stubborn boys being too cosy. I feel numb.

When I return, feeling much cleaner, my parents arrive, full of congratulations, hand-shaking and back-patting.

Mum looks over at me, my eyes start to water as I force a tired smile. I hope she can't read me.

'These are because you had to have quite a few stitches.' A new nurse hands me some painkillers and antibiotics.

I take the little plastic pot with my pills in, and swallow them with a glass of water. I'm so sore and my tummy feels like an empty sack. It's strange not to have my baby inside me anymore – sad, even.

'Are you okay, love?' Mum asks.

I nod, unsure.

'You're tired, we should go and let you sleep.'

Ian and my parents leave together after covering me with kisses, all elated and jolly, then I am left alone with Luke.

I roll over in my hospital bed, close my eyes and silently cry.

2

'Happy birthday dear Luke. Happy Birthday to you,' we all sing, out of tune.

'Blow out the candles, Lukey.' Holding the cake closer, I blow them out for him. He claps his chubby hands, grinning, showing off his perfect dimples. One year old today. Where has the time gone?

'So do you think you'll have any more kids?' my friend Jane asks, after we've finished unwrapping the last layer of paper on the pass the parcel. I stiffen. Why do people always ask this? Do I say yes, opening myself up to questions? Or do I lie?

'I think so,' I reply, without commitment.

Jane looks affectionately at her daughter, Amelia, who is enjoying eating the paper.

'You'll have a girl next time, like I did,' she says. 'It's so lovely having pink in the house and buying girly things.'

I force a smile.

'The girls' clothing is so much cuter,' she continues.

'Yes, loads more to choose from,' my friend, Stacey adds.

'Maybe I'll have a daughter next time,' I say, and change the subject before my mood shifts. This always happens. They don't do it on purpose, but what can I say? No one would understand.

'It's hot today, just like the day you had Luke. It was sweltering in that maternity room. I'm sure I lost weight with all the sweating I did!' Rose says.

Feeling saved, I laugh remembering how dreadful we both looked that day. 'I have photographic evidence.'

'Destroy them,' Rose chuckles.

Everyone leaves with a party bag. I scan the mess and take a deep breath. The tidying will have to wait.

'That went well,' Ian comments, as I run the bath, checking the temperature with my elbow. He places Luke in his bath seat.

Luke loves splashing around in the water. 'He's such a good baby isn't he?' I say.

'And a good sleeper, thankfully.' Ian swishes his hands in the bath to produce more bubbles.

'Stacey's two daughters still don't sleep very well. She's constantly tired.'

'Really? Luke's been sleeping through since he was four months old.'

I smile at my husband, I'm so lucky. I am.

We dry him off and dress him in his all-in-one pyjama suit and tuck him into his cot with a bottle of milk.

'Night, Night. Sleep tight. Don't let the bedbugs bite,' Ian says. We kiss his golden curls then sneak out of the room. 'So are we going to have another?' Ian whispers as I close the nursery door.

'Yes,' I reply, taken aback. 'Maybe we'll start planning it in the next few months?'

Ian studies my face, what is he thinking? 'Good Idea. There's plenty of daylight left so I'm off surfing now. I won't be too late,' he kisses me goodbye. The door slams behind him.

Luke cries. I dash into his room. 'Ssh. That was noisy Daddy. He's such a typical surfer your daddy, long hair, surfing at all hours. Go back to bye byes, Lukey.'

He rolls over in his cot, sucking his thumb.

As I finish tidying up, my mind whirls. What if I have another boy? How would I feel about it? I'm sure I'd be fine. I love Luke to bits, so I'll adore another boy too. I know I will, but I would just love to have a daughter this time. One of each - isn't that what everyone wants? There's nothing wrong with wanting that, is there? Luke's sound asleep, the house is tidy and Ian is still out. I go upstairs to the computer.

Can you choose the gender of your baby?

There are over three hundred thousand results to my question, all with various titles.

Baby Gender selection kit

It looks as though you have to buy it. I carry on scrolling down until I come to PGD. It says it stands for Pre-implantation Genetic Diagnosis and it is the only guaranteed method to work with a hundred percent accuracy. It is basically IVF but the embryos are tested for gender before they are implanted. That was what that debate was about, on the TV, just before I had Luke. Designer babies. I wish I'd recorded it now.

MicroSort

A technique for separating X (female) and Y (male) chromosomes but with a lower success rate than PGD.

It's all so expensive, I feel disheartened. I scroll down further.

Natural Gender Selection Methods.

If you ovulate before you conceive, it's girl timing and if you conceive right on ovulation it's boy timing. You need to learn to detect your ovulation date. Sounds easier said than done. I wonder when I conceived Luke? No way of knowing now. I didn't take notes! There are different positions which favour a boy or a girl. And a couple of timing methods which contradict each other called *Shettles* and *O+12*. I scroll down again.

Diet Swaying.

You have to alter your body's pH – higher for a boy with potassium and sodium and a lower pH balance to have a girl with calcium and magnesium. I'm not keen on milk, but I love hot chocolate! There are also different astrological calendars and moon theories. Full moon for a boy, new moon for a girl. I wish I knew during which one Luke was conceived.

I click on the diet method and find a forum full of people from all over the world, and a new section:

Gender Disappointment

You're not alone. Supportive, welcoming forum. Is it wrong to want one or the other? Secretly sad – how to overcome it. It appears to be based in America, but I can see there is also a UK page. I click on forums and blogs, and scroll down further.

At Home Gender Swaying

Lots of people have posted questions about various acronyms I don't understand, such as CM, TTC - I think that stands for trying to conceive? DH – darling husband, DD – darling daughter. It's like another language! I find a list of acronyms and jot a few down. The funny ones are BFP - Big Fat Pregnancy, and BFN is Big Fat Nothing. Now that I've kind of got my head around the more simple ones, I click back.

At Home Gender Swaying

There are questions about the diet and about testing their pH – pH of what? Oh I see, of CM, which stands for cervical mucus – nice! I'm not sure that any of this is for me?

I look up the diet. Out of the relatively small list of foods, it looks like I would have to make everything from scratch, and no shop bought foods at all, and reduce my salt intake. You have to drink lots of milk and cranberry juice. This conjures up a sickly thought of all that curdling in my tummy. Tahini, I think I've bought that before – I'm sure it's the sesame seed paste I once put it in a curry recipe, and then threw the pot away, months later, having never used it again. There is a whole list of supplements they recommend you and your DH take, I scribble calcium, magnesium, acidophilus and B6 down. I've heard of acidophilus – I think it's in yoghurts to neutralise you, or something?

The list goes on. Ions – positive equals boy and negative equals girl. I'm sure I learnt about Ions in science class, when I was in high school. Is it something to do with electric fields? I wish I'd paid more attention now!

I've got a headache. I decide to bookmark the page and go to bed. I feel like my brain is going into overload from all this crazy information. Crazy, surely none of this will work? Ian will think I've gone insane. I think I've gone insane! I hear the door open. Oh my God, it's late! I've been on the internet for three hours! I quickly shut down the computer.

'Good surf?' I call out.

'Yes, it was pumping. Would you like some hot chocolate before bed?'

'Yes please.'

Would I be able to drink it on the gender diet? I hope so. I decide not to tell Ian what I've been researching. Not yet anyway.

The morning rush is on. Ian has already left. I pack Luke in the car and drive him to my mum's house, on the way to work. I'm five minutes behind schedule. I hate being late. It makes me feel bad, although no one's ever said anything.

Chloe has stayed on at the surgery full-time. I work three days a week now with Marie. On the days I work,

26

Chloe helps the new hygienist, Sally, in her surgery. I like Sally. She reminds me of my mum, but with curly auburn hair.

'We have a root canal treatment in first,' Steph the receptionist says. She pushes her spectacles back up to the bridge of her nose. Chloe has already put all the instruments out and ready in the surgery for me, which is kind.

'How's Luke?' Marie asks, 'Did the party go well?'

'It was wonderful. The weather was lovely. We played pass the parcel, although that was more for us than him. He's a bit young for it really.'

'I'm sure he loved it. They grow up so fast, and before you know it they fly the nest,' she says, resting her arms on her large tummy. She eats too much, living on her own.

'Marie, did you ever want a daughter?'

'I've never thought about it. All children are a blessing, You can't choose, can you?'

'Mum and I are so close. We do so much together. She loves my brother, but they don't have the same connection. I would love to experience a mother daughter relationship.' As I try to explain, I feel a little ashamed. I wish I hadn't said anything. Of course I should be grateful for whatever I get. Some people don't manage to have any children.

'You know what they say, a son loves you until he finds a wife, a daughter loves you for life,' she chants.

Maybe I'm taking Marie the wrong way, I'm too sensitive, but that saying isn't helping me to rationalise my feelings.

'I don't know if it's true or not. I've only experienced the son side of things,' she continues. 'You'll have to ask Sally. She's got one of each.' She struggles up from her swivel chair. I think she's lonely. Maybe if she'd had a daughter her life would be different?

The root canal treatment goes to plan, then we have three check-ups and one extraction. I sterilise the instruments, clean and disinfect all the surfaces, and get everything ready for the next set of examinations booked in for after lunch.

I stroll down to the town during my break feeling excited. I am going to take control and do the best I can to have a daughter. I am. Sitting on a bench on this bright afternoon I lower my sunglasses. I can smell the traffic fumes from the nearby car-park mixed in with the tangy fragrance of vinegar from the fish and chip shop across the road. I pull out the notes I wrote last night and look through the list of 'allowed foods.' What could I possibly eat if I were to do this diet? Definitely not fish and chips. My mouth starts to water. I decide to draw up a daily food list, which consists mainly of risottos and pasta bakes, really boring ones with not much cheese.

Would Ian have to go on the diet too? I'll have to look that up. I'm going to be sick of leeks and green beans by the end of it. That's if I do it. Can I? I did read last night that you can't have breakfast. It's best to eat after eleven, as fasting sways towards girl. Seeing as you've already fasted while asleep, skipping breakfast stands to reason.

I unwrap my cheese sandwiches, adding crisps in the

middle and eat them quickly, finishing off with a giant sized snickers bar, then stroll back to the surgery.

The rest of the day goes by quickly.

'Before you go, Char,' Marie says, 'I've got something I want to say.'

Oh no, I hope it's not because I'm often late in, since having Luke? Chloe, Steph and Sally all come into the surgery.

'Thank you, for your ten years of service,' Marie says. 'You have been such a loyal member of staff, hardly a day off sick, always in on time.' Maybe she hasn't noticed? 'And very hard working. I consider you a friend as well as an employee. So I've got a little something for you to show my appreciation.' She hands me a box.

I open it quickly. My emotions bubble over and tears trickle down my face. 'Oh, Marie, thank you.' It's a silver necklace and pendant. Marie knows how much I love this design. I have the matching bracelet and earrings. Expensive, but worth it, I think, and it's something I can pass on to Verity-May, when I have her.

'Let's have a look,' Chloe says.

I hold it out to show everyone, my smile broad. What a lovely thing to do.

'Here, I'll put it on you,' Marie says. 'I really mean it, I do appreciate all the hard work you do, and I missed you so much when you were off on maternity leave, although Chloe took most of the strain.' Marie smiles at Chloe.

I feel so happy. I needn't have worried about not being wanted or needed when I came back. It seems so silly now, but I'm sure everyone feels worried that they'll be replaced by the person covering them.

'I actually have some news too,' Chloe says. We all turn to look at her. 'I'm sorry, maybe I should have told you this first, Marie, but I'm pregnant.'

I gasp.

'It was a real shock,' Chloe stutters. 'Jenson and I weren't planning it.'

I feel like I've been punched. She's only twenty-one. I was kind of planning on this diet thing, now I'll have to delay it. I'm being selfish. 'Congratulations.' I say and hug her. The others follow my lead.

Marie looks a bit flustered and red in the face. She takes off her glasses and wipes them on the hem of her tunic, then repeats the process over.

We say our goodbyes, and all head off to our cars. As I drive back to Mum's to collect Luke, I feel really pissed off. I bet she'll have a girl, which means that I'll have another boy. It's stupid, I know. Whatever Chloe has will have no bearing on what I have, but I can't stop thinking it. I hope she has a boy. I can't explain it. I just do.

After giving Luke his tea and bathing him, I cuddle him close. I love his tiny legs and cute knees. I tickle his feet now and again, making him wriggle and laugh. Kissing the top of his head, I close my eyes and inhale the baby shampoo and talc. I should be so content.

Later that evening I sit down with a glass of wine. I haven't even shown Ian my new necklace yet.

'What's up?' he asks.

'Chloe's pregnant.'

'And? That's good isn't it? She'll have a little playmate for Luke?'

'We were going to try for another. Now we can't,' I run my finger up and down the seam of the sofa cushion.

'Why can't we?'

'Marie couldn't replace both of us, it wouldn't be fair.'

'It's not up to her.'

'I suppose,' I get up and place my glass on the table, 'I think I'll go to bed now, read my book.'

'Okay. I'll be up in an hour or so.'

The computer is still on, Ian must have been looking up something. I click on the gender website again, and start re-reading the menus and looking at the forums.

'What's this?'

I jump, I hadn't heard Ian come up the stairs. 'Oh nothing,' I frantically try to escape out of the website.

'I know what it is. Your history popped up. You know it's crap, don't you? You can't actually have a girl doing some stupid chanting, or witchcraft, whatever it is.'

'It's not witchcraft!' I feel hot and shaky, angry even. 'What were you doing looking up my history anyway?'

'I didn't look it up. It popped up, and it's a load of crap. Any doctor will tell you. It's not possible!'

'Actually there is a lot of scientific fact behind it.'

'Where did you read that? Don't tell me! On the website. They're con-artists, Char, I bet they want money for their advice, don't they?' He paces around the room.

'No, actually they don't!' I switch the computer off, climb into bed, and turn my bedside light out.

'Don't be mad at me, angel.'

I hear Ian fumbling around in the dark, discarding his clothes on the floor and climbing into bed. He doesn't touch me.

'I'm not mad. I'm disappointed.' I inch further away over my side.

'That's serious then.' He tries for humour, and fails. I can't stop myself, I burst into tears.

'Oh, angel, I'm sorry. I know you really want a little girl.' He shuffles closer.

'Do you?' I sniff.

'Of course I do, I've always known. How could I not?' Ian switches his lamp on. We both blink, adjusting our eyes. 'Look, I tell you what, I'll try it. Whatever this stupid website says, I'll do it. For you. If it makes you happy.'

'Thank you.' Another bout of tears start to erupt. I wipe them away, and snuggle up to Ian. 'Thank you,' I say again, and fall into a deep but restless sleep.

3

'I'm also trying to pinpoint my ovulation by taking my temperature every morning. I never realised your cycle could be so complicated,' I say.

'Goodness, love, it sounds err ... what's the word ...' I grip the phone, anxiously anticipating what my mother's description of my madness will be. 'Surreal.'

Silence. I don't know what to say.

'Does Rose know?' Mum asks in the awkward break.

'Yes, just the four of us, I'm not telling anyone else.'

'Probably for the best.'

I agree, feeling slightly stung, and say my goodbyes. Placing the phone back, I stand and ponder for a moment. Mum has taken my plans better than I expected. She wants me to have a daughter, like she did. I walk back into the breakfast-room feeling empty. My sister's no longer here. Suzy. I don't even remember her.

'That was Mum,' I say, looking over at Ian's plate of

dinner. I sit down and take a mouthful of mine.

He takes another spoon himself of the tasteless risotto. 'Is this one of your special recipes?'

'Do you like it?'

'It's bland. It's that crazy girl diet you want me to do, isn't it?'

'Maybe,' I say, trying not to look him in the eye.

'I can't live off this food all the time. But it's better than that pasta thing you did the other day, that's for sure.'

He's still eating it, so it can't be too bad.

'I've met lots of people in the same situation as us online, from all over the world. There's also a whole UK forum.'

'I know, you said already.' Ian scrapes the remains to one side of his plate.

'Some of the brand names the Americans talk about, you can't get over here,' I continue, faltering slightly.

'Like what?'

'Crystal Light. It's a powder you add to water to make into a soft drink. It has lots of aspartame in it, which helps to lower your pH. One of the women I've befriended is going to send me some.'

'Should you be giving out our address?'

I ignore his question and carry on with my talk of American brand names. According to the website Ian also has to do the diet, but there are a few more food groups he's allowed. He can have breakfast, which is good. I know he wouldn't be able to function at work with an empty stomach!

At last the evening arrives and the moment is here. I'll just have to blurt it out.

'Ian.' He looks up from his surfing magazine.

'I just need to test your pH,' I whisper.

Rolling his eyes, he puts down his magazine. 'How do you test it?'

'I just need a sample of your sperm.'

'What?'

'If you could just deposit it in this... err... pot, then I'll know what pH you are before you start the diet.'

'For Christ's sake!'

'Luke is asleep, he's soundo. I just checked on him.' I hold out the container.

Ian pushes himself out of the chair, reaches back for his magazine then takes the pot from me. He huffs a bit and trundles upstairs.

'What are you taking that with you for? I call up.

'What?'

'The surfing mag? You'll need something stronger than that.'

He pauses, 'Do you want me to do this or not?'

I wish I hadn't said anything.

'The computer's upstairs,' he says awkwardly, then continues on up, his surfing magazine still tucked under his arm.

I don't want to think about what he's looking at. I pace up and down the hallway, stopping to view Luke's photo hung on the wall, his wide grin with his new teeth showing. It makes me smile, then I continue my anxious pacing. Why is he taking so long? Maybe he needs some help? I hesitate, then head up the stairs. Rocking on my feet, unsure if it's a good idea, I slowly and silently open the door to our bedroom. I peek my head round.

'What the fuck?' Ian clicks the mouse in the corner of the screen and pulls his shorts up.

'Sorry. I just thought maybe you wanted some help?'

'No. Now I need to start all over again. Thanks for that.' His face is red and sweaty, his shoulder length hair swept back off his forehead.

I feel hot too.

'Sorry.' I cross the room towards him.

'Just go downstairs, Char. I'll be twenty minutes. Leave me to it, please.'

I walk away, glancing over my shoulder before I get to the stairs. Ian stands there, waiting for me to go. He looks pissed off. I wish I hadn't disturbed him.

Half an hour later, he emerges. I take the pot from him.

'Thanks,' I say, carefully dipping the probe in. After a few seconds it registers, 7.5.

'Good reading?'

'Yes. It's in girl territory. Which is better than mine.' I have a sinking feeling, maybe it's me that's the problem. I'm the boy friendly one, not Ian?

After washing out the pot, I go upstairs, log on and start trawling through all the forums again, as I do every evening.

'Rose is here,' Ian shouts up to me. I'd forgotten she was calling in tonight. Thank God she didn't arrive earlier!

'How's Daisy?' I ask.

'Still lame. I've had the vets out again. Bloody horses, they cost a bomb!'

'You should try kids instead.'

'No. Four legged and furry. They're much better.'

I smile at Rose. The number of pets she has I'm sure it does cost a fortune!

'So how's the swaying going? Does your mum think it will work?'

'Mum says it's fifty fifty. She doesn't believe you can determine what you have with a diet.' I take a sip of my peppermint tea.

'Sorry, Char, but I have to agree with her.'

I don't want to hear this. I want encouragement and support, not a debate.

'When I first ordered my pH reader it seemed so complicated with the buffer and calibration solutions, but I'm getting used to it now.' I say, marginally changing the subject.

'Is Ian interested in the scientific bit?'

'Yes, he is actually. He was really helpful when I was close to tears trying to understand how to calibrate the thing. He's 7.5 which is girl territory for him. I tested myself and I'm 7.5 too, but that's boy territory for me.' Embarrassment creeps across my face as it occurs to me what this admission involved.

Rose subtly ignores my beetroot complexion. 'That's good he's helping. You've not started the diet yet though, have you? So it could change.'

'I suppose. But I've been downing cranberry juice and

adding fake sugar to everything to try and lower it, but it just won't shift.'

'Really?' Rose is looking at her hands. I'm boring her. I'm boring myself.

'The lowest I've got it down to is 6.5, which isn't good enough. It needs to be 4 or 4.5! The other girls seem to manage. What am I doing wrong?'

'Maybe this Crystal Light will help?' Rose says reassuringly. She looks like she wants to say more, what is she suppressing?

'I really hope so, this is stressing me out already and stress equals boy.' I state in the hope she will get the message.

'Why are you doing this, Char, is it to try and replace your sister?'

My stomach churns. I knew this was coming. 'No. Of course not, I want a daughter, someone to be close to and share girly things with when I'm older.'

'You might have been really close to Suzy. Maybe there is something in it. What does your mum think? Does she talk about her?'

'I don't like to bring her up, but maybe that's why Mum's supportive. Although she doesn't believe in it, she does back me up. I'm not sure she understands completely how I feel. She said she wanted a girl first time round. That was Suzy. I came next, then John, so I expect she was pleased to have a boy after two girls?' I flinch. How can I think about my mum being lucky having one of each after losing her firstborn daughter. I'm so appalling. I'm sure Rose thinks this too.

'Sorry, Char. Let's lighten the mood. So Ian's sample...' Rose says pulling a face.

I laugh.

'I'm so pleased I've got you to confide in. I'm fine talking to you about pots of sperm and cervical mucus, I couldn't even say those words to my mum. Who could?'

Rose thanks me for the cuppa before she leaves. I stack the dishwasher then I head upstairs to the computer again.

Ian walks into the bedroom. I don't hide what I'm looking up anymore, unlike him.

'Now what's the magic site say?'

I ignore the sarcasm in his voice. 'I'm looking up temperature charting. It's not working for me. I've been doing it for a whole cycle now.'

'Oh,' he says, uninterested.

'It's the thing I've been doing every morning, taking my temperature while trying not to move. My chart is all over the place, it's because I don't sleep well.'

'You never have,' he says.

'No, plus Luke's teething.'

'I guess getting up to him doesn't help?'

I smile at Ian. He is listening to me. But sometimes I feel so alone. I'm scared I'll get it all muddled up and it will be my fault that it's failed. I can't tell anyone this though, especially not Ian, or he may not cooperate!

'No, ideally you're supposed to have a completely undisturbed night, so I'm giving up with it! I've found out on the website about ovulation prediction kits.'

'Oh?'

'I ordered some, they are strips that you pee on and –'

'Okay okay,' Ian says abruptly cutting me off.

I exhale loudly.

'Don't spend too much online,' he says.

I look up at him. I feel exhausted. I try to read his expression. He looks resigned and tired too. He walks over to me and kisses me on the head, then swiftly leaves me to it. I decide not to dwell on it any further.

Charlie123

Diet, pH, timing, position, ions, new moon. Anything else I should be concentrating on to try to conceive a girl?

That's my online name, Charlie123. I have a picture of a cat as my avatar – Ian helped me to put that on. Within minutes, I have a reply, from someone called Bella27. She has a photo of herself on there, brave girl. Oh my God, I recognise her. I can't believe this, perhaps she still lives on the Island?

Bella27

Hi Charlie, I'm in the same position as you. I have been trying to conceive using Swim to Top method, this is the very best at home swaying and I strongly recommend you consider it. Have a look in the Extreme Swaying section and you will find all the info about it there. We also have a buddy group to help everyone along with any questions and stuff. It takes a lot of commitment but I really think it will give us a higher chance of getting a girl. I have been trying for ten months now, but there are many who have fallen pregnant much sooner than that. Hope to see you in the buddy group x

What shall I reply? Shall I tell her that I know who she is? I'm not sure what to do, but I'm intrigued with the Extreme Swaying and Swim to Top methods. I look it up – how have I missed this before? There's so much information on this site, I don't think I could possibly read it all. Then again...

Wow, putting sperm in test tubes and incubating it, then syringing it in. Is this for real? Is it even safe? What will Ian think?

After deliberating for half an hour, I decide to reply to Bella and not let on just yet, that I know who she is.

Charlie123

Hi Bella, I just looked up swim to top, it sounds very complicated I really didn't expect it to be that involved. The turkey baster sounds like the easy bit, that wouldn't bother me, but the rest seems quite hard? Maybe it's not once you get going? Do you do the diet as well as the incubator method? I hope you don't mind all the questions. Charlie X

Feeling guilty, I wait impatiently for Bella's response. I should have told her that I know her.

Bella27

Hi Charlie, yes it is complicated, but it makes sense once you get your head round it. You need to get all the equipment first-incubator, microscope, test tubes etc. There is a list on the forum. And then start practicing to get the egg white to float on top of the semen- this can be the tricky bit, but there are things to try if it doesn't float. You then incubate for an hour, in which time the majority of Ys will have swum up to the comfort of the higher pH of the egg white. You then discard this portion of the test tube and use the remaining, (which will have the majority of Xs in) for turkey basting. Does this make it seem any simpler? Or have I confused you more! X

4

The next day, after another sleepless night, my brain running through it all, I get up half an hour early and send Bella a private message before leaving for work.

Charlie123

Hi, I've been racking my brain all night, you won't believe this, but I know you. My real name is Charlotte Jackson. I was a couple of years above you at school. I think you used to play with Rose's youngest sister, Georgina? Who would believe that I would meet someone I know on here! I promise I won't tell Rose about you being on the site as I understand it is private, and I hope you too won't tell Georgina. Did you sway with your second boy? I'm thinking about trying this method in January, there's so much to take in. I hope we can help each other, and that you can advise me where to buy things on the Isle of Wight. As I said this is completely confidential, only my husband, my mum, and Rose know. Have you told anyone? I told my husband briefly about what

you have to do, he said it sounds like witchcraft and potions!
Hope to hear from you soon, Charlotte x

I log out and go downstairs, Luke is still asleep, lazy boy. The smell of cooking consumes me.

'You okay, angel? You've been on that computer for ages.'

'I know. I'm sorry. Something really strange happened.'

'Oh?' He rocks the frying pan from side to side.

'I recognise a girl online. She used to go to my school.'

'Really? That's crazy. What did she say when you told her?'

'I haven't had a reply yet.'

'You're sure it's definitely her?'

'Yes, it's her,' I say, starting to doubt myself. Of course it's her, unless she has a double.

'So she and her husband, I assume, are doing this diet stuff too then?' Ian cracks an egg against the side of the pan. I stare at it as it slops in amongst the oil.

'Yes, and more.'

After explaining everything to him, he bursts out laughing, actual full belly-hugging laughter. I can't help but smile too as he cracks another egg.

'You use an incubator. Are you planning on hatching out a baby? This is unreal, Char. Madness.' Ian picks up the broken shell and lets the left over egg white run out and into the other halve.

'It's not a joke,' I say, trying not to smirk. My cheeks hurt from the strain of keeping the laughter in. 'What are you doing with those shells?'

'Practicing separating the yolk from the white, that's what you want me to do, isn't it?' He's taking this well, judging by his jovial expression.

'Stop it, be serious,' I say, trying not to sound irritated. 'Real people are doing this, and it's not just a couple of people, it's lots, hundreds, thousands, and that's just in the UK.'

'Hundreds and thousands, do we need to add sprinkles to the sperm?'

'Stop it,' I say laughing along while reining in my annoyance. 'I've not read the boy information, but they have to do a different diet and methods.'

'Oh, what type of eggs do they use, duck?' he teases.

'Actually I think they do the same, but use the top layer. I really want to try this. Bella says it increases your chances greatly, she believes it, and I do too.' I hold my breath, I shouldn't have said that.

'Well, if this Bella says it works, then it must do.' The humour has gone from his voice.

'Please, Ian.'

'Sorry, Char. It's just all so insane. Fried egg?'

'No thanks I can't stomach a cooked breakfast, you know that.'

'Stop twisting your hair. You always do it when you're fretful.'

'I'm not fretful,' I say indignantly.

'Look, I'll think about it. You sure you don't want any eggs?'

Work in the surgery drags, but at least it's Friday. All I

want to do is get home and check my messages. I wish I had a smart phone, then I could check my emails wherever I am. I must get an upgrade! I feel apprehensive. I wonder how she will feel about being recognised?

'Bye Char,' Marie, my boss says as I leave, 'see you Monday.'

'Bye.' I say to everyone and rush back to my car as fast as I can. I drive home way too quickly. Ian will have collected Luke from my mother's already. I burst through the door, it will have to wait though.

'Come to Mummy, my little Lukey.' Luke crawls over to me with a charming grin on his dimpled cheeks.

'Mum Mum,' Luke says, I smile at my perfect cherub. I'm so pleased he came to me, I hope he's not affected by my determination to have a daughter. Of course he's not. He's too young to notice anything, I reassure myself.

After Luke has gone down for the night, I quickly check my emails on the gender site while our tea is cooking. A quick and easy fast food - fish fingers, frozen chips and peas. I won't be doing quick and easy soon, not once we start the diet properly.

I have a reply from Bella. My heart races.

Bella27

Wow- that's so crazy! Who'd have thought it! I do remember you. Wow - I can't get over that! What are the chances of me replying to your question? Mad! No, don't worry I won't tell anyone, I understand how lots of ladies like to keep it private, it personally doesn't bother me, I feel proud to be doing this, and to try my best to get what I want! Why sit back and do nothing if you have the chance to improve the odds. You can tell Rose about me if you like, I haven't seen Georgina for years! I was totally gutted when I found out my second was another boy, I cried for days, but I didn't know about swaying then. It's hard, because it feels like everyone around me has the perfect pigeon pair or just girls, so it's really nice to meet you on here - someone close to home who understands! I got all my equipment from eBay. You need the microscope to see how good a sort you have. After a while you can tell the difference between the Y and X sperm. It's really fascinating to see. Tell your hubby that it's not witchcraft. In America there is a process called MicroSort, we're doing the same but for a fraction of the cost. I feel it's the environment that is the most important factor, and timing is secondary. My pH was a high 8, but now with diet and supplements, it stays around 5. Of course ask me any questions you like and I look forward to seeing you in the buddy group! Love Bella X

Without stopping to catch my breath, my fingers fly over the keys like a blur.

Charlie123

Thanks for your reply. What eggs do you use? Did it float on the first attempt? I find the diet so tough and I'm not properly on it yet, you I guess, have been on it for ten months! Loads of questions again, sorry! Anyway, hope you get pregnant soon, you deserve it for keeping all this up for so long! Take care, Charlotte x

I stand up and stretch my legs, as I'm heading towards the door I notice I have another message. Bella has replied already. I click it open and sit back down to read. The smoke alarm beeps loudly, startled, I jump at the shrill sound. Luke! I hope it doesn't wake him up.

'What the hell!' I hear Ian shout. I run downstairs to find him waving a tea towel over the smoke detector. I quickly switch off the oven and take out our burnt dinner.

Ian opens the windows and doors and looks at me with disgust.

My heart sinks. 'I'm so sorry, Ian. I got waylaid.'

'You're always on that damn computer. I'm getting really sick of it!' he hisses.

5

'Okay okay, I'll do it,' Ian mumbles through kisses.

'You know how much I love you, don't you?'

'I think you just showed me that.' He chuckles.

I cuddle up to him. I don't want to get out of bed, but Luke won't stay asleep all morning.

'I'll miss Lukey's naps when he grows out of them.'

'Me too.' Ian nibbles my ear making me giggle.

'Are you still horse riding this afternoon?'

'Yes if that's okay?'

'Of course, it will be good for you to go out with a proper friend, rather than emailing your cyber one.'

I don't know what to say to that. I nod, without commitment.

I've not had a chance to read Bella's last email. I keep my mouth shut, I don't want to ruin what I've mended for burning the dinner!

'Be a good boy for Daddy and Granny.' I kiss Luke goodbye as he holds on to Ian on their way out.

'Ian, Don't forget this.'

'Oh no, I won't get far without it,' he says taking the day bag I packed.

'Have fun.' He gives me another peck on the lips.

I wave as they drive off, then head towards the stairs to read my email. It's no good, I haven't got time, I'm already late. Damn it, that old computer takes so long to fire up. I grab my car keys and riding hat and stride out, feeling frustrated.

Rose is putting a saddle on Dylan's back, as I arrive at the yard.

'Hi Rose,' I call out to make my presence known. I step on the dry patches of grass, picking my way through until I reach the concrete path, much like a child avoiding the cracks in the pavement.

'Hi. Daisy's still lame so you're on Jolly today. Have you ridden him before?'

'No,' I reply warily. I like Daisy, fat, friendly and reliable. I'm not sure I want to ride another.

'You'll be fine, he's a big softy.'

'Anything you want me to do?' I ask, feeling a little reassured.

'Jolly's in the stable. Can you tack him up for me, please.'

'Sure.' I grab the head collar from the tack room and let myself into his stall.

'God, he's massive.' This is going to be a challenge. I hope I'm up to it? 'Hello handsome,' I say running my hand down his chestnut nose. He nuzzles me. I put his head collar on and walk him out, tying the lead rope to the worn piece of baling twine on the stable door. I give his body a brush and comb through his mane. Standing on tiptoe, I place his saddle on his back, then I reach under his belly and grab hold of the girth and do it up.

'How big is he?'

'Sixteen hands, my big gentle giant,' Rose gushes.

After securing Jolly's bridle and adjusting the stirrup leathers to the correct length, I hesitate, then tighten the girth another notch. He turns his head to me, but keeps his ears forward and doesn't try to bite. I hope he's as gentle to ride as he is to handle.

'All set?' Rose calls out as she mounts Dylan.

'Yep, ready to go.' There's no way I can get on from the ground, so I lead him over to the mounting block and heave myself on. I'm so high up, falling from here would really hurt!

We trot through the village of Porchfield. After we pass the pub, waving to the locals, I relax and quicken Jolly's pace so we can ride side by side, seeing as there doesn't seem to be any traffic.

'Ian has agreed,' I announce.

'What! You're kidding. He's going to let you look at his sperm under a microscope, then incubate it?' Rose sniggers.

I laugh. 'I know it's not the usual method.'

'No it sure isn't.'

I don't say anything. Is she being critical? I listen to the hooves clatter on the road then fall back to ride behind her to enable a car to pass.

Rose turns in her saddle to look back at me. 'Sorry I know how much this means. I'm happy for you.'

'Really?'

'Yes, really.'

We trot on for a bit, then Rose turns to me again as we slow down to a walk. 'Are you going to meet up with Bella then?'

'Yes, I hope so.'

'At least we know who she is. You wouldn't have met up with a stranger, would you?'

I think for a moment. I don't know, maybe I would have if they lived on the Island.

'No,' I say.

'So when are you doing all this then?'

'Meeting Bella?' I question, trotting up beside her.

'No, I mean incubating. Have you got all the gear already?'

'No, I've not got anything yet. We're going to start trying in January.'

'In three months?'

'Yes, I guess it is.'

When we get to the bridle way, Rose and Dylan start to canter, so Jolly does the same. I hold on tightly, I hadn't asked him to. That's not right. I'm supposed to be the one in control, why am I not in control of anything in my life? He throws his head up. He can sense my unease. I try to make myself relax into the saddle and breathe deeply as he strides on. It works. I go from feeling scared to exhilarated. Young and free again. This must be how

Rose feels all the time, I wonder idly to myself as we slow to a walk. I laugh, the cold air stings my cheeks. Autumn is nearly over. Rose pointing out to me, that it is only three months away until I start attempting, is beginning to sink in. I hadn't realised it was so soon; time is flying.

'Will Luke start riding next year? He'll be old enough.' Rose says as she pats Dylan's neck.

'He can if he wants to.' I wonder if he will? Riding always seems like a girl thing. I raise my eyes to view the beautiful countryside. Rooks feed in the field of stubble where the maize crop has been freshly cut. A couple of round bales are still out, covered in black plastic sheets.

'Do you teach any boys?'

'No, I don't actually, although I mainly instruct adults on their own horses, I only tutor a handful of kids on mine.'

'That's another reason, it would be so lovely to share a hobby like riding. I know it's stereotyping and Luke may come out riding with me, but I've always envisaged a daughter.' I think of Rose and her mother out together on their horses when Rose was a child.

An abandoned hay baler, behind the gated field startles Jolly, he raises his head in alarm.

'Come on. Ssh.' I reassure him, trying to push him past, but he refuses. He spooks again. My heart accelerates as he starts to back up.

'Jolly, come on,' Rose shouts. I squeeze my heels in and urge him forward even harder. I don't want to end up in the hedge, worse still, the ditch!

'Good boy, good boy,' I soothe as he finally goes past

the baler. He regains composure. I don't.

'You okay?'

I nod, feeling unsure.

'Where were we? Oh yes, I'm sure you'll have a girl next time, what with all this diet and incubator stuff. I know you, Char, you're such a determined person, you go for what you want, and you get it. You always have.'

'That's what I hate about this, I'm not in control. I can't choose it, or make it happen. All this crazy stuff I'm embarking on, there's no guarantee, but I have to do something. I hate not having a choice.' My voice is shaky. I take a deep breath.

'If selection were legal here, would you and Ian go down that route?'

'Without a doubt. I'd give it at least one go. It would be so much easier, even if we had to travel up to London for all the appointments. It's too much hassle going to America. And it's something I'd want to keep private, especially from my mother-in-law.' I pause, realising I hadn't considered if Ian would agree to it, if it were an option. It's not, so it's irrelevant.

Jolly jumps again, as a crisp packet rattles by in the breeze. This time I handle it better.

'Sorry, he's not usually this skittish,' Rose says. 'He's got a lovely temperament really.' She waits until Jolly is calm again. Then she asks, 'Would Viv disapprove then?'

'God yes, she'd judge me and have such an opinion on it. Thinking I was wasting money we don't have and all that.' An image of Ian's mum forms in my mind. Yes she would disapprove.

A dog in the front garden of one of the stone houses barks loudly. I brace myself, but the horses walk by without so much as a flinch.

'It would be impossible to keep it from her. I expect you and Ian would have to fly abroad two or three times?'

'Yes, and who would look after Luke? I'd just look like a selfish cow, off on holiday all the time without her son!'

'I can't pretend that I can relate to your feelings, but Viv's only got boys, surely she'd identify with it?'

'She wanted a daughter herself, she makes comments sometimes, but she'd never admit it. She once said she's lonely, and although she's close to her sons, if she had a daughter she would have someone to go out for lunches with or have coffee together. She admits it like that sometimes, but I don't think she'd outright say it.' Why doesn't Rose understand? Although, why would she, she doesn't want children.

'Do you think Viv feels left out, where you and your mum are so close?'

I swat an irritating fly on Jolly's back, he stops twitching, relieved. 'I try not to exclude her,' I say, 'especially where I may only have boys, and then I'd be the paternal grandparent, being left out.'

'I remember at your wedding, you feeling like you needed to include her as much as possible, where she didn't have a daughter, but at the same time it was yours' and your mum's day. I guess I can understand you wanting to experience it that way round, it's such a shame you can't get it done here. Maybe in a few years things will change, you never know, it could be legalised here?'

'Very unlikely. It could be ten years away. I'd be too old by then, I can't wait for something that may never happen.'

Jolly impatiently shakes his head up and down, pulling the reins through my fingers.

'True. Come on I'll race you back up the field.' A mixture of excitement and fear ache in my limbs. No. He's not beyond my skills. I can do this. Clicking our tongues to encourage the horses on, we canter up the homeward bound, giggling like we used to as teenagers.

Later that evening, relieved that Ian has gone surfing and Luke is asleep at last, I finally get to read the email from Bella. I smile as I remember how I made it up to Ian, after burning our tea, then promptly read the message.

Bella27

Hi Charlotte, where we are changing our environment such a lot, it makes a big difference, so I wonder if that's why I'm not pregnant yet. I think my body naturally favours boys, which is why I fell so quickly before, but where I'm making it girl friendly, it seems to take longer to get pregnant. As for eggs, I have tried every single egg on the Island! I'm not joking either! The problem is finding one with a high enough pH, they tend to be 8.5 to 9 but really you want one 9 or above. 9.8 would be ideal. The best I have found are the Garlic Farm eggs. What you do is get the egg, wash it with soapy water (as this opens the egg shell up a tiny bit), and leave it on the counter for up to a week. This raises the pH slightly. I normally end up working with a pH of 9.4. As for floating, everyone is different, and it can change from attempt to attempt, depending on what hubby has eaten, what he's been doing and when he last released. It can be very tricky. At first it floated for me, but as hubby had more of the supplements and diet the less it floated, but without these his pH is about 9, so I really need him to have them. I have tried adding sugar water to the semen, (the idea is that the sugar increases density so the egg can float), this did not work for me. I now use the mesh method, there's lots of info about how to do this. It involves putting some kind of mesh as a barrier so the egg doesn't sink, but the sperm can still swim through. For the diet I just try and eat low fat, no salt, and I always let myself eat whatever I want in the two-week wait. I'd be insane by now otherwise! I hope that helps to answer a few of your questions, love Bella x

Oh God. Now I've got to think about the pH of a bloody egg, as well as my own, and Ian's. This is getting very complicated. I sigh. It looks like I'll be subtly suggesting a trip out to the Garlic Farm next weekend...

6

'I don't know why you're fussing. The Queen isn't coming for lunch.'

I stop cleaning the kitchen cupboards and glare at my husband.

'Okay, Queen Bella it is,' he says.

'I've been meaning to do them for a while now.'

Ian grins.

'I have,' I protest. 'Look, they're filthy.'

I continue wiping down the doors.

'I'll put the buggy in the car. Mum's expecting us at one and he's still asleep,' Ian flaps.

'Lazy boy, I'll wake him by half twelve at the latest.'

'Mum's doing a roast. I wish you were coming.'

'I will next time, but Bella wants to meet up. It will be wonderful to actually see her in person.'

'I know, I'm just worried.'

I look up from my kneeling position and cease cleaning

the kickboards. 'Why?' I ask, puzzled.

'I have noticed all the parcels arriving you know.'

'They're Christmas presents.'

Ian looks doubtful.

'They are.'

'What, all of them?'

He's rumbled me. I'll have to confess. 'Well no, not all, but most.'

'I know about the incubator, what else?'

'Just two salt rock lamps?'

'What rock lamps?'

'Salt rock. They produce negative ions.'

He rolls his eyes. 'I'm wondering what else this Bella will come up with?'

'What do you mean?' Oh please stop.

'Next thing she'll be suggesting that I stand in the garden on one foot, butt naked.'

'Don't be silly,' I giggle, 'you can wear a rubber glove on your head.'

Ian laughs and helps me up from the floor. My legs feel stiff.

'So all the other parcels are Christmas presents?'

'Yes. It's only three weeks away, we'd better get the decs out of the loft.'

'I'll do that tonight. Luke will love all the lights and baubles.'

'He will, he'll be into it all this year.'

'What do you want for Christmas?' Ian asks. 'Nothing swaying or baby related,' he adds.

I bite my tongue.

'Um, I'd quite like an indoor water fountain for the conservatory.'

'Oh okay, that would look nice.'

No need to mention that flowing water produces negative ions.

Ian heads out to put the buggy in the car. I frantically continue my cleaning. I want the place spotless before Bella arrives.

After Ian and Luke leave I get the 'girl friendly' quiche I made yesterday out of the fridge, and place it in the oven in readiness. I then buzz around the conservatory setting everything straight. I put some drops of lavender oil in my burner and light the tea-light under it.

There is a knock at the door. My heart races.

I switch the oven on, on my way past, and quickly fling the dirty cloth I was using earlier into the washing machine.

'Hiya,' I say as I answer the door to Bella.

She is taller than I remember and very neatly dressed.

'Nice to finally get round to meeting up,' she says taking off her expensive looking leather jacket and handing it to me. She leaves her Ugg boots in the hall, and follows me through to the kitchen. I feel quite frumpy compared to her tiny frame in her designer jeans and cashmere jumper.

'You look just the same as I remember, back in high school,'

'Thanks, you too,' I agree.

'Apart from my boobs,' she says.

'Oh.' I don't know what to say. I try not to stare at her

bust, but my eyes won't budge.

'I had them enlarged – I was a small A cup before.'

'Oh right.' I'm an A, what's wrong with that? 'Have a seat, I've put lunch on ready.' She looks like a C cup, or maybe a D...

'Lovely,' she says, parking herself down on my wicker sofa. Her hair is cropped to just above her ears and is blonder than it was at school.

'It's from the girl diet list – the pine nut and parmesan quiche. Have you tried it before?'

'No.' She looks around the room.

'I've made some Weetabix biscuits too.'

Bella is so skinny, I wonder if she bothers with puddings.

'Lovely,' she says again. 'Is that lavender I smell?'

'Yes.'

'My house reeks of lavender too. I use lavender everything – shampoo, conditioner, body wash, and perfume. I even use lavender scented furniture polish.'

'Ian hasn't asked why I've gone lavender mad. I've got the soap and body lotion – my gran gave it to me when I said I liked it. She hates it, says it's for old people.'

Bella laughs.

I relax.

'Lots of plants, that's what you need in here.' I look around my conservatory, the shelves are a bit sparse.

'Yes, my mum said that.'

'Not just in the conservatory, in every room, for the ions.'

'Oh, I see.'

'Asparagus fern, they produce the most. I even have some by my bed.'

'I'll jot that down.' *Asparagus fern* I write on the back of my shopping list.

'Also salt rock lamps.'

'Got them, they arrived yesterday.'

'I sit next to mine for half an hour a day,' Bella says. I didn't know you had to sit next to them?

The timer on the oven beeps.

'That's lunch.' I jump up.

Bella sits at the table while I serve. We chat during our meal and she didn't leave much so she must have enjoyed it. I take the plates away and bring over the tin of homemade biscuits.

'I think I'm going to have to delay my attempt by a month or two, until I can get my pH down,' I say as she picks at the monster sized Weetabix mound.

'I wouldn't have the patience to wait, but then I have been attempting for a year and a half now.'

'What's your husband like on the diet? Ian's sick of it.' I take a bite of my biscuit. God it's dry.

'My hubby, Joe, doesn't complain, well, not anymore. I used to get so upset with him, I'm sure when he's at work he throws away the packed lunch I've made for him and goes down the shop and gets a pasty. What can I do though? He knows it's so important to me, and it won't be forever.'

I nod, trying to keep in a potential coughing fit, I quickly take a sip of Crystal Light. 'It must be so hard, after all this time. No luck this month then?' I manage to croak out.

'No.'

Silence. I wish I hadn't asked, how insensitive of me.

'Let's see your incubator.' Bella says, swiftly changing the subject.

'It's in the kitchen,' I get up from the table and take it out of my newly cleaned cupboard.

'It's polystyrene?' she remarks.

'It's a fan heated one, I got it from eBay.' I open up the lid on the incubator and get out my test tubes and pipette.

'You need four of those.'

'Do I?'

'Yes, one for the egg white, then there's lime juice, one for the top layer and another for the bottom.' I look at her with a blank expression.

'If you use the same one, you'd mix the Ys and Xs, which is completely defeating the object of a good sort!'

'Oh of course.' Why didn't I think of that? 'What do you use as a mesh, you said your egg whites don't float anymore?'

'Don't laugh, but I bought a cheap bra, a lacy one, and use the lace from that. I've got a bit of it in my bag to show you. I find this easier than netting as it's hard to get the exact size so that the egg white won't filter through. You don't want it to just sit on the top either.'

I roll the bit of lace through my fingers. I hope my egg whites float.

'So have you had a go with the incubator yet?' Bella asks.

'Not yet. We're going to soon, once Christmas is out of

the way. I got some eggs from the Garlic Farm and tested them.'

'They're definitely the best,' Bella replies as I pack away my incubator. 'You can also add gradient density spinning to your sway.'

My heart sinks, what more could you possibly do to the sperm? 'How do you do that?' I ask, feeling defeated.

'Spin it really fast with sugar water. This also separates the boys and girls, you then use the top layer to incubate and carry on with that.'

'I have heard of someone online doing that, I've just not taken much notice,' I admit, sitting back down at the kitchen table. Bella sits opposite me.

'I bet that's Bex, she spins a test tube on her food mixer.'

'Yes, it is.'

'She's got five boys, how dreadful,' she says with a hint of smugness. Now I'm being unkind, just because I don't want to hear about gradient whatsit.

'I hope she gets a girl.' I say.

'Who, Bex? Poor woman,' Bella looks at me. It seems as if she wants to say something further?

Silence. What is it?

'There's one girl online, well, probably more than one, who found out what she was having at twelve weeks, by having a CVS test.' She hesitates and twists her manicured fingers together.

'CVS?' I repeat. Where is this going?

'Yes it stands for chronic something or other, it doesn't matter,' she waves her hand. 'You have to have it done privately. They put a needle in your tummy and take a sample of your placenta, like an amniocentesis, but earlier.'

'Why did she pay out for that, couldn't she wait for the twenty week scan?' Oh God, I'm not sure I want to hear this?

'It kept her options open, if you know what I mean?'

'So she could terminate?'

'Yes, and she did.'

'I didn't know you could do that?' I don't know where to look so I keep my eyes firmly on my fidgeting hands.

'Well you're not supposed to. She just said it was an accident, lots of women do it. Look in the Extreme Disappointment section.' I don't say anything. After a while I realise I'm fiddling with the lacy bra material. I hand it back to her. 'I'm not saying that you should do it or anything, but it is something that others do,' she says, flustered, taking the lace from me.

'Are you planning on doing it?'

'I'm not sure?'

'What about your husband, Joe?'

'I wouldn't tell him, best not to. I'd just say I'd miscarried, that's if I even did it, that is. Also, if it's a girl, you wouldn't have to.' She wrinkles her nose.

'I guess not.'

The air is thick with awkwardness.

'Thank you for lunch, Charlotte. It's been lovely to see you in person. I still can't get over how we both kind of knew each other, it's so mad!' she laughs, nervously, 'You think I'm awful, don't you.'

'No, Bella, I don't. I just didn't know things like that went on, that's all. I'm surprised.'

'I only said I might do it.'

'It's none of my business what you do. I couldn't do it, I know that.'

'You only have one boy though. My boys, Adam and Si, have a brother in each other, so it's not the same.'

'I guess so,' I say, dazed.

Bella visibly relaxes. She finishes her water and stands to leave.

'Thanks for coming.' I show her to the door.

'We'll have to catch up again soon.'

I agree, waving her out. My mind is spinning and not in the gradient density kind of way. I don't know what to think of Bella anymore. She was so lovely, how can she think of doing something like that?

'So how did it go?' Ian asks, passing a tired Luke to me.

'Hello Lukey babes.' I plant a kiss on his head. 'It went fine,' I half whisper, I'm not going to tell Ian her plan. 'I'll put him to bed, he looks tired.'

'Yes he is. He's been crawling around with Granny and Grandad all afternoon, running them ragged.'

'I hope they didn't mind?'

'No, angel, they loved seeing him.'

'Did he do any standing practice?'

'Yes, loads.'

I smile. 'I'll get him to bed now.'

Luke stirs as I pull his cord trousers off and change his nappy as gently as I can. I put his pyjamas on and fasten him in his sleeping bag. Gently lifting him into his cot, I cover him with another blanket and tuck him in at the sides. Gazing at him as he sucks his thumb, I stroke his head. How can anyone plan to get rid of a baby before they're even conceived?

Luke's too tired for me to bother brushing his teeth. It'll be fine just this once says the mother in me. Slippery slope says the dental nurse. I twist the dial on his cot mobile and leave, dimming the lights on my way out.

7

Christmas passes in a blur of excitement. I feel a little deflated now that the New Year festivities are over and I am packing away the last of the decorations.

'Crystal Light?' Ian calls out.

'Yes please, kiwi flavour if there's any left.' We've finished all the powdered drink Marnie from Texas sent me, but I managed to find an online shop that stock American products.

Ian downs his glass. 'I love this stuff.'

I'm glad someone does, I hate it. I can practically feel it eroding my teeth with every sip I take; not that it's helping with my pH much. I'm fully on the diet now, as well as the drinks, and it's barely shifted. It's so far off 4 it's unbelievable. Why does it work for everyone else? I'll post the question online later, and see what suggestions they come up with. I can't be the only one having this problem, surely?

'It's snowing' Ian calls out, excitedly.

I hurry into the conservatory. Ian has the door open and is catching snowflakes for a bemused Luke.

'Let's go outside, Lukey.' He clings to the doorframe, watching his father. All the cold air is entering the house.

'I'm glad your mum bought him those wellies,' Ian calls in. I slip the boots on Luke's feet.

Ian comes back inside. Impatient. 'He's learned to walk just in time for the snow.' He passes me his coat and hat. I smile and do up Luke's coat buttons.

We make footsteps on the snow covered decking. Luke points and laughs, inquisitively touching the white covering.

Half an hour later I take my cold damp cherub back inside to thaw out. Ian stays outside to play on his own, like the big kid he is.

'Got any carrots?' he shouts. I leave Luke sat by the fire watching "The Muppet Christmas Carol" and go to the fridge. Yes we do, surprisingly. Only Luke eats carrots now, we're not allowed to. I pull out a bag of raisins from the cupboard, that will have to do for the eyes, mouth and buttons, unless Ian can think of anything better.

The snowman is now just a mound, and the raisins are few and far between, thanks to the birds.

'I'm off now, Ian. Bye bye Lukey. Be good for Daddy.' I give them both a kiss.

I really don't want to go into work after the long holiday. I wish I'd booked today off, like Ian.

After de-icing the windscreen, and letting the car warm

up, I take a slow apprehensive drive to work, trying to avoid the black ice. I get there safely after a couple of hair-raising moments. Chloe is in already, setting up the surgery.

'I find out what I'm having later,' she says. 'Marie said I can go early, as you're here today.'

'Wow, that's come round quick.'

'I know, Jenson is so excited, he's meeting me at the hospital.'

'Text me when you find out.'

'Will do.'

I just know she's going to have a girl.

Time passes slowly after Chloe leaves.

'Are you okay?' Marie asks.

'Yes, I'm just a bit tired that's all,' I lie. Marie adjusts her spectacles and pauses, studying my face. I look away feeling awkward.

After the next couple of patients, I clear up and put the used instruments in the autoclave to sterilize them ready for the morning. I then disinfect all the surfaces and mop the surgery floor.

'I've got a text from Chloe,' Marie says.

I quickly fish around in my bag, I hadn't heard my phone. I have a text too.

HI ALL, IT'S A GIRL!

My heart sinks and I feel a little nauseous.

'That's lovely,' Marie says.

Steph, the receptionist comes down to the surgery. 'It's a girl,' she says, looking really happy.

I smile.

'Great news,' I say. I'm sure my face is giving my jealousy away, my neck and chest feel hot. I bet it's red, that always happens when I'm feeling stressed or anxious or if I've been crying, or am about to…

The incubator is set up, the egg is separated and all the pipettes are laid out on the counter. I get the bottled lime juice out of the cupboard and pour some into a cup, and put it in the incubator so that everything is the same temperature. The microscope is ready. I'm just waiting for Ian. I'm not going to offer my help, not after last time.

Ian comes down the stairs with the pot in his hand. 'What do we do first?'

My mind's gone blank.

'Where's my pH reader?'

'Calm down angel, we're bound to make mistakes first time round, that's why we're practicing. Here it is, by the sink!'

Our kitchen looks like a science lab. Tension creeps up my spine, I just want it all to be so easy.

'7.8,' I say as I take the probe out of the container.

'Let's write on the pipettes so we know which is which,' Ian suggests.

'Good idea.'

Ian finds a permanent marker in the utility drawer and hands it to me. I write T on one and B on another.

'What does that stand for?'

'Top and bottom.'

Ian looks blank.

'Layers of the sperm,' I clarify.

I continue and write E and L on the others. 'Egg and lime,' I explain.

Picking up the pipette marked B, I extract some sperm, slowly squirting it into the test tube.

'Oh no, Ian, it needs to be at a 45 degree angle.'

'Here use this,' he hands me a pot of nail varnish. I left it out on the side this morning, nail varnish and remover have negative ions, so now my toenails are colourful. I can't do my fingernails, it's against work policy. We put the coral coloured bottle on its side in the incubator, and rest the test tube up against it.

'Egg white. I need to put the egg white on top, before I put it at an angle.' I feel so flustered.

Ian calmly takes the test tube out, and I suck up some egg from the cup inside the incubator, and slowly squirt it out on top of the sperm.

'Is it floating?'

Ian holds the test tube up to the kitchen window and we both squint. 'I think it might be,' I say. 'What do you think?'

'Yes it is. Oh no, look at that clear bit, I think that's some of the egg white sinking into the middle, don't you?'

'Damn! I so wanted it to work.'

'It is working, most of it's floating. Quick, put it in the incubator, Char, before all the sperm die.'

I take the test tube from Ian, and rest it on the nail varnish bottle, then replace the polystyrene lid, while Ian sets the stopwatch for an hour.

'What are you doing?' I ask.

'There's still a few sperms on this pipette. Let's look at them under the scope. We've got an hour to kill after all.'

'Good thinking.'

He puts a drop on one of the glass slides, and covers it with another. It flattens and squashes out of the sides. 'Oops, I don't think we need a cover on it!'

'Is there any left?' I chuckle.

'Yes, here.' Ian repeats the process on another slide, but this time doesn't cover it. He puts the slide under the microscope and looks into the eyepiece.

'Wow this is amazing, Char. There are thousands of them swimming around, just in this tiny little drop. Look.' I lean down to the eyepiece. It is unbelievable, it's so clear.

'Incredible,' I say. 'It's so mad that just one of these could be your baby.'

'I don't mean to put a dampener on all of this, angel, but I really think it's just down to the strongest swimmer at the end of the day. There's thousands upon thousands of them. Even if you halve, or quarter them, doing all this, still hundreds of boys could be in what's left over, and one of the boys could get there first.'

'I know, I just want to up my chances a bit.'

'But what if you're not upping your chances, what if it makes no difference?'

'It's a risk I have to take, Ian. I thought you were willing to take it with me?' Glaring out the window I feel my heart sinking, I know he's right. But I can't acknowledge it. I slide the pendant on my new necklace backwards and forwards repeatedly along the silver chain around my neck.

'I am. I just want you to realise that it may not work.'

'Don't you think I know that? I think about it every day, but I can't see any alternative other than going abroad and shelling out lots of money we don't have.'

Now Ian is the one glaring.

'Please, let's not talk like this. Look how amazing it all is, unbelievable.'

The stopwatch beeps. I switch the incubator off and carefully take out the test tube. Holding it to the light of the kitchen window again, we peer at it.

'What do you think?'

'I can see the line of the egg white, so I don't think too much of it sank. Now what, Char?'

I pick up the pipette marked E, and extract the egg white from the test tube. 'Now we need to look at the top and bottom sample to see if we can tell the difference. Bella says she can. Apparently the girls swim slower and are a bit fatter, and the boys jot around zigzagging and are very slightly thinner, but much faster.'

Having looked under the scope at both samples Ian sighs. 'I can't see any difference.'

My shoulders sag as I can't see a difference either. I test the pH of the incubated sample. '8.1. It's gone up?'

'Really, is it supposed to?'

'No idea, I'll have to ask Bella. Now I just need to add some lime drops to either of the samples, and get the pH down to 4.5, then look and see if they're still alive.'

Adding drops of lime, counting as I go, and checking

the digital figures on the reader, I feel like a scientist. Only I'm not particularly confident at what I'm doing!

'Thirteen drops of lime, that can't be right, can it?'

'How would I know, Char?' He looks under the microscope. 'All dead.'

'What?'

'They're not swimming anymore, look.' I peer through the eyepiece.

The little mini tadpole like sperms are just floating around. They are lifeless, in a sea of lime. 'You're supposed to reduce them to 4.5 though, before you insert them,' I whisper. I feel sad for some reason.

'There's no point inserting dead sperm inside you, and what about the lime juice, that can't be good for you?'

'I guess not. But a lot of girls do a lime water douche.'

'What's that?'

'A solution to insert to help lower your pH. I think I'm going to have to do it seeing as I can't shift mine.'

'Sounds dangerous. You'll probably get a really bad infection, and end up having to go to the surgery, and what would you say to Doctor Spencer - I'm sore because I've been squirting lime juice up my whoopsey, Doctor!'

I giggle. 'I'll take my chances.'

'Jesus, angel.' Ian says rolling his eyes.

'It's really important to keep your pH down all throughout your ovulation period.'

'It's your call. Don't come crying to me when you've got an infection.'

'I won't,' I snap, while tipping the remainder of Ian's sperm down the plughole. I tidy away and wash up all the utensils in hot water, better not put washing up liquid in there. What if it doesn't wash off enough and it ruins the next attempt?

8

'Oh Mother,' I say half joking as she struggles in my front door carrying six leafy green tomato plants.

'What?' she says, 'I always start yours off for you.'

'But I can't eat tomatoes, nor can Ian. It's one of the biggest no no's ever for having a girl.'

'Oh poppycock.' My mother continues out into the garden and places them in my greenhouse.

'Well, if I get pregnant straight away I'll be able to eat them,' I concede. 'Where's Dad?'

'He's down the allotment, watering. It's so hot for April. Get the kettle on, darling.'

I inhale the smell of coffee. God, I wish I could have a cup. I swirl around my boring peppermint teabag.

'You got pregnant straight away last time.' She looks at me strangely as I hand her the cup.

'What?' I question.

'You're so skinny, Char, you look ill.'

'Thanks, Mum.'

'Sorry, darling, but your bones are jutting out.'

I pull my cardigan tightly around myself.

'Your clothes are hanging off you!' She places her cup on the chopping board, walks over to me and tugs at the waistband of my jeans.

'Stop it.' I step back, annoyed. There are tears in her eyes. 'I'll put the weight back on once I'm pregnant.'

'What if you don't even get pregnant? Being this thin, you may not be able to? That Bella isn't yet, is she?'

'No.'

'Well, perhaps if she ate some food, she would be.'

'You haven't even met her.'

'You pointed her out to me in town a few weeks ago, remember. She looked like a drug addict, she was that skinny.'

'I thought you understood.' I walk over to the kitchen window and pick a dead head off of one of my many plants and deposit it into my vegetable caddy on the side.

'I do, love, I do. I'm just dubious about whether it actually works. And people are talking about you.'

I turn to face her, 'What people?'

'Gran, for a start. She says you look anorexic.'

I roll my eyes.

'She saw you tip your tea into her pot plant.'

I laugh.

'It's not funny, Char, everyone's worried.'

'I'm laughing about the tea. Gran kept on asking why I didn't want a cup. She wouldn't take no for an answer. I find it easier to accept one and tip it somewhere.'

My mother purses her lips.

'The plant was as dry as a bone. I'm sure it appreciated it.'

'Anyone else see you throwing away food or drink?'

'I don't think so. I do it at work sometimes. It's just easier. If I refuse I get questioned.'

'You're even acting like an anorexic.'

I roll my eyes and exhale.

'How's Ian?'

'Fine. Why?' I realise that I'm twisting my hair. I stop and let the strawberry blonde waves fall freely to my shoulders.

'Oh, nothing.'

'Come on, Mum, what is it?'

'He's worried about you. We all are.'

'You've been talking about me... to Ian?' I pour the brown mint liquid from my cup down the sink and try to hide my irritation.

'It's just that you're a bit... what's the word.'

'What?'

'Obsessed.'

'Of course I am,' I say raising my voice and stomping over to the table. 'I do want to have Verity.'

'Verity?'

'Yes. Verity.' I hold my mother's gaze. Why is she doing this? 'I can't just do nothing. I have to try.' My tummy rumbles, giving me away. I look down, ready for my mother to go on and on about eating again. She doesn't. There's just silence.

I look up at the clock. My stomach lurches. 'God I've

got to pick Luke up from nursery.'

'I'll come with you.' Mum follows me as I madly dash out the door.

The pattering sound of rain on the conservatory roof is usually relaxing. I don't feel relaxed on this wet Sunday morning, lying here on the wicker sofa, I feel het up and annoyed. I ball my fists and sit up. The burning beeswax candle combined with the lavender scent is making me feel dizzy. I have my water fountain running and my salt rock lamps on in the hope of reducing my stress and soaking up the negative ions. So much for chilling out, I'm like a tensed up patient, lectured to floss, then mouth forced open being probed and tutted at. I can't believe Ian has been talking about me. And Gran!

I punch Rose's numbers in my phone and listen to the rings, hoping she's in.

'Hello.'

'Hi it's Char, I just wondered what you're up to?'

'No plans. I can't ride this afternoon, it's hammering down.'

'Come round if you like? Ian's out surfing, and Luke's asleep.'

'Okay, I'll just finish up here, won't be long.'

'See you soon.'

I lie back down and try to make myself relax while I wait for her to arrive.

'What's wrong?' she asks as I stand to one side to let her in.

'I feel like everyone is watching me all the time, and

noticing what I'm eating or not eating.' I follow her down my hallway, through the kitchen and into the conservatory.

'You've lost so much weight and in such a short space of time. What is it, a stone in two months?'

'Around that.' It's probably nearer two but I keep this to myself. It won't be forever. I nestle on the sofa, Rose on the matching wicker chair.

'Everyone's bound to comment, you were small to start with.' Why did I phone her? This is not going how I wanted.

'Marie's the worst.'

'Your boss?'

'Yes,' I say, picking the paint off my toenails. 'It's so annoying, I wouldn't tell her she was overweight and should watch what she's eating, but she says to me that I look skinny and ill and need to eat more.'

'That's just the way it is. Maybe you need to buy some smaller clothes?'

'I would if I was going to stay like this. But I'm not. I don't want to waste money on a new wardrobe. It will only be for a few more months.'

'I'll put the kettle on,' she says getting up.

'Oh, sorry, Rose, I didn't think.' I follow her to the kitchen and watch as she fills the kettle and switches it on.

'How's it going up the yard?'

'Daisy's much better, the laminitis is gone now.'

'That's good, but that's not what I meant.'

Rose's cheeks colour the same as her crimson jumper.

She laughs, tucking her light brown hair behind her ears.

'Well...' I say, 'has the blacksmith been out?'

'He may have...'

We sit in the conservatory and have a good gossip. Rose with her coffee, me with my glass of milk.

'It's so nice to have something else to think about. Mum says I'm obsessed.'

Rose doesn't say anything.

'Don't tell me she's phoned you, too?'

'No she hasn't.' Rose fiddles with the hem of her jumper. My heart sinks. She has.

'So how's your pH?'

'Not shifting,' I say, thinking about the shift in conversation. I won't think about that now. I don't need stress, it's bad for me.

'Bella came round again.'

'Oh.'

I can tell that Rose is biting her tongue.

'Is she pregnant yet?'

'No, hopefully next month.'

'What do you think of what she said about people online aborting?'

'It's up to the woman, isn't it? I wouldn't do it.' I avoid her gaze.

'I certainly couldn't do that to a baby.'

'It's not a baby. And you don't want kids anyway,' I say, defensively.

'No, but if I did, I'm sure I wouldn't care what I had, so long as it was healthy.'

I feel annoyed and frustrated. I don't know what to

say. Sometimes I wish I hadn't confided so much in my best friend.

'So, how accurate is the CVS test?'

'One hundred percent. You get the results four days later,' I answer numbly.

'I bet that would be nerve wracking, waiting.'

'Yes.' I force down a sip of milk, trying not to wretch. I hate milk. 'A girl online said about a doctor in Kent who advertises that he can tell the sex of your baby at twelve weeks with a scan.'

'Really?'

'Yes. It's called a nub shot. But it's only eighty percent accurate.'

'That's not high enough. You wouldn't be sure.'

'No,' I agree.

'Have you looked at his website?'

I cheer up at this question. Maybe I took Rose's earlier comments the wrong way. I'm too sensitive. 'Yes, do you want to see?'

We head up the stairs, I switch the computer on in my bedroom. 'It'll take a good five minutes to fire up.'

'How long does Luke sleep?'

'Two and a half hours or so, we've got time.' I turn the volume up on the baby monitor then type in the name of the website. 'He's called Doctor Thompson.'

'Is the scan just for finding out the gender?'

'No, it's for abnormalities, but it says if he can see the nub he'll look for you if you want.'

'Nub?' Rose questions, looking over my shoulder at the picture of Doctor Thompson. He's wearing a tweed waist jacket and he looks stiff and stuffy with a comb-over attempting to hide the fact that he's balding. He must be at least fifty-five going on a hundred.

'It's a line that goes parallel to the spine if it's a girl, and up at an angle if it's a boy. There's a gallery.'

'Let's have a look.'

I click on the nub gallery and scroll through the black and white scan pictures.

'So those are the girls,' Rose touches the screen with her fingers, trying to expand the picture.

'It's not a touch screen,' I say, dragging the corners of the scan with my mouse.

'Sorry, I'm used to my iPad. You really should update from this dinosaur.'

I continue scrolling down all the girl nubs then view the boy ones.

'I can see now, so it's that bit pointing up.'

'Yes, if it was a girl it would be parallel.'

Later that evening, I place some semen on a slide and put it under the microscope.

'You never know what people get up to behind closed doors,' Ian says.

I smile, 'I still can't distinguish between the Xs and Ys.'

'It's a cheap microscope. It doesn't magnify enough, that's if it's even possible to tell them apart.'

I add lime drops, one at a time until the digital figure reads 4.5. 'The lime freezes them.'

Ian glances up from the eyepiece, 'They still look dead to me.'

'If they're dead, they appear black, that's what they all said online. They said lime juice freezes them because it has a low pH. If you add bicarbonate of soda, mixed with water to the sperm, they come back to life.'

'We'll see,' Ian says with disbelief.

I add the bicarbonate mix to the test tube and gently shake it back and forth, mixing in the white liquid. Taking a pipette, I place a drop on a glass slide and stand back for Ian to look under the microscope first. I can see he's itching to prove the online buddy group wrong.

'I can't believe it. They've started swimming again.'

'Let me see,' I say impatiently.

We freeze them with lime, and then awaken them with the bicarbonate, over and over again, watching them stir then dart around in a manic fashion.

'So, even if they look frozen and dead, when you insert them, they apparently wake up inside you because your pH is higher than the lime,' I explain.

I'm so happy that he seems fascinated by the science.

After washing up, and packing it all away, we sit out in the garden, in the dark with our patio light on, drinking cups of peppermint tea.

'How was Luke today?' he asks.

'A bit whiny, he's teething again. But Rose came round so that broke the day up a bit.'

'She's not really child friendly, did she talk to Luke?' Ian chuckles.

'Yes. We played hide and seek. Luke was so excited, laughing and clapping, until Rose jumped out from behind the curtains and startled him.'

Ian laughs and I join in trying to erase Rose's 'so long as it's healthy' comment from my mind.

'Look at that massive full moon. I've never noticed it so much since having to know which is full and which is new.'

'It's so big at the moment and we have had crazy tides for surfing.'

'It looks closer.'

'It's beautiful and dramatic isn't it?'

I nod and lean into Ian's embrace thinking about how care free our love making used to be. What am I doing?

9

I wake up to the deep humming noise of foghorns. The red digits on my alarm clock say 5:30am. I used to love the sound when we first moved to the seafront village. I roll over and squeeze my eyes tightly shut, annoyed. I need to rest, we have a few early starts ahead of us.

Sleep evades me, so I get up feeling tired and frustrated. I pass the hours away by researching, the computer doesn't wake Ian. I look at magnified sperm and more scan pictures, before the chaos of breakfast.

'Don't forget your sups,' I say, handing Ian the eight tablets and popping the lids back on the various containers. I take my red ones first, then my white, with a glass of water, in between spoon-feeding Luke his cereal. He mashes his Weetabix covered hands on his highchair, then rubs them in his blonde curls as if he's shampooing his hair. Great, just what I need.

After dropping Luke off at Mum's house, I park the

car in my usual space. I'm running late. On the way in I pass the bakery. I inhale the beautiful baking bread fragrance and my mouth floods with saliva. Fingers crossed, I might be pregnant next month. I'll have my own bun in the oven. I smile.

Chloe has the surgery set up ready for the first patient.

'Doesn't look like Mrs Stanley's going to turn up,' she says walking down the corridor to reception.

'She's always delayed. It's a filling isn't it?' I take off my cardigan and place it behind the desk along with my handbag and my sealed carrier bag.

'Yes.' Chloe looks at the record card.

'So have you thought of any names yet?' I ask.

'A couple. We quite like Sophie, or Rosie, but I think we'll wait and see when she's born.'

'We would have chosen Verity-May for a girl. I love that name.'

'You only have a couple of months or so left at work now,' Steph the receptionist says, emerging from the storeroom, tightening her auburn ponytail.

'I know. It will soon fly by,' Chloe says, 'Where's Marie?'

'In the yard, watering the plants.'

Chloe and I head to the surgery.

Marie waddles in, 'No show?' she questions as she plonks herself down on her swivel chair.

'Looks like it.' I write on the record card and file it away.

The morning passes, at lunchtime I walk to the park and sit on one of the benches. I munch away at my boring rice cakes with sesame seed paste and unsalted butter on. God I'm sick of all this food. Our first real attempt is in the morning. I watch the mothers pushing their children in their buggies to the play park. One mother has two boys with her, and is pushing a pram. I strain to see if the baby has a pink or a blue blanket. Pink. I hate the fact that I have to know what other people have, but I can't help it. Another lady passes. Her little girl has a scarlet headband on. Someone else goes by with a double buggy, is it one of each? I can't see...

When I get back to work I nip into the toilet with my carrier bag and handbag. I pee on an ovulation prediction stick and wait impatiently for a minute. There is no line. Relief floods through me. I need a line tonight. Now would be too early. I take the container with the lime solution out of the carrier bag, it didn't leak, surprisingly. Carefully opening it up, I take out the lime tampon I prepared this morning. My pH has to stay low. After all that business is attended to, I go behind the reception desk and get my Crystal Light drink from my drawer, secretly adding ten fake sugar tablets to it. I down it in one.

'What's that?' I jump and dribble some of my pink drink down my white and yellow trimmed tunic.

'Jesus, you scared me, Chloe!'

'Cup of coffee?' she says, her eyes lowered, looking at the stain on my uniform, then she looks at my face, scrutinising.

'Uh, yes please.'

Chloe sips her coffee while chattering on about girly

nurseries, pink bedding, princesses, flowers, hearts...

'Sounds lovely,' I say.

'You didn't drink your coffee. It's gone cold now.'

'Never mind, I'll make us one later. I didn't really fancy it anyway.' I take the full cup with me into the kitchen and tip its contents away. I rub the stain on my top with a wet-wipe and exhale. I feel uncomfortable, the lime tampon is irritating me. It's all going wrong.

The rest of the day passes slowly. After collecting Luke and giving him his tea, I bath him then read him his bedtime story.

'Night night,' I say, kissing his head. He's already asleep, sucking his thumb and cuddling his favourite teddy. I stand and listen to his gentle snores, smiling to myself. My mind wanders thinking about the spare room, I can't wait to paint it pink. I gently close the door to Luke's blue nursery, just as Ian opens the front door.

'Hi, angel.' He takes off his overalls and hands them to me. 'It was so busy at work.'

'They'll need soaking,' I hold the overalls at arm's length and take them through to the conservatory. 'Tea's in the oven,' I call out.

I get the incubator out of the cupboard as Ian finishes his meal, and set it out on the work surface. Microscope, test tubes, pipettes, I check to myself. Then I notice it.

'What's your wetsuit doing there?'

'I'm surfing.'

'When?'

'In the morning. I'm doing a dawny. The wave buoy says it's pumping.'

'But we're attempting in the morning?'

'What!'

'I told you.'

'I can be back for seven.'

'That's no good. You have to be showered and ready by six.'

'Showered?'

'Negative ions.' I say, as if I'm talking to a child.

'I'll be back around six then.'

'That's still no good. I have to check when I'm ovulating, so the time may vary a bit. You can't go surfing. Not for the next three mornings. Go in the evening.'

'Three mornings? I'll go when the tides right. I'm going in the morning.'

'You know we're attempting over the next three days. I told you.'

'Tough.'

I can hear my heart beating loudly. I can't be stressed, he knows that. Why is he doing this to me?

'Please, Ian, this is our first go at it, we've had three months of planning this.'

'Yes, and don't I know that...' Ian slams down his knife and fork.

'Why are you doing this then?'

'I've not been surfing in weeks-'

'I haven't stopped you.'

'I know, but the tides were wrong and there was no swell. My brothers are meeting me there. I can't let them down.'

'But you can let me down.'

'Look, Char-'

'Of all the weeks, please, not this week. And you know I can't be stressed.'

'I'm not doing it. I've had a fucking gut full. I've done your stupid diet, taken your stupid pills. That's it. No more!' he gets up from the table, the legs on the chair make an ear-piercing screech.

'But we've not even tried yet.'

'What the hell have we been doing these past months then?'

'Preparing, you know that. Stop being difficult.'

'I'm surfing, Char. I'm God damn surfing. You're not going to stop me.'

'How can you be so selfish?'

'Selfish! Do you think any other husband would do all this? Put up with all this shit.'

'We've not done it yet. And Joe would, Bella's husband.' I regret bringing Bella into it, but it's too late, it's passed my lips and there's no taking it back.

Ian storms off, grabbing the car keys on his way. I feel numb and shaky. I look around the room in disbelief, then run to the door and pull Ian's arm.

He shakes me off. 'I'm sick of it, Char, I need some space.'

'Don't do this.'

He doesn't look at me, and leaves. I slam the door. The stained glass panels crack into a thousand pieces, the noise makes me jump. The lead pattern between the green, blue and burgundy glass holds the shattered pieces in place, bar a few shards that fall to my feet. Ian would have heard the noise, but he still left. Shattered glass and a shattered attempt.

My heart sinks, my sway is ruined and so is my door. We'll never replace that glass, it's so old fashioned, I doubt they even make it like that now!

Crying. Luke's awake, crying. Great...

Ian comes in and passes me a box of chocolates. 'Forgive me?' he says. Chocolates, he's so thoughtless.

I move them to one side. I can't speak to him. I stare at the TV screen, not seeing or hearing.

'Talk to me, Char.'

'I've taped the glass together.'

'You slammed it, not me,' he says accusingly.

I glare at him, then look back, unseeing at the telly.

'Sellotape, seriously? I'll get some wood from the shed.' He stands up.

'Don't bother, I phoned the insurance company. I said the back door was open too, and the wind caught the front one. A guy's coming out in an hour or so to do a temporary repair.'

'I'm sorry, angel. I forgot the plans and was looking forward to surfing, I've not been in ages.

'That's not my fault.'

'I know it's not. I shouldn't have blamed you.'

'I can't eat chocolate. You know that. Unless the plan's all off?'

'Of course it's not. I'll do it.'

Tears fill my eyes. Why did he put me through this?

'I'm not supposed to have stress, stress equals boy.'

Ian puts his arms around me. My back heaves as I surrender to the upset and tension I've been holding in.

'I'm going to bed. We've got an early start in the morning,' I numbly state.

'What about the repair guy?'

'You can wait for him.'

'What was it you said to him again... what's the story?'

'Say whatever you like, I'm past caring.'

10

'How long will you be like that?'

'Ten minutes, that's all. Luke's still asleep anyway.'

Ian huffs and sits on the edge of the bed. I look up at my feet, feeling ridiculous, lying with my legs in the air. This could be it.

After the time is up, I insert a lime tampon, and rifle through my wardrobe for something to wear. I stand still, staring numbly.

'What's up? You're not still upset about yesterday are you?'

Long sleeved tops, dresses and skirts of all colours and textures drape on their hangers, tightly packed in, and fighting for room.

'I said I'm sorry. I wish I could rewind the day and do it all differently, but I can't,' he says.

'I shouldn't be stressed,' my voice is cold.

Ian looks me in the eye and gives me a weak smile.

'It's not about yesterday and the door incident. I've lost so much weight, I don't look good in anything. Everything just falls off me.' As I hold my old faithful denim skirt up to show Ian how big it looks now, I reminisce. Ian glances at me.

'I wore this skirt on our honeymoon four years ago. Remember how hot it was in Las Vegas?'

'It was sweltering, two days were more than enough.'

'I loved Yosemite the most, it was so beautiful and peaceful. It would have been great to have spent more time there.' I slip the skirt on over my black leggings and find unsurprisingly that I don't need to undo the button to pull it up, it still feels so familiar and part of me. I used to live in this skirt. Life was so carefree back then. Now look at me. I'm stressed out and skinny. I mentally shake myself. I will be happier soon, and I'll fit in this skirt again. When all of this is over, I can go back to just living a normal life.

'Here, put this on,' Ian says, handing me my brown leather belt. I look at it and see the mark is on the third hole, it will have to be on the first now. Ian gives me a hug, I lean into him. 'Those were the days,' he whispers into my hair. A tear runs down my cheek while I remember my life before all this madness.

Half an hour later, Ian leaves for work. I take Luke to toddler group and carry on my day as usual. If this is it, I could finally eat some chocolate. A Cadbury's Wholenut bar, that's what I want. I can feel my mouth watering.

'Isn't it too soon?' Ian looks concerned.

'Bella always tests early. If I get a slight line, we could take Luke to Pizza Hut or something, have a big stuff out.'

'Sounds great, but you said you're not due on for three days,' he continues. 'Don't get your hopes up.'

'It says it's a first response test.'

I take the white stick to the bathroom and pee on it. Replacing the cap, I wait the agonising three minutes.

'Negative,' I say, with tears in my eyes.

'Let's have a look.' Ian holds the test up to the light and squints at it. 'Never mind, angel, it was only our first attempt.'

'I know. I'm more disappointed because I wanted to eat something. I need to be pregnant so I can be normal again. Plus, Marie is organising a surprise meal out to say goodbye to Chloe. She's on maternity leave next month. I really want to go. I have to go. It would look so bad if I didn't. But what am I going to eat?' I splutter through tears.

'It might work out okay?'

'I've already looked in my diary, it's a few days before our second attempt. What on earth am I going to do?'

'We'll think of something.' He hugs me. 'You will enjoy the cinema tonight, wont you? It will make a nice change.'

'I'm looking forward to it,' I say burying my head in his chest.

I pull up in the cinema car park. Rose is already there with our friend Stacey.

'Aren't you buying any popcorn or anything?' Stacey

asks, shovelling a handful of hers to her mouth.

'I've brought some with me. I'm trying to save money,' I lie. I have got some popcorn in my bag, I popped the corn kernels in the microwave with unsalted butter, and added fake sugar to it.

'Taste okay?' Rose whispers during the horror movie.

'It does actually.' I take a sip of cranberry juice, enjoying the film and the normality of it all.

'That went well,' I say to Rose after Stacey leaves. 'I actually got to do something ordinary. Didn't look too conspicuous either.'

'We'll have to go again now that we've thought of something you can do without having to make excuses for not eating,' she puts her hand on my arm and smiles.

'We'll pick a better film next time though, it wasn't very scary!'

'Char, I'm worried about you. How much do you weigh now?'

'I'm fine, Rose. I've never felt better. I like being thin.'

'You're too thin. You're not eating enough protein, you're not eating enough of anything. And you've not answered my question.'

I stare at her.

'You don't look good, Char, you look older.'

'Thanks,' I say, annoyed. She knows why I'm doing this. Why does she keep on about how I look? I can't help it. I'm sure all the comments from Rose and others are mainly due to jealousy. Everyone wants to lose a few pounds deep down. I think I look fine. If my clothes fitted better then I'd look quite good, all the celebrities are a size zero after all!

I pace around the lounge unsure how to broach the subject. I'll just blurt it out. 'I think we need to do some practice tries at spinning.'

'Oh?' Ian grunts.

'Density Spin. It's the thing where you whizz the sperm around on a centrifuge.'

'We haven't got a centrifuge.'

'Other girls use food blenders or mixers, I've got the Kenwood Chef I never use that Rose gave us as a wedding present. We could tape the test tube to that.'

Silence.

'We don't have lids for our test tubes though, it will fly out everywhere,' I continue.

Still silence. I need to stop talking, but I don't.

'That girl I told you about, Bex, the one with five boys. She's doing it.'

'Don't you think we've got enough to do?'

'I just thought where the egg white keeps sinking, other girls add sugar water to the sample, so if you're doing that you may as well spin it seeing as you have to add sugar water anyway.'

'Fine, I've got nothing else to do. You want me to jiz in a pot then?'

'Please.'

He stomps upstairs, shutting the door behind him.

I set up the microscope and incubator, then stir different amounts of sugar water in three cups. I add a drop of green food dye to the lowest amount, blue to the medium and red to the highest. Placing the three separate cups of coloured liquid in the sink bowl with hot water in, I stir until the sugar dissolves. I pour the biggest amount of red liquid in the test tube, slightly less blue, and even less of the green, all layered on top of each other, then position the test tube in the incubator to keep it at body temperature.

'Here,' Ian grunts, handing me the warm pot. I place it in the sink of hot water.

'What are you doing?'

'You have to liquefy it. Take a look at the test tube.'

'Do I have to?' he carefully takes the test tube out of the incubator and holds it up to the kitchen window. 'What am I looking at now?'

'Can you see a clear line between all the colours?'

'Yes.'

'Good. I'm using food dye to check it layers correctly. Bex suggested it.'

'So it's Bex now, what happened to Bella?'

'She's doing it too.'

Ian returns the test tube to the incubator and replaces the lid.

'Apparently the girls are heavier than the boys. By spinning them, the G force will make the girls sink to the bottom.'

I add the liquefied sperm to the test tube with the green, blue and red solution and try to sellotape it to the K beater on my Kenwood Chef.

'I hope it works.'

'I've got some gaffer tape. Hold on, Char, I'll get it.'

Ian goes out to the shed and comes back with a roll of silver tape.

'We can stick some of this on the top of it as a lid,' he suggests. I've got his interest...

'Good idea. Here you do it.'

Ian re-tapes my useless attempt and sticks a makeshift gaffer tape lid to the top.

I switch it to spin on its highest speed, and set the stopwatch. 'It needs to whizz around for fifteen to twenty minutes, but I'm going to check it sooner.'

After ten minutes, Ian cuts the test tube free, and we hold it up to the window again.

'I can't see any rays of light,' I say.

'Is that what you're supposed to see? You can still distinguish the different colours though. I thought they'd all mix in,' Ian says while re-sticking the test tube to the K beater.

'Yes, but apparently you're supposed to see rays. This is the girl sperm descending, I think? There's also supposed to be sediment at the bottom. God this is so confusing!'

'This is a pile of shit. It's all crap. Come on, Char! Even you must see this is too much!'

I switch on the food mixer. I can see Ian grinding his teeth as the loud noise blocks him out. He leaves the room.

After a further ten minutes of spinning, I syringe out the top two layers into a cup, to look at under the microscope later. Then I put the bottom bit into another test tube, and add the egg white I separated earlier.

'It's floating, Ian,' I call out, 'the sugar water has made the egg white float, it usually sinks.'

He doesn't reply. I can hear the telly on in the lounge.

I set the timer for an hour and double check the temperature of the incubator, then put the spun product in my new wooden test tube holder inside it.

He's right, this is too much of a performance to add to an already surreal way of conceiving a baby.

'Ian?' I hope I haven't pushed him too far tonight...

I pour some more of the mixture into a clean test tube. I'll just whizz it around once more while I've got everything set up... I've not seen the elusive rays yet. I re-apply the tape and twist the dial to full speed again, then turn to look under the microscope at the remaining sperm. My eye firmly in the eyepiece, hair tucked behind my ears, I watch the tiny tadpoles manically swim.

A juddering sound startles me. Immediately my attention is drawn towards the Kenwood.

The test tube catapults across the kitchen, hitting the cupboard door above my extractor fan. A mixture of colours and bubble like solution runs down the units.

'Oh my God!'

The glass test tube crashes onto my kettle. It breaks into three sharp jagged pieces. Blind panic. The noise of the food mixer is intrusive. I switch it off. It's all over the cooker hob. The colour has mixed to make a dirty brown. It's everywhere. What a disaster. No point in calling out to Ian. I sink to my knees and cry.

11

'You've fitted in so well. Such a help when Char was on maternity. Now it's your turn,' Marie says to Chloe, passing her the gift we all clubbed together to buy.

'Thanks, guys. Can I open it now?'

'Of course,' Marie says.

She pulls the ribbon and starts to undo the sides of the pink wrapping.

'It won't be bad luck, will it?' Chloe asks, pausing.

'Of course it won't,' Steph, our receptionist, chimes in.

I smile at Chloe as she reveals the beautiful purple dress with cerise appliquéd flowers. A knot of jealously tightens in the pit of my stomach.

'It's lovely,' she beams. 'It even has matching knickers. Thanks, guys. Thanks so much.'

'There's more,' I say, handing her another beautifully covered present.

Her eyes well up as she unwraps the silver picture

frame and first year album.

'Shall we order?' Marie says, picking up the menu. The Three Crowns, just a short walk from our practice is newly re-opened. What was once a dark olde-worlde pub, is now a modern, clean restaurant.

While everyone looks at the menu, I feel flustered. How am I going to pull this off?

'Are you ready to order?' the waitress asks.

'I'll have the beef wellington, with new potatoes and vegetables... no, make that chips,' Marie says. 'Char?' she turns to me.

I can feel the blood creeping up my neck. 'Um... I'm having the special macaroni, I phoned yesterday,' I stutter.

'Ah, yes. We have that ready,' the waitress says, scribbling on her notepad and turning to Steph to take her order.

Everyone is staring at me. I take a small self-conscious sip of wine.

They're still staring. Rummaging around in my handbag, for something to do, I flip open my phone and switch it to silent mode. By the time I've placed my handbag back down by my feet, the waitress is gone.

'You already ordered?' Chloe asks, folding up the baby dress and placing it in the bag with the other gifts.

My stomach lurches, it was Bella's idea. Say you're on a salt free diet, for medical reasons, she'd said. So that's what I did. 'I looked at the menu online. Wasn't keen on much and it said you can make a request. I thought it would be quicker to phone it through,' I lie.

No one says anything. My face is hot. I can feel four pairs of eyes on me. I'm on fire.

'Top up?' Sally our hygienist says re-filling everyone's glasses. Mine's still full. I reluctantly take another sip. She adds an extra drop to it. I really shouldn't be drinking wine.

My special macaroni arrives. It looks lovely. While everyone tucks in, I eat what I can, then scrape the rest around the plate. I shouldn't eat too much salty cheese, and I can't touch the side salad. I ignore the glances at my relatively full plate as it is taken away.

'Who's for dessert?' Marie says as soon as the waitress leaves. She scans the chalkboard to the left of the table. I dissect a beer-mat. There's no way anyone's going to allow me to refuse a pudding.

'Chocolate torte. Apple crumble,' Marie reads, adjusting her spectacles and standing up for a clearer view of the board. Her large belly almost knocks her wine over. She's a funny shape, Marie, like an upside down triangle. Her legs are small but her top half is humongous. I know she's had two sons, but that's no excuse. Being alone, no husband, boys have flown the nest, I guess she's lonely. I don't want to be lonely. If I had a daughter, I'd be like me and my mum... 'Banana split. Spotted dick. Pancakes with strawberries and fresh cream,' she continues.

I look up. Yes. I can have that. I couldn't have asked for a better pudding.

'Splash,' Luke says jumping in a puddle. The muddy

brown water squelches up the sides of his Spiderman wellies.

'We're going to meet Mummy's friend, Bella, at the park. She's got a little boy for you to play with called Simon. That will be fun, won't it?'

Luke nods, unsure, then jumps in the next pool of dirt.

The lemon coloured sun is warm on my back. We walk the short distance from our house, down the hill, stopping for every puddle en-route. The wind is stronger along the seafront. The beach huts to the left are freshly painted, ready for summer. Walking over the lush grassy hill, we reach the park. The play area has been modernised and expanded since my childhood. It now has a large pirate ship complete with wooden sails and portholes. There are fewer trees and shrubs, but the sea views remain stunning. The grey green waves are choppy. I can hear them lapping against the sea wall.

'Hi,' I call out, walking towards Bella.

'Hello, Luke. This is Simon,' she smiles.

'Ello,' Simon grunts as he dismounts from the swing. He pulls down the hood of his jumper.

Luke clings to my legs.

'Go have fun,' I say, taking his hand. 'Come on, let's look at the big boat.' I gently coax him into the wooden ship.

'I'm a pirate!' Simon shouts, climbing aboard. Luke bravely clambers on, following Simon to the helm.

'Aren't they cute,' Bella says, watching the boys turning the wheel. 'Luke's so little compared to Si. Simon starts school next year.'

'Really? He doesn't look old enough.'

'August baby. He's looking forward to being all grown up like his brother.'

'Do they get on well, Simon and Adam?' I ask, watching him as he turns the wheel faster and faster, making Luke step back.

'Not really... well sometimes they do. Adam's dreadfully boisterous. Likes rough and tumble. Simon's the easier one out of the two.'

I decide to keep a keen eye on the boys.

'I'm attempting tonight, Joe's working late, so the timing isn't ideal, what about you?' Bella slides down her sunglasses to cover her eyes. I've never met her husband, Joe, I wonder what he's like? Perfectly neat and fashionable, similar to his wife I expect...

'I got my period this morning. A day early!' I say.

'Oh no. Maybe next month.'

'All that fussing around with the menu, at my work's meal. I could have relaxed a bit and enjoyed some food after all. It's so annoying!'

'It will be worth it in the end.'

'I hope so. I'm so disillusioned with it all. If I don't get pregnant in the next couple of months, I'm going to drop the incubating.'

'You'll regret it. Why not drop the spinning instead?'

'I don't spin.'

'Oh, I thought you did?'

I look over at the people entering the gated area. A mother and a grandmother, with two girls. 'I did a practice run,' I lower my voice to not much louder than a whisper, 'and it sprayed up my cupboards. I gave up.'

Bella laughs, 'You should try it again. I've really got the hang of it. It's just practice.'

'Ian went berserk. I can't. It's just too much.'

'I know what you mean. It is hard. But you have to be determined.'

We stroll over to a wooden bench, made from a tree trunk and watch the boys playing. Luke giggles as Simon kicks a stray ball under the slide. 'Weather turned out nice after all,' I say, changing the subject. Determined? I am bloody determined!

'It said rain on the news.'

'They always get it wrong. I wish I'd put my washing out.' Damn. I'll hang it out as soon as I get home.

'Wouldn't it be terrific to have pink dresses on the line?'

'And tights,' I say, 'I love little girls tights, stripy ones and spotty ones, they get me the most.'

'I know what you mean,' Bella muses.

'Silly isn't it. It's not about tights or dresses. It's later on, the different relationship.' I watch what I assume is three generations of women playing. Grandmother, mother and daughters. I wonder if she wants a son?

'No one understands,' Bella runs her hands through her blonde elfin hair. 'I was talking to my mum the other day about it. Trying to make her comprehend.'

'Oh?' My eyes revert from the family of women, to our boys playing on the roundabout.

'She has three daughters. And she loves the grandchildren to bits. If she'd had all boys instead, she wouldn't have what she's got now.' Bella takes a deep breath. 'It would be completely different. She might not have any involvement at all with her grandkids.'

'No,' I say, 'daughter-in-laws aren't the same as a daughter of your own.'

'She didn't want to hear it though. If I could just make her see it my way...'

Simon is pushing the roundabout too fast. Luke is clinging on.

'People who have girls just don't under-'

I dart across the playground. 'Stop now,' I shout.

Luke is crying. I pull at the bars to slow them down. Thank God he didn't fall off from that speed. Simon stomps away. 'Lukey, it's okay,' I envelope him in my arms, hugging him close.

'Too fast,' he mumbles into my shoulder.

'I know, never mind, you're all right. Do you want to go on the swings?'

He nods.

'Sorry,' Bella says. 'Simon, that was naughty. He's only little.'

'Baby,' he taunts.

Bella apologies again, and attempts to grab Simon. He runs off to the climbing frame. She gives up.

I carry Luke over to the infant swings with the closed in bars and lift him into it, pulling his wellies through the divider. I gently push him. 'Weeee,' I say. Luke copies, happy again. The moment of fright forgotten.

Later that evening I scroll through the posts on the

buddy group. Completely engrossed with all the information to-ing and fro-ing between Marnie from Texas, and someone called Mountaingirl, about biorhythm charts.

'Hey.'

I jump.

Ian kisses me on the head.

'You startled me.'

'That looks technical,' he peers over my shoulder at the graph with blue and red line readings.

'If both lines are in the top half, it's girl timing. It's calculated to predict –'

'Stop.'

I exhale and close the link. It will be saved on my history, I'll read more later. Best not mention to Ian about the baby wish the women are typing about. At only six pounds, even if you don't believe in psychics, it's still worth a try, surely? I'll read more on that later too. I log out and turn my attention to my husband.

'Come on, angel, let's, you know...'

I follow Ian's gaze to our bed. 'You know we can't.'

'But you're not pregnant. We won't be attempting for a couple of weeks.'

'Don't you listen to anything I say? I can't orgasm before ovulation. Or at all, it will mean boy.'

'Can I then?'

'You can't release until our attempt.' I sigh.

Ian looks defeated. He sits on the bed, his head in his hands. 'Fine. Can I kiss you? Or is that against the rules too?'

'Of course not,' I soften, and walk across the bedroom, ready to embrace him.

A text alert sounds out.

'Leave it.'

'Hold on,' I walk back to the computer desk, locating my mobile. Flipping the screen open, I touch the picture of the envelope.

CHLOE AND JENSON ARE PLEASED TO ANNOUNCE THE SAFE ARRIVAL OF VERITY-MAY BORN TODAY AT 7.15PM WEIGHING 7LBS 2OZ.

'Oh my God!'

'What's up?'

'I can't believe she took my name!'

'Who? What is it?'

'Chloe, from work. She never once mentioned the name Verity. She knew that was my name. She's even taken the whole of it. Verity-May.' I feel so hurt and jealous. I want to scream at the top of my voice. 'I have to text back.'

'It can wait. Come here,' Ian pats the bed.

CONGRATULATIONS. I type. I'm tempted to write LOVE THE NAME but I resist the urge.

'I need to phone Mum,' I say with tears in my eyes. Ian visibly deflates as I head downstairs to the landline.

Dialling the number with shaky hands, I can hear my heart beating.

'What's up darling?' all she would be able to hear is my jagged breathing.

'Verity-May. Chloe called her baby Verity-May.'

'Oh dear, Char. Did she know you were going to use that name for Luke, had he been a girl?'

'Everyone knew.'

'Perhaps you should have kept it to yourself?' My throat is dry. I can't speak. 'It doesn't matter, you can still call yours Verity.'

'No I can't', I croak, 'and the reason I told everyone is because I thought then they would steer clear of that name.'

'But she doesn't even know you're trying, does she?'

'No, but I'm so upset, Mum, how could she.'

'You'll be okay, Char. There are plenty of other lovely girl's names, you'll think of a different one when the time comes.'

'I know, it was just such a shock, but at the same time I kind of knew. I can't explain it, as soon as I heard my text, I knew it was from Chloe, and that it would be that name.'

'Don't be silly, darling.'

I feel so numb and betrayed, and stupid for feeling like this. I'm not even pregnant, I may never have a girl.

I say my goodbyes, slam the phone down and hysterically cry. Ian's slippers are abandoned in the hallway. He knows that pisses me off. I pick them up and hurl them across the room, barely missing him as he emerges from the stairs.

'What the fuck's the matter with you?'

'It's your bloody fault. If you could have given me a girl in the first place, none of this would be happening.'

Ian stares at me with a bewildered expression. I push

past him, up the stairs, wailing uncontrollably.

12

I hear the sound of mail dropping to the floor. Dashing to the door, I pick it up and stash it behind the bread bin. I know what it is. I'll look at it when Ian's gone.

'Bye, angel,' he waves at me and Lukey as he leaves the house. As soon as I'm certain he's driven away, I grab the bubble-wrapped envelope. I hold it to my chest. Is this really going to make a difference? I tear it open and unfold the cream embossed pages of the wish I bought online. Enclosed is a funny looking silver fairy, not real silver I'm sure, along with a small rose quartz stone. The instructions say I have to read the chant aloud then make my wish and hide the paperwork. Once my desire has come true I have to retrieve it and read out the completion chant. I take off my silver pendant from Marie and place it in my jewellery box. I feel resigned, I love that necklace. Rummaging through the box, I find an old tarnished chain and link the fairy onto it, along with a heart shaped purple stone I bought for my girl sway, and fasten it round my neck. I look down at my wrist and squeeze my Kiflow bracelet. The ion crystals inside make a crunching sound between my fingers. Twenty pounds for something that looks like a rubber band... another thing I've kept from Ian. I slip my personal ioniser round my neck. There will be negative ions aplenty.

Feeling self-conscious, I start my crazy chant. God this is so stupid. Luke looks quizzically at me from his playpen. I close my eyes. 'Healthy baby daughter,' I say and fold the paperwork up. Carefully lifting the loose floorboard section in the hall, I place the wish in the hole among the cobwebs, then I gently position the board back in place.

'Isn't Mummy silly,' I say to Luke as I lift him out.

The next couple of months go by slowly and hungrily.

'I'm giving up on the incubating. I'm just not getting pregnant.' I rant to Rose.

'Are you going to try naturally?'

'Not quite. I've convinced Ian to still do turkey baster method and lower the pH to five.'

'Are you sure it's not the lime that's stopping you from conceiving?'

'I don't know, Rose. I'm so sick of it. Ian has lost two stone!'

'Really? Maybe I should go on this diet,' she jokes, taking a bite of one of my homemade Weetabix biscuits. The crumbs drop. She scrapes them into a neat pile on my polka dot tablecloth that hides my old beaten pine table in the breakfast-room.

'There's someone called Chicklet online. She went to that nub doctor in Kent, Doctor Thompson.'

'What did he say she's having?'

'I don't know. She's disappeared. I've sent her a private message but I've not heard anything.'

'Strange?' Rose questions tucking her light brown hair behind her ears.

'Umm, I have a theory.'

'Oh?'

'I think it's a boy and she's terminating.'

'The same plan as Bella. Jesus, that's terrible.' Her hair falls loose again, she roughly tugs it back in place, annoyed.

'She might not be,' I say defensively. 'I've texted Bella to see if she's heard from her but she's not replied yet.'

'She's friends with her then?' I detect a dislike towards Bella.

'Yes, online. She's not met her. I could be completely wrong about it all.'

Rose looks at me, then looks away. 'How's Ian?' she finally asks.

'Fine. Why?'

'No reason. Tammy saw him the other day.'

'Oh?' I wonder where he would have bumped into her little sister?

'She's started surfing lessons.'

'What did she say?' I have noticed Ian's been wearing aftershave recently. Now I'm being stupid.

'Not much. Just that he gave her some pointers.

Nothing interesting.'

'It's a funny time for Tammy to start surfing, mid-October? You'd think that as a beginner she'd have learnt in the summer?' An image of Tammy's face springs to my mind. I wish she was plain, like me. She's not. Her face is similar to Rose's only rounder and her hair is thick and curly. It's so long, almost to her bottom and is the shade of a hazelnut. I'm sure her expertly applied make-up covers a multitude of sins. No one's perfect!

'I guess so. Plus you're limited with the daylight hours this late in the year.'

I nod, deep in thought. I hope he doesn't chat to her about our situation. No, he wouldn't.

'Char?' I look up and realise that Rose has been speaking. I didn't hear a word. 'Luke's party? How did it go? Sorry I couldn't make it.'

'It was fine. Err, lovely. Really easy having it at the soft play zone, rather than at home.'

'No mess ay.'

'Yes,' I say distracted. I take a sip of cranberry juice. 'Bella came with her boys.'

'Oh right.'

'Ian got to meet her, and my mum.'

'Did they like her?'

'I think so. I can't believe Luke's two now.' Was Ian wearing his wetsuit when he got back yesterday?

'Are you okay?'

I look up from my drink. 'I'm fine. Tired, that's all.' I'm being ridiculous.

Rose leaves. I have an uneasy feeling. I shake my

thoughts away, I can't go there. After reading my text from Bella I fire up the computer and log onto the swaying site, searching for recent posts.

Chicklet

I am sorry to say that I have had a miscarriage. It is a very difficult time for me and my husband, so I won't be posting on here again for a while. Thank you for all your support and friendship over this last year. Goodbye. Chicklet x

There are lots of replies from the online buddies. I add my condolences, although I know that she terminated. Bella confirmed my suspicions. I wonder who else online knows? Bex, the girl with five boys has recently found out she's pregnant with her sixth, she could be planning to do the same?

'I'm so tempted to test now,' I say to Ian a few days later.

'Go on then, but try not to be too disappointed.' I jog upstairs to the en-suite bathroom where I keep all my paraphernalia.

'Negative,' I shout down, after the obligatory three minutes pass. I toss the white plastic stick into the wicker bin in my bedroom.

'Never mind, angel,' he says as I slope down the stairs. 'Your phone beeped.'

I have a text from Bella OMG I'M PREGNANT.

'I'm really pleased for her,' I say, 'so jealous though.'

'Our time will come. I'm surprised you got a negative, where we dropped all the crazy stuff, or most of it at least. Maybe you are pregnant? It's too early.'

'I didn't add too many lime drops. But I still took all my supplements and did the douches, maybe it's that?'

'We could just try naturally?' he suggests.

'Perhaps, and still do the douches before and after? Even though we did turkey baster, it was such a relief not getting the incubator out.'

'You could say that!' Ian says heading into the other room.

'Are you surfing later?' I call out.

'Yes.'

I hesitate. 'Is Tammy going?' The question burns my lips.

'I'm not sure.' I follow him to the kitchen. He doesn't look edgy. He meets my eyes as he gulps back his milk. I hope he's not thinking about her. I picture her youthful face, long silky curls and a smug smile.

I pick up my phone, re-read Bella's message and type. CONGRATULATIONS, YOU REALLY DESERVE IT. DID YOU DO SPINNING AND INCUBATING? As I wait for Bella to reply I flick the kettle on. My phone beeps.

I DROPPED THE SPINNING BIT, BUT I DID INCUBATING. I ALSO DROPPED THE DOUCHES. JUST BOOKED MY CVS TEST 1ST DECEMBER NERVOUS ALREADY!

'Bella's booked a CVS test, you know the needle in the stomach one they do at twelve weeks.'

'Where's she going for that?'

'Cambridge.'

'Do you want to do that, when it happens for us?' Ian swipes his too long hair out of his eyes and leans on the grey marble effect kitchen work surface.

'I don't know? Do you?' I study his face. She's too young for him.

'I think maybe we should. It will give you more time to get your head around having another boy, if that's what it is.'

'I agree.' I ponder for a moment. 'I'll get sleepy head up now. Rose is expecting us in an hour, he'll need lunch before we go.'

We eat our scrambled eggs, Luke has toast with his, we have rice crackers, then hurriedly stack the dishwasher and walk out to the car. It only takes ten minutes to arrive at the yard in Porchfield.

'This is my new horse, Apple,' Rose says.

'Apple,' Luke repeats.

'Apple the appaloosa – that's the name of her colour. Do you like her, Lukey?' he nods at Rose.

'She's beautiful,' I say. 'White with black spots, like a Dalmatian dog.' Luke claps his hands. He looks so cute in his Spiderman wellies and matching rain mac.

I sit Luke on Apple, bareback. Rose leads the mare around with a head collar while I hold him in place. Ian squelches in the mud, taking photos.

'He's a natural rider,' Rose says, 'his posture's perfect.'

Ian lifts him off and takes him for a walk around the stables to look at all the other horses.

'Tammy still enjoying surfing?' I question. Tammy's hair won't look so perfect when it's wet and salty. I wonder if she wears all her make-up in the sea. Black mascara running down her face...

'I don't think she's been for a few days. She didn't mention it when I saw her this morning.'

I breathe a sigh of relief.

'Bella's pregnant,' I stroke Apple's nose.

'That's good, what about you? Any news?'

'No, nothing again.'

'Maybe you're too thin. Not healthy enough?' she picks up a comb and runs it through Apple's mane.

'I look dreadful, don't I?'

'Not dreadful,' she says unconvincingly.

'Do you think Ian's having an affair?'

'What? Where did that come from? No. Do you?' she ceases combing.

I sit down on a hay bale. 'I don't know. It must be hard for him, not having sex. And he has been seeing your sister a lot. You don't think...'

'Oh God, Char, is that what you're thinking? No Tammy wouldn't do that. Not to you. She's practically married.'

'Sorry,' I say, feeling stupid. Although I've never thought she was particularly suited to her boyfriend, Max.

Rose doesn't say anything. Awkward. I pull a few strands of hay from the bale and twist them around my fingers. I wish I hadn't said anything...

'I met a girl online, Nicole, she sent me a link to an Australian website. It's a similar diet to the one I'm on but the dates to attempt on are worked out for you. They do an individual plan.' Why am I telling her this? I want to know about Tammy.

'Oh? Are you thinking of doing that instead?'

'It's more of a kit. You have to pay for it.'

'It's probably a con then.'

'Probably,' I concede, pulling a few more strands of hay loose.

'Look. Don't worry about Tammy. I'm sure you're wrong. I'll keep my eyes peeled but I know Ian wouldn't do that. Neither of them would.' She pats my arm. 'When you do get pregnant, will you go to that doctor in Kent for what was it... a nub shot?'

'It's only eighty percent accurate. Ian and I spoke about it, we're going to do the needle in the tummy one in Cambridge. Like Bella.'

'Ouch.' Rose screws up her face.

'I know, scary. And there is a one percent risk of miscarriage.'

'Sounds dangerous. Couldn't you just wait for the twenty week scan?'

'I could, but what if they got it wrong, what if they say girl, like they did to your cousin's friend, Tracey wasn't it?'

'That's right. I remember her going out and buying loads of girly stuff, she even got pink curtains. She found out it was a boy at an emergency scan, two weeks before she was due. She was really upset actually. Turned funny. I've not seen her for years, so I've no idea how she's doing now.' I refrain from asking her to define funny.

'I've still not come on,' I say to Ian two days later.

'Oh?' I'm sure he's feigning interest.

'I'm going to take another test.' He rolls his eyes as I head upstairs. I must be quick, I don't want to be late for work. I squint at the test.

'Ian,' I shout urgently. He slowly walks up the stairs. I wait impatiently. 'Is that two lines?' I try to suppress a smile.

'It is. We're having another baby.' Ian picks me up off my feet and twirls me round laughing. 'We can eat,' he says.

'I can't believe that first response test came up negative.' I pick it out of the wicker bin. 'There is a faint line on it.'

Ian takes the test from me. 'How could you have missed this, Char?'

'I'm sure it wasn't there before? How annoying, we could have had a feast.' I thought he looked at it too? Even if he had, I doubt he looked closely, just trusted me.

'We'll indulge tonight. What do you fancy?'

'I don't know?'

'What do you mean you don't know? I've been thinking about food for half a year. And other things... I'll surprise you, when you get home from work.'

'Work, oh God, I'm going to be late! Don't tell anyone I'm pregnant yet, will you.'

'Of course not.'

'And remember, I can't eat any funny cheese, now that I'm pregnant, or prawns, pate... and some other things, I can't remember.'

'Okay, now get to work.'

I feel so happy. I decide not to take my rice crackers with me. I'll go to the shops in my lunch break. If I'd had more time, I would have had some Marmite on toast for breakfast... Salty Marmite oh how I've missed you...

I kiss the two men in my life and dash out. All worries of Tammy put to the back of my mind.

13

'I'm due July 23rd.'

'That's great news, Char,' my mum hugs me tightly, relieved that I'm no longer starving myself, no doubt.

'When can you find out what you're having?'

'December, when I'm twelve weeks. I've booked a CVS test at the hospital in Cambridge, where Bella's going.'

'Are you going together?' Mum asks as we sit down at the breakfast table.

'No. Bella's due tenth of July, so she's two weeks before me. Are you able to have Luke for the day while Ian and I drive up there?'

'Of course. What time are you leaving?'

'Early, around seven in the morning, and we won't be back until late, around ten. Our appointment isn't until four. With the boat it will probably take three and a half hours each way.'

'That's fine, darling. Don't panic,' she leans across the table and pats my arm. Her hair is clipped back off her face. She smiles, there are small creases under her eyes and laughter lines around her mouth. A hint of mascara, no more, she still looks and acts youthful, we could pass as sisters, almost.

'I'm so scared, Mum, what if it's another boy?'

'I think you're having a girl. And we'll all adore a boy if it is one. Luke will love having a little brother.'

'I bet Bella has a girl.' I feel like a child saying this.

'You don't know that, it could be the other way round, or you may both be lucky, you never know. I had a mix, I expect you will too, whether you'd done all this diet stuff or not.' Memories of Suzy, my dead sister, my mother's first born hang in the air.

'I hope we both get girls.' I say, filling the silence.

'Let's have a nice cup of tea.' My mother walks over to the kitchen and chooses two matching cups, deep in thought.

'I'm off tea, coffee too, typical! I can only keep down water.'

'You weren't as sick as this with Luke, it's definitely a girl.'

A sudden thought occurs to me as I watch my mother filling the kettle. I need to do my completion chant for my girl wish. After the tea – water for me - we get Luke up from his nap and give him a snack.

As soon as my mum leaves, I place Luke in his playpen. I wobble the loose floorboard, until I manage to lift it and take out my chant. I open the instructions and re-read them. 'Praise to the angels and the stars,' I begin. Fiddling with my fairy charm and heart necklace, I feel ridiculous. I continue reading the final verse, then return it to its hiding place. I will need to get it out again once my baby girl is born. I know I'm clutching at straws, and that this is all a load of rubbish, but I've come this far, I may as well complete it.

During my lunch break at work I meet up with Bella.

'Have you told anyone you're pregnant?' I ask while picking at my chips in the Three Crowns.

'I'm not telling anyone, not until I know if I'm keeping it or not.'

'Not even Joe?'

'Oh, he knows, I wasn't going to tell him, but I couldn't help myself, although he thinks I'm keeping it regardless,' she states in a matter of fact tone. 'Only two weeks to go.'

'Scary, it's four weeks until my appointment, well just under. I phoned them the other day, they said the only reason they may not be able to do it is if I have a low lying placenta.'

'They said the same to me. I looked it up, it's not that rare actually,' Bella nibbles at a chip while I stuff mine in, I'll soon be the size of a whale! 'I'm getting really paranoid about it. The nurse on the phone said where I'm coming all the way from the Isle of Wight, it may be an idea to have my NHS scan first, so they can check where the placenta is lying. I agreed, but obviously I can't. I've not got a midwife or anything.'

'You've not told your doctor that you're pregnant?' I ask, stunned.

'No, I can't, can I? If I need an abortion I'll make out that it was an accident. The doctor thinks I'm on the pill, that way I can say that it didn't work, or I must have missed one, and only just realised I was pregnant.'

'Oh, I see.' I dip a chip in some sauce and look around. It's quite busy for a Wednesday. Picking up the Christmas menu, I flick through the pages, unseeing. 'I've started telling people. I've not told my boss yet though. I'm worried what she'll say where Chloe's off. I might tell her this afternoon.' I put the menu back in place and finish my chips. Maybe I shouldn't have told anyone either? It's too late now, the doctor knows and it makes no difference to me anyway. I'm keeping the baby.

Bella leaves most of her chips. The girl diet must have been easier for her. It certainly wasn't for me.

'Remember your proof of blood group,' she says as we leave.

'What? Oh no, what can I use?'

'I'm going to take my donor card.'

'I've never donated blood before. What else could I use?'

'Maybe phone them and join? They give you a card proving what group you are. You'd have to have a finger prick test first to see if you're anaemic.'

'I am anaemic. Plus I'm pregnant. What am I going to do?'

'Don't panic, I'll think about it and text you later.'

'I am panicking, start thinking.'

I stroll back to the surgery feeling dejected. I'm seriously considering cancelling the appointment...

After the last patient of the day has left I mentally calculate when I think Chloe will be back at work. If she takes the full nine months off then she should be back in May. I'm due July, so I'd probably just be leaving as she comes back.

'Could I have a word before we go, Marie?'

'Of course, is everything okay?'

My insides knot together.

'I'm pregnant. I know it's not good timing,' I stammer, 'what with Chloe being off, but I've worked it out, and I think if everything in the pregnancy goes well, Chloe should be back in time.'

'Congratulations,' Marie gives me a hug. 'Don't look so nervous, I thought you'd have another one soon. Chloe's I didn't expect, it was a shock. I'm really pleased for you, and Ian. A little brother or sister for Luke.'

Sister, please let it be a sister.

'When are you due?'

'July 23rd.'

'That's great news, Char, a summer baby.'

We switch the surgery lights off, lock up and walk to our cars, saying goodbye.

I drive home deep in thought. What could I possibly use for my blood group proof? Is there a way of forging it? No that would be too dodgy. I could get in trouble.

'Lukey,' I say, catching him in my arms as soon as I get in the door.

'Mum Mum.'

I lift him up and hug him tightly. I love him so much. Running my hands through his golden curls, I feel guilty that he's not enough. But he is. It's not that I don't want him, I just want a daughter too.

After tea and the bedtime routine, I settle down on the sofa for a cuddle with Ian.

'What's up?' he questions.

'I need proof of my blood group, for Cambridge.'

'Won't they do it without?'

'No. Bella's using her donor card. What shall I use?'

Ian rubs his temple. 'Oh, angel, couldn't they just test you while we're there?'

'But the results aren't instant. Did I hear my phone while I was reading Luke's story?'

'I don't know.'

'It might be Bella.'

Ian sighs as I get up and collect my phone from my handbag, which is hung on the kitchen door.

THEY GAVE ME PROOF AT MY GP'S WHEN I HAD A BOOB OP PRIVATELY. SAY YOU'RE HAVING THAT DONE.

I read the text aloud to Ian. He roars with laughter. 'You wouldn't get breast enlargements done while you're pregnant. Trust Bella to come up with that.'

I stare into space, my ears ringing.

'How embarrassing would it be to say that to Doctor Spencer,' he continues.

'It might just work.'

'What? You're not serious?'

'What other options do I have?' I say exasperated.

'I suppose you have got small boobs,' Ian jokes.

'Thanks.' I fling a cushion at him as I sit back on the sofa. Tammy's got big boobs... no, I'm not going there. Ian's not mentioned her surfing lately. An image of her smirking springs to mind, followed by the one of her beautifully made up face with mascara running down her eyes, hair like rats tails, drenched in sea water. I laugh. Ian cuddles me – obviously thinking I'm laughing about the breast enlargement suggestion. I can't think of an alternative, although Ian is right – no one would have that type of operation while pregnant. I wish I hadn't informed the doctor already!

Thursday, my day off. I pick up the phone, hesitate, then dial the number I now know by heart.

'Hello Medical Centre, can I help you?'

'Hello. I'd like to make an appointment with Doctor Spencer.'

'We have a slot free this afternoon due to a cancellation. Can you make three thirty?'

'Yes that's perfect,' I say looking over at Luke playing with his train set.

'Can I take your name please?'

'Oh yes. It's Charlotte Jackson.' I place the phone back and immediately call Mum.

'Hello, darling.'

'Hi, Mum. Can you look after Luke for half an hour this afternoon, please?'

'Sure. Why?'

'I've got a doctor's appointment.'

'Is the baby okay?' she asks in an urgent tone.

'Yes fine, it's just a routine check,' I lie, feeling ashamed. I don't want to go into specifics with my mum, she'd laugh too, and if I don't do it now I'll talk myself out of it. Lucky they had a space today.

'Okay, darling, I'll come round after lunch, I want to see my chubby little grandson anyway.'

I take Luke to toddler group at my local church hall, all the while my mind is elsewhere. How embarrassing it's going to be saying I'm planning on enlargements. I won't mention that bit, I'll just say I'm paying for a private operation, it could be my nose? But my nose isn't big? My ears? Hopefully she won't ask...

I sing along to the wheels on the bus, speak to the other mothers and make Play-Doh snowmen and glitter cards. I try to concentrate on Luke and my surroundings. God, what am I doing? Why am I doing any of this, I'm keeping the baby regardless, aren't I? I'll wait until I'm twenty weeks. I can't do this. I'm cancelling. Fishing around in my bag for my phone, I flip it open and text Bella, telling her about the appointment and that I'm not going. Why am I texting her? I know she's going to talk me into it, maybe that's what I want?

I was correct, moments later my phone beeps. YOU'LL BE FINE. YOU'LL REGRET IT IF YOU DON'T. She's right, what's a moment of humiliation. I want to know what I'm having at twelve weeks, I can't wait until I'm twenty. I'd go insane.

Sitting in the doctor's waiting room I feel shaky and

stupid. Doctor Spencer has been my GP for as long as I can remember. She says hello to me in the street, what will she think of me after this?

'Charlotte Jackson to room six,' the speakerphone announces. Here goes nothing...

Doctor Spencer gazes at me over her half-moon spectacles. She's wearing a twin set and pearls and has a very old fashioned outlook on life. I knew this was a bad idea.

'How can I help you, Charlotte?'

'I just wondered if I could have proof of my blood group?'

Doctor Spencer narrows her eyes then turns to her computer screen. She clicks the mouse and pauses. Will she give it to me? Heat soars up my chest, scolding my cheeks. She turns her gaze back to me, her deep brown eyes look huge through her glasses. She's got a girl and a boy, a perfect pigeon pair. Just give it to me, I will her.

'Ah, yes, I've found it. You last had a blood test when you were pregnant before. A positive, nice and common.' She smiles.

Silence.

'If I could have a copy?' I stammer. I feel sweaty.

'I'm sure I could do that for you. What's it for?' she questions, her finger hovering over the mouse.

'I was thinking about having a private operation.'

'Oh?'

I look down. Just press print my mind screams.

'May I ask what type of operation?'

'A boob job.' Oh my God, did I just say that? I should

have said breast enlargement.

Doctor Spencer lowers her glasses to the bridge of her nose. 'You're pregnant, are you not?'

'Yes.' Ian was right. I wish the ground would swallow me up. 'But not for yet... um... now, I mean, I'll have it done after I've had the baby.'

'Not too soon after, I hope. I assume you'll be breast feeding.'

'Ah yes, I am going to feed my baby. I'm just being organised, that's all. I'd like to have it ready in case I do it. I might not. It's just-'

The sound of the printer churning stops my rambling. I smile awkwardly and take the printout from her outstretched hand. 'Thank you,' I murmur and hastily retreat.

What an ordeal. I hope persuading the doctor in Cambridge that I'm worried about the possibility of Down Syndrome is easier, and more convincing than that unbelievable charade that just occurred. Breast-feeding. I should have thought about it more thoroughly, but it's done now, and I've got the proof that I wanted.

14

'Thanks for coming with me, Mum.'

'I'm delighted. Such a shame Ian couldn't take the time off work. He's really missing out,' she says from the passenger seat.

I agree while strapping Luke in the back of my car. Once I've buckled myself up, I drive to the hospital for my NHS scan.

Circling around the car park, I eventually give up on finding a space and bump up on the grass verge.

'Perhaps they'll be able to tell you what it is,' Mum says.

I sigh, we've already discussed this. 'They can't, Mum, not here. And I'm only ten weeks, not quite that even.'

'It's the twelve week scan though isn't it?'

'Yes. I managed to get in early. I said I was on holiday next week.'

My mother purses her lips.

'What?' I say, 'I need the scan early so I know where my placenta is lying ready for my CVS test.'

I pick Luke up and carry him through the car park. We enter the maternity wing, pass my notes to the receptionist and sit ourselves down in the bright yellow waiting room.

'I'll take him,' my mother's arms are outstretched to Luke. He rests his head on my shoulder.

'You're all right, Mum.' I cuddle him tightly, kissing his golden locks. 'Mummy's cherub.' He hugs me and I kiss his head again, inhaling the smell of baby shampoo.

'Mrs Jackson.'

Looking up, I smile at the tall nurse. Lifting Luke up with me as I stand, she still towers over us, 'Is it okay if we all come in?'

'It's entirely up to you.'

We follow her into the next room. What if there is a problem and I have Luke with me? I didn't think this through.

Mum takes Luke and sits down while I recline on the chair which is very similar to the dentist's at work, and lift my jumper up.

'I've heated it,' the sonographer says as she squirts the clear jelly on my tummy. Pushing the probe in circular motions, spreading the gloop around, we finally see my baby on the black and white screen.

'Sorry, the sound doesn't work.'

'That's okay.' I squint trying to detect a nub, all I need is a parallel line. No angle. 'Can you tell if the placenta is high or low?'

'Let me just take the measurements then I'll have a look for you.'

After a lot of clicking and typing, the nurse scrolls through the middle of the baby and kind of flips it upside down. I'm completely lost and have no idea what I'm looking at. Nothing seems to resemble the nub shot scans I've viewed online.

'It's positioned on the posterior wall. Nice and high in the uterus.'

I breathe a sigh of relief. 'Look Lukey,' I say pointing to the screen. 'It's the baby in Mummy's tummy.'

'A little brother or sister for you,' my mother says. 'Can you tell what it is?'

I'm secretly overjoyed that my mum has asked the question, even though I know it's not possible.

'It's too early,' she dismisses.

I keep my alert eye on the screen, trying to observe the area of deep interest for me before she removes the probe from my still too skinny tummy, eradicating the view.

I sit in my conservatory with the radiators on full, it's so cold outside. Mum thinks it's going to snow, so long as it's not during my trip to Cambridge, I don't care.

The doorbell rings.

'Bella hi, come on in,' she follows me through the hallway. Her make-up and hair is perfect. I on the other hand, look washed out and rough. 'Would you like a drink, tea, coffee, peppermint tea?'

Bella laughs, 'I'll pass on the peppermint and have a

coffee, please.'

'I gave all my mint teabags to Rose, she seemed to like it. I'm never going to drink it again.' We sit down at the breakfast table.

'Are you okay?' she asks.

'Yes, fine. Just tired. I was up twice in the night being sick. I don't know why they call it morning sickness.'

'You're having a girl. The old wives tale says the sicker you are, the more likely it's female.'

'Have you been sick?'

'No,' she frowns and looks down at her French manicured nails. She wishes she was the one up in the night, vomiting. It's strange what we envy.

'So how did the CVS go on Friday?'

'It was awful. The doctor really grilled me about my reasons, I'm sure he didn't believe my story.'

'Oh no, really?' my heart races, God, I wish mine was over and done with.

'Quite a few of us online have gone for the same thing, and I'm sure we all look like mumbling idiots, that's how I felt anyway.'

'Did it hurt?' I ask, taking a sip of water.

'No, it was just a bit uncomfortable. I had to stay really still while they inserted the needle, but they numbed me up first. I was told to take paracetamol afterwards, but I didn't need it. You'll be fine, Char.'

'I'm worried. There are loads of us, all paying for the same thing, and spouting off the same old reasons. Did you mention Down Syndrome?'

'Yes. I said my sister's kid has it. The doctor said

something about how it's not hereditary, but he still did the test. Probably just wanted his five hundred smackers.'

'Probably,' I agree. 'When do you get the results?'

'In two days, I'm dreading it. They've got my home number, and my mobile. The boys will be at school so I'm just going to sit by the phone all day.'

'Do you fancy going for a drive, when Luke gets up?' What am I doing?

'Sure. Where do you want to go?' Bella looks confused.

I look down at my polka dot tablecloth. I've not told her my suspicions. 'I want to check if Ian's surfing.'

'What?'

I take a deep breath. 'It's probably nothing. It's just, you know. Oh, I don't know,' I run my fingers through my lank hair. I feel like I'm going to spew up.

'What is it, Char? Tell me.' Bella pleads with a concerned expression.

'Since I've stopped swaying, and timing and all that, we can obviously have sex now. Ian's not interested.'

'I'm sure it's nothing to worry about. Look at you.'

'Thanks.'

'No, I didn't mean that, you look fine. But you're you know, a bit pale. It's because of the morning sickness. He probably doesn't like to try it on while you're fragile.'

'I guess so,' I concede, staring over her shoulder at my wedding picture hung on the wall in a silver frame. Ian and I are looking lovingly at each other. It was all a pose, I remember the photographer instructing us. My face was so stiff from smiling all the time.

'Char, what is it?'

Shall I tell her? 'Rose's sister, Tammy. She's sniffing around.' The words tumble out before I know if I really want to admit my paranoia.

'What?' Bella exclaims.

'She's started surfing lessons. They meet up at the beach. It's Ian's day off work today. I just wondered if her car's at Compton Bay too.'

'Do you really think Ian would cheat on you? Especially now that you're pregnant?'

'No. I don't know. I hope not, I just have this nagging feeling that I can't shake off.'

Bella stands up. 'Come on. Let's get Luke up, I'll drive. He won't recognise my car.' A red BMW convertible. Not too conspicuous.

After transferring the baby seat into the not-so-spacious soft-top shoebox, I wait impatiently for Luke to awake.

'Can't you just wake him?'

'I would, but he's got another half an hour or so left.'

'Stuff the routine,' Bella barges into the nursery while I follow in pursuit. Too late, he's stirring.

'Ssh,' I gently open the curtains, 'let him wake naturally,' I whisper.

Bella folds her arms. I can't believe she did this.

'Hello, Lukey,' I say in a quiet voice. He stretches his body and rubs his eyes. I lift him out of his cot, un-popper his sleeping bag and change his nappy. I give him his beaker of water, while zipping up his winter coat and placing his woolly hat on his head. Bella stands there, it looks like she's on a mission. Maybe I should have kept my mouth shut, what have I got myself into...

When we're on the road, heading to the back of the Island, I unwind the electric window and heave.

'My car,' Bella yelps.

'Sorry,' I rummage in my bag and find a baby wipe. Bella looks really pissed off. She did offer to drive...

'I hope it doesn't take the paint off.'

I ignore her comment. 'If we see Ian, I just want to say that we came out for a walk, that's all. Oh but we didn't bring the pram, shit.' I put my hand to my mouth and look back at Luke. He didn't repeat it, thank God.

'There's no way it would have fitted in my tiny boot anyway.'

'I hate this!'

'What?' Bella glances at me, then looks back at the road ahead.

'I don't like what I'm turning into. I never used to be jealous. Let's turn around. I don't want to do this.'

'We're here now.' Bella turns into the Bay car park. My heart races. 'Is that his van?' she points.

'Yes,' I feel like I might be sick again at the sight of his silver Ford Transit with the surfboard decal on the blackened window. 'Park over there,' I point to the far corner, 'this was a bad idea with Luke with us.'

'Can you see what's-her-face's car?'

I scan the car park for her light blue Ford KA. 'She's not here.'

'Are you sure?'

I nod, relief floods through me. I feel stupid and irrational.

'I'll just drive round a bit.' We slowly crawl through the maze of vehicles. A few surfers wander around, looking frozen to the core. I look about, praying that Ian is in the sea. I really don't want to bump into him. Once we have satisfied ourselves that Tammy's car's not there, we drive home.

'Thanks for that. I feel much better.' I look back at Luke. He's fallen asleep, I knew he hadn't had enough nap.

'Anytime.'

'I'm so paranoid. It was nothing after all. I trust him, I do.'

'It's probably just the hormones.'

'Yes,' I agree. I feel as if a weight has been lifted. And I no longer feel sick.

'If I hear boy, on Tuesday, I'll phone my doctor up and schedule an abortion. I've looked it up already. It has to be done in Bournemouth and I have to go twice.' Bella suddenly announces.

'Twice?' Oh no, not this again. She's been so nice to me, I'll keep my thoughts on this to myself. Things like this are easy to say. She won't follow it through.

'Once for a consultation, then they send you home so you've got a chance to change your mind, then you come in again the next day.'

We stop at a mini roundabout and wait our turn. I don't know what to say. 'I'm sure it's a girl. You won't have to do any of that. It's a girl. I know it.'

'I wish I was as sure as you. I've already phoned the abortion clinic up in readiness. So long as my doctor faxes them straight away, they can fit me in on the Thursday and Friday.'

'It won't come to that. You did such a good sway, unlike me. I wish I persevered with the incubating, like you did.'

'But I'd dropped the lime, at least you still did that. Your pH will have been on target.'

We dissect our attempts at length during the rest of the car journey. She won't terminate. I know Bella, she wouldn't actually go through with it.

That evening, after reading Luke his story, I sit on the floor in his nursery, hugging my knees to my chest and silently cry to the rhythm of his gentle breathing. The events of the day have taken their toll on my emotions. Guilt over my feelings for a daughter combined with relief that Ian wasn't with Tammy reverberate through me.

Tuesday is here. Ian is at work, and Luke is quietly playing. I find myself pacing around, anxiously waiting for news from Bella.

It'll be a girl. Shall I text her? No I'll wait, I don't want to disturb her when she's finding out her results. I spray some polish on my mantelpiece and wipe it over with my yellow duster. Loud ringing makes me jump, my heart is in my mouth as the anticipated telephone call startles me. Which way will it go? I drop the cloth on the floor and dash to the phone in the hallway.

'Bella,' I answer.

15

'I'm having an abortion.'

'Oh my God. When?'

'Thursday.'

'It's definitely a boy, they're sure?'

'One hundred percent!'

'Won't you regret it?'

'Char, I can't have another boy. It's not what I want. I want a girl.'

'I'm worried for you.'

'Thanks. But don't be. Once I've got rid of this baby, I'll be fine. Can we meet up? I really need to talk to you.'

'Ian's back in a bit, it's his early finish today. We can't talk in front of him. I could come to yours?' I've never been inside Bella's house before, she always comes to me. I'm intrigued to see what her home is like.

'Um... can we meet at the coffee house?'

'Okay. I'll leave now so I don't have to explain to Ian.

I'll be about half an hour, Luke will nod off in his buggy.'

'Fine. See you then.'

As I put the phone down I feel numb. I can't believe she's actually going to go through with this. And why can't I go to her house?

Just popped out, back soon. I hastily scribble, and leave the note by the kettle.

Bella is already there, waiting for me. She smiles through the glass door as I try and manoeuvre Luke's buggy in without waking him.

'I got you a latte.'

'Thanks,' I say wrapping my hands around the cup. 'Hopefully it will warm me up. It's started snowing out there.'

'Will you come with me?' Bella asks.

'Oh.' I look down at my milky coffee, stalling.

'That's a no then?'

'Won't Joe come?'

'He doesn't know. You know that.'

'I'm not sure I can book time off work, that's all.'

'Can't you pull a sicky? It's really important. I can't drive myself, I'm having a general. No one else knows, only you.'

I fiddle with the button on my jumper. I can't meet her eye. I don't want to do this. 'Yes, fine. I'll drive you.'

'I know you don't agree with what I'm doing, but it's my choice.'

'I just wish you'd tell Joe. He has a right to know.'

The noise of Bella's chair startles me as she gets up. 'You know why I'm not telling him. Don't start on me,

Char, I can't take it at the moment.'

'Sorry,' I look up at her crumpled face. 'Sit down. Please. What time do you need picking up?'

'Seven in the morning. We should be home by teatime. The same on Friday, but we'll be home a bit later then.'

I try to avoid the stares and glances from the other customers.

'Let's hope the snow stops.'

Walking home up the white frosty hill, I look down at Luke's face through his weather shield. Sound asleep. Completely unaware of what's going on in the world around him. Lucky thing. Could I do what Bella's doing? I'd like to think not. But she does have two boys, it's only natural to want a girl. 'It's not like Adam and Si don't already have a brother.' Bella had said, 'they have each other.' That was her way of rationalising it. So now I have to take time off work. What am I going to say to Ian?

'You all right?' Ian asks while I'm stood at the kitchen counter chopping up the vegetables for our tea.

'Yes, I'm fine.' I lie. I'm not fine, I'm trying to choose the right moment to tell Ian my plan. Each time I decide to say something, I stop myself. I'm going to burst.

Evening comes, it's now or never. I can't put it off any longer.

'You're driving where?'

'Ssh, Ian, you'll wake Luke up.'

'Shopping? I thought you'd finished getting all the Christmas presents?'

'I've not got Mum's yet, nor yours.'

'I don't understand why you have to drive on the mainland? It's snowing and you're both pregnant for Christ's sake, go shopping in town instead. It will be safer.'

'We'll be fine.'

Ian shakes his head and mutters something under his breath.

'Oh and the next day, Marie has asked me to come into work early. We have a root canal treatment booked in that needs doing before Christmas.'

'I'm off that day, so that's fine, I'll be here for Luke.'

I smile at him, he doesn't return the gesture so I head up to bed alone, feeling paranoid and miserable.

The next day Ian leaves for work, barely uttering a word to me. Does he suspect something?

I text Bella - MAYBE YOU SHOULD RING THE CLINIC AND ASK IF THEY WILL DEFINITELY BE THERE IF IT'S STILL SNOWING THURSDAY?

It looks like it may settle. What if it's snowing when Ian and I need to drive to Cambridge?

My alarm clock rings. I quickly switch it off. Ian stirs as I sneak around the room, picking up my clothes I laid out in preparation. I tiptoe down the stairs and pop some bread in the toaster. I force my breakfast down, retching in between, then grab the car keys on the way out, careful not to wake Luke.

'You can't drive in this,' Ian emerges from the stairs in his blue chequered pyjamas. 'It's dangerous, you're putting our unborn baby in jeopardy for a shopping trip.

I can't believe you sometimes.'

'I'll drive really slowly and I'll stick to the main roads.'

'Main roads,' Ian whispers through clenched teeth. 'You're driving through the bloody New Forest, there are no main roads!'

'Of course there are,' I say unconvincingly. 'I've programmed the sat-nav to lorry routes, we'll be fine.'

'Do what you want,' Ian splutters, not even looking at me, or saying goodbye as I leave. Feeling torn, I slowly make my way to Bella's house. She's outside sat on her garden wall, waiting.

'Hi' I say as she clambers in.

'Thanks, Char, for taking me.' I smile, I don't want to let on to her how much grief this expedition is causing me.

Driving as steadily as I can, I decide to avoid Porchfield on my way to Yarmouth, they never bother gritting the roads out that way. Rose is always complaining about it.

Bella hardly says a word as we sit on the Wightlink ferry. I get my book out and flick through the pages trying to block out my own turmoil.

The loudspeaker tells us to return to our cars, we follow the herd of commuters down the metal stairs back to our vehicles and I drive slowly and carefully off the ferry. The sat-nav takes us left and we follow the traffic. Everyone is driving slower than usual due to the remaining ice, thankfully. I don't like driving on the mainland, especially when I don't know where I'm going.

'Jesus,' I say as we go over yet another cattle grid. 'This

is set for trucks, it seems to be taking us all over the show.' Bella doesn't answer, I wonder if she's changing her mind?

We finally find the clinic and park in the adjoining car park. It looks like a large Victorian house from the outside. We open the front door and find ourselves in a clean reception area. Bella speaks to the lady at the desk while I hang back to give her a bit of privacy. She emerges with lots of forms to fill in and we are ushered into the waiting room. While she fills in the questionnaire, I have a good peer around. There are ladies of all ages here. One of them only looks about twelve, whereas the majority are probably mid to late thirties. One in particular catches my eye. Long dark eyelashes, possibly false, thick lip gloss and totally caked in foundation. I would guess her age at around twenty. She doesn't seem worried or nervous at all, you'd think she was waiting for a hair appointment or maybe getting her nails manicured, perhaps she's done this before? Another girl who also looks about twenty is so obviously pregnant. Her stomach is huge. Her straight blonde hair is ironed within an inch of its life, but she's very smart in appearance, wearing a suit you'd see an estate agent or solicitor wear to work, apart from it's the maternity variety. I wonder how far gone she is? I overhear her talking to the make-up girl.

'My boss is expecting me back at work in two hours, I hope this doesn't take too long,' she says. Work, how can she be thinking about work? I suppose it is just the consultation, but still.

After an hour and a half Bella is finally called.

'Can you come with me, please,' she asks.

'I'm sorry it's partners only,' the nurse replies.

'Charlotte is my partner,' she lies. I climb the stairs behind Bella up to the next waiting room, feeling self-conscious.

'This is as far as partners are allowed,' the nurse says in my direction. I blush and nod in agreement. I didn't want to come this far to start with! Another hour or so goes by then finally Bella is called. I can't concentrate on my book so I spend the next hour sifting through crappy magazines full of drivel about which reality TV celebrities are having affairs. I stare at the words, but none of them process in my brain.

The door opens. It's Bella. She looks normal. What did I expect? Tears maybe?

'You okay?'

She nods.

We walk back downstairs and out to the car. 'How did it go?'

'Fine,' she says. 'They just asked my reasons, I said I was on the pill and it didn't work. They did a finger prick test, for my blood group, I guess, and that was it.'

'They didn't try to talk you out of it?'

'No, she just asked if I was sure, and I said yes, that was it.'

'Oh.' I concentrate on driving. The journey home seems shorter than coming here. We don't even have to wait for the boat.

'Thank you,' Bella says as I pull up outside her house.

'See you tomorrow,' I say as she closes the passenger door. I drive back home feeling tired and weary. A fluttering of snow sprinkles on my windscreen. Great.

Opening the gate to my front garden, I pray that Ian's not moody with me.

'Luke's already in bed,' he says as soon as I get in the door. 'Your mum said he didn't have his nap so he's completely zonked out.'

I enter his room and watch him softly sleeping in his cot. My little cherub with his blonde angelic curls.

'Where's your bags?' Ian whispers.

'What?'

'I thought you went shopping?'

'Oh yes, Bella took all the bags out of the boot by mistake, so she's got all my stuff too.' My heart accelerates.

Ian frowns as I quietly leave Luke's nursery. He closes the door and follows me through the hallway. 'Buy much then?'

'Yes, a bit.'

'What did you get?'

'I don't want to ruin the surprise. It's for you.'

'Bournemouth, is that where you went?'

'No, Lymington. It was very Christmassy.' I take a deep breath. Please stop questioning me, I don't know how much longer I can keep up the lying. What am I doing? 'Um, remember I'm leaving for work early in the morning. And I'll be back late too.'

'Late? Why's that?'

'I've just got a couple more presents to get. It's late

night shopping in Newport, I thought I'd pop into town after work. That's okay isn't it?'

'You won't have seen Lukey awake for two days!'

My heart flips. 'I know, I'll make it up to him, I just want to get everything sorted.' Will I get away with this, what if Marie phones? I can't get caught out.

It's so dark first thing in the morning. Donned with my woolly hat and scarf, I leave the house, yet again before I should even be awake. Breathing out white mist into the cold air, I walk as steadily as I can across the frozen pavement to my car. I start up the engine and leave it running while I de-ice the windows. Eventually, when it's safe and I actually have some vision, I slowly make my way to Bella's house. She's waiting outside in the cold for me again.

'Hi, Char,' she says quite brightly considering what the plan is. 'I checked the forecast, no snow today.'

'That's good. So you're okay then, all set?' I say as tactfully as I can.

'Yes, I've got my dressing gown, nightie and slippers, plus a book this time. What are you wearing?' she looks down at my white tunic which is poking out the bottom of my winter coat.

I lift my foot from the pedal and wiggle my white dental nursing shoe to and fro, 'I told Ian I was starting work early. I had to wear it in case he woke up again, plus I'll need it on when I get home.'

'I'm sorry, Char.'

'That's okay. What does Joe think you're doing today,

and yesterday, I forgot to ask?'

'He thinks we're both off to a spa day again, to cheer me up.'

'Does he know it's a boy then?'

'He thinks they lost the results. He tried to phone them and complain, but I persuaded him not to. I need to put five hundred pounds back in his account.'

'Oh?'

'To reimburse us for their cock up. He said they should compensate us too. Maybe I should give him six hundred? I've applied for a new credit card online, it's been approved. I'll transfer the money tonight.'

'Oh God, then what?'

'I miscarry in a week.'

I don't say anything. What can I say? I feel sorry for Joe, not that I've ever met him.

As we board the boat at Yarmouth I finally begin to warm up.

'I'm forever weeing, I think the baby is sitting on my bladder.' I instantly regret saying it.

'It's okay, Char, I know I'm not keeping mine, but I can handle talking about yours, please don't worry about what you say, I'm fine, really I am.'

'God, I need to phone Marie.' I dial the surgery number. Thankfully it goes to answering machine. I leave a message saying I have got diarrhoea and won't be in today and I'm very sorry. Why did I just apologise? I'm supposed to be sick, you can't help that after all.

The drive through the New Forest is more hair-raising than yesterday due to the black ice. We skid and slide our way to the clinic and check in. I need a cup of tea to help steady my nerves, but of course there are no tea or coffee making facilities here seeing as the patients can't eat before a general anaesthetic. I have to settle for water, just when I've started drinking hot drinks again. I have brought food supplies, as I'm sure it's going to be another long day.

Bella sits next to me in silence. She fiddles constantly with her fingernails. I feel strange sitting in my work clothes, I look like a member of staff, I wish I'd thought to bring some different shoes with me, and a change of outfit. I notice the girl I saw yesterday, the one with the thick foundation, she hasn't any make-up on now and she's crying, perhaps she's changed her mind? She takes a seat next to me wearing her dressing gown and slippers. I feel I need to say something, but what?

'Are you okay?' what a stupid thing to say.

'No, I'm not.' Well that told me.

She rubs her eyes and blows her nose. 'They won't fucking do it,' she sobs.

I wince at her coarse words, 'what do you mean?'

'The abortion. I only fucking coughed once, now they won't put me under. I've got to come back when my cough is gone. I haven't even got a fucking cough, I was just clearing my fucking throat.'

Bella makes eye contact with me then resumes picking her nails.

'Didn't they listen to your chest?'

'Yes, but still wouldn't do it, just to be safe and all that fucking bull.' She gets up and starts ranting at the receptionist. I wish I hadn't said anything. I can see some movement in my peripheral vision, but I'm trying not to stare at what's going on with the make-up-less girl. I hear the receptionist telling her she needs to get dressed and leave, her appointment has been re-scheduled for next week. Bella appears tense. After that drama has finished I try and pick up my book, but my mind is whirling about my appointment in Cambridge next week. What if I hear boy? Could this be me in a couple of week's time? No. I'll be fine with another boy won't I? I couldn't destroy Luke's brother. Destroy. What a terrible thought. I still want to have the test, just to find out what I'm having. Fortunately Ian is on board with that. Ian, all the lying and deceit. I just want to get these two days out of the way, then I can go back to concentrating on my family.

'Isabella Thorne,' a nurse calls. Bella gets up with her bag full of nightwear and gives me a weak smile. She looks like she's going to cry.

'I'll wait here. Don't be scared to change your mind, if you want to.'

Bella looks away and heads for the stairs with the nurse.

16

Hours later, and I'm starving. Sneakily rummaging around in my handbag I locate my chocolate bar and open it, trying not to be too obvious. Just as I transfer a beautifully flavoursome piece to my mouth, I notice Bella, struggling down the stairs holding the arm of a plump, red haired, nurse.

'Bella.' I walk over to them, wiping my mouth.

'She's been sick a couple of times after coming round from the anaesthetic,' the nurse says to me, 'but she's fine now. She's had something to eat, but is a little unsteady on her feet. She needs plenty of rest and is not to drive or operate machinery for forty-eight hours. Any problems just call us, all the numbers are in this pack,' she hands me a white plastic folder.

'Thank you.' I tuck it into my handbag, then pick up Bella's heavy rucksack from the floor. We link arms, and I lead her out to the clinic car park.

'Do you feel sick?' I ask as I help her into the car.

'No. I'm fine, I just feel a bit dizzy that's all.' I open the windows, even though it's cold, I don't really want to be cleaning out vomit from my car, Ian would notice the smell, and it would turn my already sensitive stomach too!

I programme the sat-nav and head left. We are directed through the narrow forest roads again. After three cattle grids, I look over at Bella, her head is rested against the window, her eyes shut. I hope she's okay?

'Shit. A horse,' I yell as I swerve to avoid a New Forest pony. I press down on the brake pedal in a panic and slide out of control. The pony trots away up the snow covered grass verge.

A car is coming towards me. I turn my steering wheel and it locks. I have no movement. As if in slow motion, I career into the side of the black ford fiesta and finally halt with a bang. My bonnet flies up, making the car jolt and there is a funny ticking sound.

Bella is crying. I wish she'd be quiet. I can't think! Putting my hand to my belly I give it a rub. We're okay. But I've crashed the car on the mainland. I'm going to get caught.

Gingerly opening the car door, I step out into the cold air. 'I'm sorry,' I say to the elderly man through his window as he struggles to unwind it.

'Just what I need before Christmas,' he says. He looks angry, I feel my stomach turn as his small pig-like eyes narrow and the grey wrinkles on his face tighten. Carefully walking over the icy road in my dental nursing clogs, I look at my car. Using both hands, I tug the bonnet down and it clips shut. It is dented in the corner and the headlight is smashed. His car is a wreck! The door is caved in and the wing mirror is lying in the road. I pick it up and hand it to him through his window. He gives me a stern look but says nothing.

'I'll just get a pen and paper, write down my details for you,' I rummage around in my handbag and tear out a blank page from the back of my diary. With shaky hands I write my name, address, telephone and registration number. I rip the page in half and write his number plate down and hand him the two pieces of paper and the pen. 'I'm sorry, I can't remember who I'm insured with, I'll phone them and lodge the claim when I get home.'

'It was your fault,' he barks, handing me his almost illegible information.

'Yes, I'm sorry, it was an accident. I skidded.'

'I'll be telling them you admitted it,' he starts up his engine and slowly drives off. No goodbye. Charming.

I glance at my poor old car. How am I going to explain this to Ian?

'I'll pay your excess, it's all my fault,' Bella says, then puts her hands to her mouth. She quickly opens her door and throws up.

'Hopefully it'll start,' I say once she's composed herself. I turn the key and the engine chugs. Pumping my foot on the gas it fires up. I slowly move forward, taking extra care to look out for horses.

The rest of the journey is fine, but I can't stop my hands from shaking. A tear is threatening to fall, I wipe my eyes with the sleeve of my coat. Bella's head is rested back on the window. Good. I don't want her to see me upset. Thank God it wasn't worse. She's had surgery and I crashed the bloody car! Ian was right, I shouldn't be driving in the ice. What if I'd lost the baby? We could both be in hospital now, and on the mainland too. How would I have explained that? In my work clothes, boss thinks I'm ill, husband thinks I'm at work. What's happening to me?

When we're back on the car ferry, Bella perks up a bit.

'Do you feel sore?'

'No, they've given me painkillers though, and anti-inflammatory. I'm also on antibiotics.'

'Was it really dreadful?' I ask as gently as I can, staring out of the window at the choppy sea.

'It was like a conveyor belt. We all had to go in one room, get undressed and into our nighties. We could keep our socks on though. They had little cubicles with curtains to get undressed in. Then we all had to lie on a bed each, and got wheeled into the other room, one at a time. It was like a factory production.'

'How strange.' Seagulls swoop and dive outside. I watch one skim the water. It must be cold.

'Then they gave me a general. That was the worst bit, I think I was quite tensed up, so it hurt having the needle go in.'

'I hate needles!' I say, fiddling with the hem of my tunic.

'And the other bad bit was being pushed through corridors on the bed, I've never had that done to me before. It was like a scene from Casualty. Next thing I knew I was being woken up in a different room. The other girls were there too. I guess we all got wheeled in, in a line.'

'The nurse said you were sick?' She doesn't seem too bad now. And not regretful in the slightest. That may come later?

'Yes a couple of times, they made me eat some toast and get dressed, then brought me down.'

'So it wasn't too bad then?'

'No. It's just all the waiting around, going to another room, only to wait further.' I don't know what to say to that, so I look out the window again. How am I going to explain to Ian about the car? And Marie, I hope she hasn't phoned home to ask how I am! Lying to my boss. Lying to Ian. I'm such a dreadful person!

'Thank you, Char, for taking me over, twice, and sticking around, it was a lot of waiting about for you too. And I'm so sorry about your car.'

'That's okay.'

I drop Bella home and walk into a quiet house. Where is everyone? My heart pounds, oh my God. My answering machine is flashing. I press play and listen to Ian's message saying he's bathed Luke at his mums and he's asleep in his pram. His brothers are there, so he will be home late. Relief. Good, now I've got some time. I search for my file I keep in the kitchen drawer with all my insurances and car paperwork in. Sifting through it I find the schedule. I want to get this out the way before Ian returns. I phone the twenty-four hour claim-line and give over all the information. Pacing around the room, apprehensively looking through the front room window to see if Ian's on his way back. He must have walked. Of course he did, his van hasn't got a baby seat, I didn't think to take it out of the car. The car. I wish I'd been firm to Bella and said no. Now look what's happened. If Ian finds out where I was he'll go mad!

After being on hold for a good twenty minutes, I breathe a sigh of relief when I'm finally off the phone. One hundred and fifty pounds excess, I wonder if Bella will actually pay it. She has to return all that money to her husband's account though. I won't ask her, see if she offers again. Maybe we could go halves? Great, I guess I'll lose my no claims bonus too.

Busying myself in the kitchen un-stacking the dishwasher, I hear the front door burst open. Ian comes rushing over to me.

'Oh my God, what happened? Are you and the baby okay? I've just seen the car!'

'Yes, I'm fine, baby's fine too. Where's Luke?'

'Asleep in his buggy, I pushed him into the spare room. What happened?'

'I skidded in the ice avoiding a cat.'

'You're okay though. Not hurt at all?' I burst into tears. 'Oh angel,' Ian hugs me. I hold on to his chest and sob. He kisses my head. 'Don't worry about the car, it's not important. I'll phone the insurance company in the morning.'

'I've already done it. It was my fault. I hit someone.'

'What?' Ian draws back, concerned.

'In the car. He's okay.'

'Where?'

'His door mainly.'

'No. Where were you? Newport?'

I hesitate, 'Yes.' Ian looks at me. I bury my head in his chest again, tension heavy on my shoulder blades. Please don't let me mess this up. I hate lying.

'Where? In the High Street?'

'Yes. No. Just on the Newport road.'

Ian steps back, scrutinising. 'Did you skid across and hit him?'

'No. I don't know. It was narrow.'

'Narrow?'

'Why are you questioning me?' Oh my God, please stop.

'I'm just trying to figure out if it was his fault. Did you admit it?'

'Yes.'

'Oh, Char, you should never admit liability.'

'It was my fault. Please can you just drop it! I feel tired and queasy.'

'Okay, you go upstairs and lie down, I'll bring us up a cuppa after I've transferred Luke to his bed.'

'Thanks.' I turn and head up to our bedroom, 'Oh, Ian,' I call out, 'we'll have to take your van to Cambridge next week.'

'It's not a four-wheel drive. It'll be even worse in the ice than the car!'

'Oh no. We have to go!' My heart races, I can't miss this appointment, it has to be done at twelve weeks.

'Don't panic, angel, the snow and ice will be gone by then.'

I hope he's right...

17

'They're on.' Ian sounds impressed with himself.

'You did read the instructions?' I look at the snow chains on his van.

'Yes, yes. We'll be all ready and set to go to Cambridge tomorrow.'

'What if the doctor doesn't get to work though?'

'You phoned them, didn't you? He was working yesterday?'

'It's a different doctor each day, our doctor may not have a four-wheel drive, or may live further away.'

'Stop panicking, Char. I'm just going to take it for a test drive.'

'Okay. I'll be back in an hour or so. Drive carefully.' Ian gives me a peck on the cheek and rubs Luke's head. Grinning as he drives off, no one else is on the road, only the odd Range Rover.

Luke and I wave to Ian and slowly trudge our way to

Bella's house. She's not returned any of my calls or texts since the abortion.

The sun is shining and it hasn't snowed for a couple of days. Please thaw out. Luke walks slowly and cautiously, laughing at the sound the grey sludge makes with each footstep.

Her curtains are drawn. I hesitantly ring the bell. After a minute or so I ring it again and tap the door. No answer. Peering through the gap in the curtains, I see movement. I knock hard with my knuckles.

'Come on Lukey, let's walk back.' He protests with a cry as we turn to leave. His nose is red. This was a bad idea.

'Char, what do you want?'

I rotate to see a small section of Bella's face through the crack in the door. 'Can we come in?'

'I'm not very well.'

'Just for five minutes.'

She sighs. I hear her undoing the safety latch. The double glazed door opens to reveal a drawn, greasy haired, make-up-less shadow.

'Ignore the mess, the cleaner isn't coming until tomorrow,' she says as we follow her through the hallway and into the huge open-plan kitchen. She has a cleaner? I can see a lot of money has been spent here. She has one of those Aga-type range cookers with a large extractor fan above. Modern lime green bar stools surround an island of cream cupboards and all the latest stainless steel appliances and a coffee maker are arranged around the copious wooden work surfaces. But the room is a tip.

Plates and pans with dried on food stuck to them are piled up in the large butler sink, a basket of dirty laundry next to the washing machine. Cups, plates and general litter strewn all about the place. This is too much for a cleaner. She needs a team of people to tackle this!

'How are you feeling?' I lift Luke onto a stool and take off his hat.

'You can't stop. Joe will be home in a bit.'

'Oh.' I re-fasten Luke's coat.

'Sorry, I would offer you a drink but it's just a bit awkward at the moment.'

'Are you having some regrets?'

'No. Not at all,' Bella glances at her tatty nails. They look as if they've been painfully bitten down to the quick. 'He found out.'

'What. Joe? How?'

'He's been checking my phone. I thought he was going to hit me.' A tear runs down Bella's pale cheek. I rub her back. 'He went mad,' she continues and wipes the tear with the palm of her hand. 'I don't know how I'm going to get through this.'

'Oh God, Bella.'

'You'd better go. He knows you took me.'

My heart jumps into my throat. 'What did you tell him?'

'Shit. I can hear his car. Go out the back door.' I lift Luke from the stool and Bella ushers us out.

'I forgot Luke's hat.'

'No time.' She shuts the door in my face. I stand there, stunned. Bella's voice is loud. She's shouting and swearing. I can't hear her husband though, and I'm not going to stick around to listen either. I pull Luke's hood up and fasten the Velcro around his neck. Carrying him, I walk as quietly as I can along her gravel side path. I look back just as a dark haired man is pulling open the lounge curtains. We lock eyes for a moment, then he is gone. I hope Bella is going to be all right with him. If Luke wasn't with me I'd go back.

I can't stop thinking about his face during the cold walk home. He didn't look angry and it was Bella yelling, not him. If she was scared surely she wouldn't be aggressively hollering like a mad woman?

As we board the boat in East Cowes, I feel butterflies in my tummy. What am I going to achieve by doing this? I've decided I'm keeping the baby regardless, haven't I?

We drive off the boat and turn left.

'What's that noise?' I ask.

'I'll pull over.' People honk their horns and make hand gestures as we bump up the kerb. My palms are sweating. Ian gets out of the van. Do I need to get out too and look helpful? I suppose I'd better show willing. Just as I'm unbuckling my seatbelt he opens the door.

'They bloody snapped,' he says holding up a metal snow chain.

'Oh no.'

'I did have to force one of them, the one that broke actually, but it just wouldn't go on.' Ian always rushes things, and refuses to read instructions.

'We'll just have to drive carefully, it's not supposed to

be too bad. No one else uses them, we'll get there.' I say, deflated. Ian passes me the chain and heads out to take the other one off. I sigh and chuck it down by my feet.

'Reverse the van back.'

'What?' I call out.

'Just a couple of inches.'

I reach over and take the hand-brake off. Cars whizz past us. I can't believe this is happening.

'That'll do.'

I pull the hand-brake up and take a deep breath. Ian rattles around then finally opens the door and hands me the other chain.

The rest of the journey goes smoothly, but I feel tense.

'It looks like we can park here for two hours,' he says pointing at the sign. I nod while not really looking. 'Let's get something to eat.'

Everything in Cambridge seems expensive. Ian spots a Burger King. I follow him in and take a seat while he orders. I feel sick.

'You look nervous, angel,' he says between bites.

'I don't think I can eat all of this.' Ian helps himself to my chips. I watch the other customers, chatting and laughing to each other. Flipping open my phone I notice I have a text from Bella.

GOOD LUCK TODAY. SORRY ABOUT YESTERDAY. EVERYTHING IS FINE BETWEEN ME AND JOE NOW SO NOTHING TO WORRY ABOUT. TEXT YOU LATER X.

Feeling relieved I return my phone to my handbag and notice Ian is watching me.

'It was just Bella, wishing me good luck.' He finishes both of our meals and we head out back to the van.

'We've been less than two hours,' Ian says, gingerly jogging up to the traffic warden, on the sludgy snow covered pavement.

'It's two hours no return,' the stern looking woman states. 'You still have to pay to park.' Oh no, I wish I'd read the sign myself, trust Ian...

'Seeing as you're here now, I'll let you off this once.'

'Thank you,' Ian says.

I smile at her. 'I can't believe you did that,' I whisper.

'What?'

I decide to keep my mouth shut, I'm stressed enough as it is. We re-programme the sat-nav and follow the directions to the hospital.

Parking the van in the hospital car park and paying the fee, we walk into the building following the signposts to the maternity ward.

After waiting for what seems like forever we are finally called into the private sector department.

'Sandra will be in to call you through shortly,' the young girl behind the desk says. After signing all the forms I take a seat with Ian to wait again, then I get up and help myself to water from the drinks machine, I need to have a full bladder.

'You okay?'

I nod as I pass him a paper cone of water. 'It will be a rush back, the last boat home is at eleven. If we get away by six we will hopefully just about make it, if we're lucky. But if we're held up and we miss the last boat, the next one's not until four in the morning, it's too cold to sleep in the van, I don't know what we'll do,' I say.

'Why did you book such a late appointment? We could have left earlier rather than hanging around.' Ian replies a little too hoity for my liking.

'This is the first appointment, the private patients are out of hours.'

'Oh, well we'd better make sure we leave by six then.'

At half past five - half an hour later than our appointment time, we are called in by a grey haired, deeply creased, Sandra.

'This is Anya, the doctor who will perform the chorionic villus sampling.' We both shake Anya's hand. She's a kind looking lady of around forty years old with dark hair tied back in a ponytail. She speaks with a foreign accent, German, I think.

'The test involves taking a sample of the developing placenta that contains the chorionic tissue. Before I perform the test, I will carry out an ultrasound scan to check your dates and the position of both the baby and the placenta,' Anya continues. 'I will give you a local anaesthetic injection to numb the area. I will then pass a fine needle through the wall of the womb. Ultrasound is used to help me to guide it into the right place.'

I nod, having read all of this online, I already know the procedure inside out. Ian however has a frown etched upon his face, which deepens when she mentions the risk of miscarriage. He shoots a look of horror at me. I glance down at my feet.

'A small piece of the tissue, which is only about the

size of a few grains of rice is removed through the needle and sent to the laboratory for testing. Now do you have your blood group with you?' I nod at Anya and extract the paperwork, which had caused me much embarrassment, from my handbag. Sandra takes the proof, checks it over and ticks a box. Pretending I wanted a boob job to my GP had worked, she had given me the printout that Sandra seems happy with, it's all going to plan.

'Why is it that you want to have this invasive test carried out?' she asks. I am momentarily taken aback as her eyes bore into mine.

'My brother has a Down Syndrome baby,' I stammer. 'It's just for peace of mind really.' I'm sure I see both Anya and Sandra making eye contact, maybe I'm paranoid?

'If you could lie on the bed, I'll do the ultrasound and check your dates,' Anya says. I do as she asks and pull my T-shirt up, lowering my jeans in readiness.

'Gosh you're very slight,' she observes.

I guess I am still thin, my normal jeans are loose even though I'm twelve weeks gone. As the warmed up gel is applied to my tummy and pushed around with the probe I try to relax and look up at the screen.

'Lovely,' Anya says. 'The placenta is in the right place.' I knew that from my NHS scan, but I don't say anything. She clicks and measures on the computer while I watch baby Jackson number two moving her little stick legs. Anya still seems to be looking about, deep in thought. I glance up at the clock, it's nearly six, and I've not even been numbed up yet.

'Well, I can see your dates are correct, but see this,' she points at a blurry grey bit on the monitor, 'this is your bowel, it's very high up, I'm worried that I would pierce it, should I try to gather a sample.'

All the air sucks out of me, I can't believe it, my placenta's in the right place, but not my bowel? No one's mentioned the bowel before. 'What do you mean? You can't do it?' I ask. Ian grips my hand.

'Go to the toilet, empty your bladder and I'll see then. Maybe it will be possible.'

I jump off the bed and dash out of the room locating the toilet opposite and hurriedly pee. After washing my hands I repeatedly bounce about like a child. Maybe I can move it? Viewing my reflection in the mirror, I look ridiculous and my face and chest is scarlet and blotchy. As I walk back into the surgery, I try not to acknowledge Ian's glum expression. I get back on the bed and pull my T-shirt up ready. It's all sticky from the gel earlier, thinking about it, I don't think I gave them time to wipe it off me.

Anya re-applies more gel – although I'm not sure she actually needs to. She shakes her head. 'I'm sorry it would be too dangerous, if I accidentally pierced it, it would be a disaster, death even. I'm not willing to risk it. An amniocentesis is available after fifteen weeks gestation, you could always go that route.' She wipes my belly with a tissue.

I slowly get up, dazed.

'We have to rush if we're going to catch the last boat,'

Ian says. I vaguely look in the direction of the clock but I can't register the time. 'Thank you,' I hear Ian say as Sandra sees us out.

'We'll send the invoice in the post, it won't be for the CVS test,' she says. 'It will be for the dating scan which is a hundred and twenty pounds plus VAT. If you decide to have an amniocentesis just telephone us, rather than paying the bill, and we can deduct the scanning charge from the total. Have a safe journey home,' she smiles sympathetically.

'I can't believe it,' I say as we head towards the motorway.

'I know, angel, but it was too dangerous, you heard her.'

I get my mobile out and switch it off silent mode. I've had a missed call from my mum, and two texts, one from Bella and one from Rose, both asking how it went.

Tears roll down my cheeks, I don't bother wiping them away. 'What a bloody waste of time,' I whine, 'and we're still being charged for this!'

'That's going private for you, they even charge you for the loo roll,' Ian laughs. I look at him stony faced. How can he make a joke?

My mobile starts playing out its tune.

'Mum.'

'What's up Charlotte, did it hurt? Or have you got the results already?'

'They couldn't do it.'

'What do you mean, they couldn't do it?'

'My bowel was in the way they said.'

'Never mind, darling.' Her words irritate me.

'Which way?' Ian shouts. I stare at the sat-nav and blindly point left. Ian takes a right.

'Got to go, Mum, I think we're lost and we can't miss the boat or we won't be back until tomorrow.'

'Get off the God damn phone and help me, Char.'

I can't believe he said that, not when I'm feeling like this. As the sat-nav recalculates I advise Ian to carry on as we are. We are then sent right and back on track.

'You're speeding Ian, slow down.'

'We have to make the boat. Shit, that camera just flashed.'

'Great.' I say.

'One day we'll laugh about this, I'm sure we will.'

'Well I'm not ready to laugh yet,' I snap back.

When the computerised voice says to carry on for the next nineteen miles, I decide it's safe to text Rose and Bella.

THEY COULDN'T DO IT, BOWEL WAS IN THE WAY. GUTTED ON OUR WAY HOME NOW. HOPE TO MAKE THE LAST BOAT. I hit send, sending them both the same message. Within a minute I get a reply from Bella.

GO TO DR THOMPSON IN KENT HE'S THE ONE THAT DOES THE NUB SHOTS BETWEEN 12 AND 14 WEEKS. THAT'S WHAT I WOULD DO. I flip my phone shut.

'Fuck. It's starting to snow,' Ian shouts.

There is a light scattering falling from the dark sky. The headlights illuminate them and I shudder, what else can go wrong?

We make it back to the boat with moments to spare. A tired grumpy looking man in his fluorescent orange tabard holds his hands up. He's not going to let us on. I put my hands to my mouth. 'Please,' I whisper. He waves his arms, directing us on. 'Thank God,' I say as we drive up the ramp. As I trudge up the metal stairs with a disappointed, tear stained face, I gently rub my belly under my winter coat.

18

I wake up to the sound of Ian leaving for work. Luke is still asleep, so I rest my head on the pillow and fight back the tears that are still threatening to fall from my sore eyes. Should I try Doctor Thompson in Kent? Will Ian agree to another mainland trip? I get up and switch the computer on. Maybe I'll just Google him first and re-read the website information. I click on pregnancy and scroll down to fetal gender. The gender can be determined at the Nuchal scan done between eleven and thirteen weeks. It says they would be happy to attempt to let you know if your baby appears to be a boy or a girl at no additional charge. I jot down the telephone number and stroll downstairs to check Ian's shifts in my diary. I hear Luke in his nursery, singing to himself, he has woken happy and chirpy as usual. I hug him close, kissing his golden locks.

'Baby,' he says poking my tummy.

'Yes, Mummy is having a baby. A little sister, or brother for you,' he laughs and repeats the word brother.

After lunch, and a couple of encouraging text messages from Bella, I telephone the hospital. The lady on the other end of the phone sounds really kind and books me in for this Saturday morning, in two day's time.

Ian comes home from work, I decide to wait until after he's had his tea to broach the subject.

'You know that doctor in Kent, the one Bella said does the nub shot gender guess?' I murmur.

'Yes,' he looks up from his surfing magazine.

'Well, we've got an appointment on Saturday.'

'What?'

'Before you say anything, we're not at work, Mum will have Luke and it says it's ninety-five percent accurate, not eighty like I originally thought. I'll show you the website.'

'I've seen it before. Fine, book the boat then.'

'Booked it already. The courtesy car is coming tomorrow, so we'll drive up in that.'

Ian nods, flicking through the pages of his magazine. I get up from the breakfast table and wander into the lounge to watch telly on my own.

'Thank God it's not snowing,' I say with a sigh of relief as we drive off the boat and on to the mainland, yet again. 'I just feel so bad that Mum's unwell.'

'Yes, she was sick, wasn't she?'

'In our front garden, before she came in for Luke. God I hope she's okay and Luke behaves for her.'

We're on our way up to Kent on the M25 in our tiny

silver courtesy car, a Nissan Micra. It's a grey drizzly day, but no sleet or snow, thankfully.

'How's Bella?'

'Fine,' I say staring out of the window at the many lanes. Why is he asking about her?

'When's she due?'

'What?'

'Her baby?'

'Oh. Um. Didn't I say? She miscarried.'

'You're lying.'

'What?' I feel hot and sweaty. How does he know?

'The insurance company rang. You crashed in the New Forest. What were you doing there, Char? You told me it happened in Newport.'

'Sorry, we were Christmas shopping. I knew you'd be mad if I was driving on the mainland again.'

'She didn't miscarry. She had an abortion, didn't she?' His voice raises a pitch. I stay silent. 'She had that CVS test, she must have had her results. What was it? A boy?'

'I'm sorry. I had to take her, no one else knew about it.'

'You had to take her?'

'She was having a general, she couldn't drive herself.'

'She could have taken the train. It was snowing for Christ's sake. You nearly lost our baby.'

'Now you're exaggerating.'

'I can't believe you lied to me. I suppose her husband thinks she miscarried?'

I stare at the scenery, it's all a blur.

Ian turns the radio up. 'You're unbelievable,' he mutters.

'Look, Ian, I'm sorry, I was put in an awkward position.'

'Don't speak to me.'

The rest of the journey is cold and silent. I could have done without this confrontation today. What the hell am I doing?

'I'm scared,' I say to Ian as we pull up at the hospital. Ian cuts the engine and the irritating sound of the lady's computerised voice on the sat-nav ceases.

'Let's just get this over with,' he grunts. 'It can't go any worse than the Cambridge trip, surely.'

We make our way to the reception area, he doesn't hold my hand. We are directed to another waiting room. Sitting in the small hallway-come-reception, I feel really nervous. Putting my hands into my coat pocket, I feel something small and plastic. I pull it out.

'What on earth,' Ian rolls his eyes as I hold up a miniature pink doll. 'Where did you get that?'

'I've never seen it before,' I say, pleased that he has spoken at last. I put my hands back in my pocket, and find a slip of paper. 'Girly' is written in my mother's familiar handwriting. I smile to myself, trust Mum, let's hope she's right!

The phone rings at the desk. I hear one of the receptionists talking. 'No, the scan is an anomaly one. Yes, if Doctor Thompson can tell what the sex is, he will. No he may not see what it is. Yes if he can, he'll tell you. Did you want to book an appointment then? No it's not a hundred percent, the scan isn't for that. It's an anomaly scan. Okay. Bye.' She slams the phone down. Ian and I glance at each other. 'It's a baby. Why do they care what it is?' I hear one receptionist say to the other.

'I know. He really should change the wording on his website. I keep getting calls like that. It makes me so mad,' the other receptionist replies.

My insides knot together. Maybe he won't be able to tell me? He obviously gets this all the time. Before I can speak to Ian, a nurse calls us in.

'Mrs Jackson, if you'd like to follow me.'

A ripple of apprehension shoots down my spine.

'Mrs Jackson, Mr Jackson.' Doctor Thompson says, shaking each of our hands in turn. 'Pop yourself on the bed.' He looks much nicer in the flesh, his website picture doesn't do him justice, and his comb-over hair suits his country tweed style. I lie down propping my head on the pillow, and watch him tap away on the strange circular computer.

Ian stands close and places his hand on my shoulder. I smile at him, thank God he's touching me. Why is he going along with all of this? I want a daughter, but does he really mind either way?

'So you are here for an anomaly scan.'

Nodding, I look up at Ian, who finally answers with a 'yes' for us both.

Doctor Thompson goes through all the formalities and statistics. He doesn't interrogate us, thankfully.

'Do you have any other children?' he asks.

'Yes. One boy.' Maybe I should have said girl? That way he wouldn't know how desperate I am? Now I'm being stupid.

'Just lift your top up a bit, and roll your trousers down slightly, and we'll get started.' I like him. The tension has almost gone and I feel comfortable. He has a kind face with a warm smile and he hasn't asked any awkward questions... yet!

He applies the gel to my tummy and I look at my baby on the screen. Doctor Thompson seems to take forever doing all the routine checks and measurements. It's amazing. Some of the scans are in 3D. He explains that it's called 4D because the baby is moving whilst in 3D and he prints a few out for us. It's a shame I'm not excited about this bit. I feel on edge.

'Can you tell if it's a boy or a girl?' I blurt out.

'Yes, I'll just go back to 2D, it's easier to tell that way.'

I feel Ian squeeze my shoulder. That wasn't difficult, perhaps it's the office staff against finding out the gender, and not him?

The doctor presses a few buttons, and it looks like a normal hospital scan now. Staring intently at the screen, I think I know the answer already. My stomach churns. The nub is pointing up. It's a boy.

I feel the squeeze on my shoulder again. Ian knows it too.

'It's a boy.' Doctor Thompson says.

'Lovely,' I mumble. I feel so hot.

Ian's hand on me is beyond irritating. I can't look at him, if I do I'll burst into tears. 'What percentage would you say?'

'I'm pretty sure, but I'd say ninety-five percent to be safe.'

I get off the bed. To avoid looking at Ian, I concentrate on tucking myself in. I don't think the doctor notices my flustered disappointment as he prints off more scan pictures.

'Thank you very much.' Ian shakes Doctor Thompson's hand once more and takes the scans.

'Don't forget your CD.'

Ian goes back in for the CD footage of our baby. I can feel the doctor gazing at me. He knows I'm disappointed. I don't care. I just want to get out of here.

We walk back to the car in silence. We don't speak until we're on a main road.

'You want to get rid of him, don't you?'

'No. I don't know. I don't know anything.'

Silence again.

After a few miles, I hear my phone bleep. Flipping it open, I see I have a text from Bella.

WELL?

BOY. I reply. One little word, three letters that sum it all up for me. I don't need to elaborate.

'Bella. Already!' Ian spits.

'She just asked how it went.'

'What's her advice? A trip to Bournemouth?'

'She's not replied.' I stare out the window on my side. Tears start to stream down my cheeks. I wipe them away with the back of my coat sleeve.

'I wish you'd never met that evil bitch.'

My mobile rings.

'Mum,' I manage to choke out.

'Oh darling, is it a boy?' Mum sounds rough.

'Yes,' is all I can manage.

Ian glances my way. Disgusted.

'He may have got it wrong?'

'He hasn't,' I say, 'ninety-five percent is what he said. I saw it myself. It's a boy.'

'Luke will love a little brother.' My mother says, sympathetically.

'I know he will.'

'You could try for another, in a year or so?'

'No. I don't want three children.' Ian snorts. 'This was my last chance at having a girl.'

'You never know what's around the corner.'

'I do,' I whine, 'that's it. Never again.'

'Good.' I hear Ian say. I look over at him, but he doesn't look at me. He just stares at the road, like he hadn't said anything.

'How are you, Mum, you feeling better?'

'Not really. Dad had to come down to help. I had to tell him, Char.'

'What? Why?'

'He thought you and Ian had left me like this, to go Christmas shopping. He was going to call you.'

'What did you tell him? Oh God, I didn't want Dad knowing anything.'

'More lies,' Ian whispers, distracting me.

'I said you were going to have a private scan, to see if it's a girl, that's all.'

'Okay, Mum, that's fine. You can tell him it's a boy if you like.'

I say goodbye to my mother. My eyes glaze over. What

183

is wrong with me? Why is this happening? It could have been such a happy journey home, excitedly phoning and texting everyone with the news. But no, it went the other way. Why can't I just be happy?

19

Drowning in a sea of sorrow. Devastated. Self-pity. Loathing. I hate myself for feeling this way. I can't eat. I can't sleep, and I have a permanent headache from all the crying I've done over the past two days and nights.

'You are going into work this afternoon, aren't you, Char.'

'No,' I say from under the duvet.

'I've put Luke down to sleep. I'm just going to pop out for a few hours.'

'It's your day off. Do you have to go out?'

'I'm surfing, sorry, Char, but I've not been in ages.'

'Enjoy yourself, maybe Tammy will be there!' The fact that Ian doesn't say otherwise makes me believe she will.

'You can't wallow forever.' He turns and walks down the stairs.

'I'm not wallowing,' I mutter as I hear him leave.

I'm still functioning, although phoning in sick at work.

I'm doing all the things I need to do. I cook dinner and I play with Luke. But I can't talk about the baby. I've not let on to anyone that I know the sex. As far as everyone knows, apart from Mum, Bella, Ian and Rose, I'm blissfully unaware. I wish I was. I'm ashamed to admit that I have looked up abortions. But I can't do it. Not to Luke's brother. Ian hasn't mentioned Bella's termination and my lying. He doesn't talk about the baby either. He's worried, but not enough to stay home with me today. I feel numb. I'm living, but not living. I need to get a grip. A grip on reality. I just can't. Not at the moment.

I take a shower while Luke is asleep and give my hair a much needed shampoo. Mum's well again now, fully recovered. The sickness bug is yet to spread around our house. Fingers crossed it spares us.

My doorbell rings, I'm not expecting visitors.

'Hi, Hun,' Bella says, giving me a hug as I open the door. 'God you look bad.'

'Thanks.' As we walk down the hallway, I catch a glimpse of myself in the mirror. My wet hair, scraped back in a ponytail makes my features look harsh. Ugly. No make-up, pale, but blotchy. I hastily look away, and carry on down the hall and into the kitchen. The roles have been reversed, Bella looked like me two weeks ago.

'Tea?' I reluctantly offer.

'Please.' She settles herself at the table as I fill the cups. 'You've not been answering my texts,' she says, taking a sip.

I look down at my cup. The floodgates I'd only recently managed to close, re-open. I can't stop. Heaving shoulders, full on, sorry for myself, gut-wrenching sobs emerge. Bella puts her arms around me. I shrug her off.

She walks back to her seat with her hands up in a surrender position. 'I know you're upset, Char, but you could always do what I did.'

'What? Kill it?'

She winces at my harsh words.

'I'm sorry. I didn't - I know you mean well, it's just not for me, that's all. No one knew you were pregnant. Everyone knows I am.'

'Lots of people miscarry. Why don't I phone the doctors for you? Just book the initial appointment. Or if you went private, you wouldn't have to even tell your GP.'

'I can't do it, Bella. It's... he's Luke's brother. Ian's son. I'd never forgive myself. I'll just have to have him. Get used to only having sons. Forget my dreams. I can do that.'

'Are you sure? I know I couldn't. And I don't regret what I've done. Not in the slightest. It's family balancing, that's all. Luke will never know, nor Ian, if you didn't want him to.'

'He would know. He guessed you terminated.' She takes a sharp intake of breath. I shouldn't have divulged that, 'I'm devastated that my last chance at having a girl is gone,' I continue, 'my life isn't going the way I thought it would. But I still can't do it,' she nods. 'How did you imagine your life?' I ask, releasing my hair from the tight band.

'Just one daughter. That's all. I wouldn't have had any

more kids. I look at people with one child, a girl, and it annoys me. That's all I wanted. It's so difficult with two, arguing and fighting all the time. Boys stuff everywhere, football. I hate bloody football. Now I feel forced into having three children, so I can have my daughter. I won't stop until I have her. But I refuse to have more than three, that's why I did what I did.'

'But you do love Adam and Si, don't you?'

'Of course. I wouldn't be without them now. I just saw myself with a girl, shopping, make-up, girly chats. Dance lessons, I wanted her to do ballet like me. And later, helping her choose her wedding dress, all that stuff. I feel so cheated. What about you? How did you see yourself?'

'I don't know why, but I always thought I'd have two girls.' I run my fingers through the damp tangled nest on my head. 'It's not that I didn't want a boy at all, I just couldn't see myself with one. Silly really. If I'd had a daughter first time round though, I wouldn't be disappointed having a son after, or a daughter. It wouldn't bother me either way. But I have always known that I'd have two children. Not three. This is it for me.'

'I've been looking online, I want to go abroad and have PGD,' Bella says.

'Really. Would Joe go for that?'

'I'm sure I could persuade him. It's not like we can't afford it.'

'What does Joe do? For a job?'

'Oh this and that.'

'Like what?' Why is she being vague? I can't believe I've never asked about his work before.

'Stocks and shares, boring stuff. I don't ask.'

Bella doesn't work other than an hour's cleaning for her neighbour, which I find quite strange considering she has a lady come in to do her housework for her? It's probably mainly shopping and helping her as opposed actual cleaning, but I wouldn't think she earns much? She always has the latest clothes and accessories, Joe's obviously doing well.

'So all is forgiven then, for the abortion?'

'Yep. We don't talk about it.'

'You said he knew I took you, and he was checking your phone.' I give up with my hair and tie it back up.

'Honestly, Char, everything's good now. Don't worry. He realises how determined I am to have a daughter. He respects that.'

I look down at my bump, it reminds of my own misery. 'I wanted to do girly stuff. Mother and daughter craft shows, plaiting her hair, horse riding. Mum says one of my boys may ride, she's just trying to make me feel better. She knows how I feel really, she wanted a daughter too, only she got one.' I wince, thinking about my dead sister, Suzy. Poor Mum, I'm sure she still grieves for her. I'm so selfish.

Luke wakes up. I place him in his highchair with some Marmite sandwiches and slices of apple. After finishing a second cup of tea, Bella persuades me to go for a walk.

It is energising going outside. Refreshing. We walk down to the seafront, Bella pushes Luke for me. I watch grandparents playing with their grandchildren. Granddaughters, and grandsons clad in their hats, mittens and scarves. The snow has melted now, but it's very cold. I can see my breath each time I exhale. Luke runs around. Bella does most of the playing while I stand back, watching.

'You put your decs up yet?' I ask Bella as we head home.

'Yes, ages ago. Only a couple of weeks to go now. I noticed you haven't got yours up yet?'

'I really don't feel like Christmas. But I have to, for Luke,' I look down at his innocent face through his weather shield, he is beautiful, 'I'll put them up tonight. Maybe when Ian gets back, we'll go and get a tree.

'Yes, real trees are lovely. I've just put a fake one up, always do.'

Later that evening when Luke is asleep, I lug out the box of Christmas decorations from the loft. I tried to contain my relief when Ian said he didn't feel like getting the tree today. Too worn out from surfing I guess. I picture a bubbly, carefree Tammy. I expect he had a stimulating conversation with her. God, he wouldn't tell her how disappointed I am, would he? Or mention the hospital appointments? Of course he wouldn't!

We don't talk like we used to, just the basics. All this baby planning has changed us. I can't remember how we used to be.

'You shouldn't be lifting all that,' he says when he sees me precariously carting boxes and bags full to the brim down the stairs.

'Why don't you help me then?' I snap back. 'Neither of

us wants to do this, but someone has to!'

Ian takes over. I'm beginning to feel nauseous.

'You okay?' he asks.

'I don't feel right.' I run as fast as I can to the bathroom. Heaving and retching. After vomiting the whole contents of my stomach, lining as well, I head to bed with a sick bowl. My mother's germs have finally spread around. Great.

Ian decides to sleep downstairs, I don't question him. I'm past caring about anything at the moment. I awake in the night, yet again, to be sick. I have been so ill, I am beginning to feel scared. I've never been this unwell before. Poor Mum, having Luke that day. As the sickness continues I grow increasingly anxious for my baby. My little boy inside me. Will he be okay? Terror trembles down my spine as I vomit again. I stumble down the stairs to Ian. He's asleep so I curl myself up in a ball in the bathroom. But if I lose him, all this will be over. I'll have another chance at having a girl. I mentally shake myself, I'm ill, I'm not thinking straight. I'm worried for him. I want him, I do. I'm delirious.

Hours later, I awake, curled up by the toilet, shivering and trembling. I slowly make my way into the lounge where Ian is still sleeping.

'Ian,' I croak.

'What's up?' He rubs his eyes and stretches. 'What time is it?'

'I feel dreadful,' I say squinting at the clock.

'God, you look terrible. Get back to bed, Char, I'll bring you up some tea and toast.'

'I don't think I can manage food, or drink at the moment. I'm worried, about the baby.'

'We'll call the midwife later, I'm sure it's okay, loads of people get sickness bugs all the time. You're past the dodgy stage, he'll be fine.' He'll. Him. He. I'll have to get used to that.

'I'm sure you're right, I'll drink some water.'

'Yes, angel, get plenty of fluids down you.'

I start to feel better as the day goes on. Mum has taken Luke out for a bit, so I can rest. After reassurances from the midwife on the telephone I start to calm down. I don't want to lose him, I don't. It was just a stupid thought, I didn't mean it, I tell myself.

20

Charlie123
Why am I not allowed to have a girl?

I type in the heading box and pour my heart out online about my failed swaying attempt and my recent scan.

It sounds so bad as a friend of mine had a daughter who died, I'm sure she would have given anything for her to have been a boy instead and have lived. Plus my sister who passed away, I can't remember her as I was only young, she was my mother's first born. I also had a friend who had two daughters and she herself died of cancer a few years ago, so she missed out on all the things I was looking forward to doing with the daughter I never had.

Should I type this? Am I trying to justify my feelings? I start to delete it. Shaking my head I re-type the last sentence.

I thought I was feeling better, putting it into perspective after I had a scare when I was sick.

Feeling ungrateful I type all my inner thoughts, spilling them out, opening myself up to being criticised and judged by strangers who I hope will sympathise. I also find myself typing that I'm only having two children so this was my last chance. Will anyone want to take the time to read such a long essay, do I really want them to?

My twenty week scan is in a couple of months and I am praying that they will say it's a girl this time, but I know they won't, I saw with my own eyes that it is a boy. I am no longer looking forward to Christmas, I'm not enjoying this pregnancy, I wish I wasn't pregnant! My first trimester has been so different, I was so sure it was a girl, why am I not allowed to have a daughter? Sorry to go on but it's still so raw. I love my son to bits and wouldn't swap him for anything, I'm sure I will feel the same about the next son but I just wish it wasn't happening! Does anyone have any thoughts on this which will help me?

Wiping tears from my cheek, I hit send and log off. It is the same website that I go to for swaying information, but I posted on the gender disappointment page, a section I've never visited before. I feel so guilty. Bex, from online, is having her sixth boy after a failed sway. She must be feeling worse than me? Maybe she's not? She's probably a kinder person than I am.

I hastily dress myself in my dental nursing uniform and head down the stairs to the sound of Luke waking up. Ian has been going into work early, apparently they're really busy at the garage and have a backlog of MOT's due.

In the evening, when Luke is asleep, I check my online post. Sixteen replies. Wow. I hope no one has had a go at me and tells me I'm a hateful bitch. Although that's what I deserve.

Why can't I be happy with what I've got? Feeling anxious I start to read through them all.

Justoneboy

I'm like you, only I would have given anything to have a little boy. After my second daughter was born, I was so upset, I seriously thought about ending it all. I know life is very fragile and fleeting, and that there are more important issues to be dealt with, besides the gender of your children, but I guess since we're human, we all have desires and dreams. I felt for sure I would have at least one little boy in my lifetime, but it didn't work out that way. Somebody on this forum, and I'm sorry, I would like to give her credit, but I can't remember her name, said that we don't regret the children we have, just the ones that we didn't get. I think that sums it up pretty well. It does get better with time, but for me, the disappointment and upset still rears its ugly head now and again.

I scroll down to the next reply.

Daughterdreams

I'm so sorry you are going through this. I could have written your post six years ago. My pregnancy was totally different, and while I didn't really sway, I thought the timing was in girl territory. I was stunned to hear I was having a second boy, and I wished it would all just go away. My little boy will be six years old tomorrow. He is the light of my life. I would not trade him for all the girls in the world. It is so beautiful to watch the relationship my two boys have, and to know they will be friends for life. But I'm not only happy my son has a brother. I'm happy I have this incredible, sweet little person in my life. I still want a daughter as desperately as ever. We can love the children we have with all our hearts and still feel like something is missing. Please don't beat yourself up over other people's situations. I'm sorry to hear about your sister, but this is what is real to you, and right now it is very painful. It's important to give yourself time to grieve. When I had my second boy, I also thought we were only going to have two kids. I knew I still wanted a daughter, but I didn't think it was ever going to happen. It took us years to reach a point where we were ready to have another child, and I am now pregnant with a baby daughter conceived through PGD, which stands for Pre-implantation Genetic Diagnosis. I'm not sure which country you live in, your status doesn't say? In the US it varies from county to county if they allow it, so I'm lucky where I am. I don't want to give you false hope if you are absolutely certain that you will only have two children. But in a few years your heart and your financial situation may change, and you might find yourself in a place where you could consider it. I'm glad you found us here. This is a wonderful forum to find support. I hope that your second little boy will be every bit as much of a blessing to you and your family as mine is to us.

I smile, what kind responses. Much of them are in the same vein, although one has been deleted. A few of the replies mention a 'troll' I wonder what she had written?

Do I really want to know? But at least I'm not the only person in the world feeling this way. I scroll through the remaining two replies, the first of them being a bit of a holy 'life is life' patronising email which gets my back up slightly, the last one reads:

Texmex

I understand the pain you are going through. I have been there so many times myself. For me the only thing that helped was time. When they handed me my babies I always loved them. But after my fifth, I was bitter. I always tell myself never say never and everything is in Gods time, not mine. I may not understand why this is happening, but it must be for a good reason. I understand your sadness, it feels like a physical pain at first but I can say from experience that time changes everything. Give yourself a chance to grieve the little girl you were wishing for and then day by day that pain eases and is gradually replaced by excitement, and when you finally meet your baby you will know that he was meant to be yours and you will love him beyond words. I too have struggled with the issue of why I am not allowed to have a girl and I am beginning to feel that this greatest hardship could prove to be my greatest blessing. I am very seriously looking into fostering which I would never have done if I had my own biological daughter, so you just never know where life can lead you. Remember too that all those crazy pregnancy hormones make everything seem worse, so be gentle on yourself. Best wishes.

Feeling overwhelmed, I hit reply. My fingers fly over the keys, typing faster than I can think.

Charlie123

Thank you for that, it does help to know that I'm not the only one going through this. Every five minutes I change my mind as to whether or not to try again, but I shouldn't be thinking that now as I've not even had this baby yet. I live in England and gender selection isn't performed here. I know I will get over having a second boy but I don't think I will ever get over not having a girl. It's not just the girly hobbies and pretty clothes, it's also in twenty years time we would be going out to lunch like I do with my mum - my brother doesn't do that with her. Also being more involved with wedding stuff and her children. I still can't believe it!

I hit send and shut the computer down. Feeling angry at the world, I storm down the stairs, wrench up the floor board, not even trying to be careful about damaging it or loosening it further. I pull out the wish sheet and grabbing a lighter from the kitchen drawer, I dash outside. Stuffing the cream embossed paper in the chiminea, I light it and close the wire mesh. It starts to smoulder.

'What are you doing?' Ian's voice startles me.

'Burning,' I reply.

'Burning what?'

'A stupid wish I bought online.'

Ian looks at me like I've gone mad. I peer through the grate in the ceramic chiminea as the fire ignites in a golden blaze then I race back into the house.

'Now where are you going?'

'I forgot something,' I call out. I walk through the hallway and grab my coat off the peg. Rummaging in the pockets I locate the ridiculous pink doll that my mum put there, along with the note inscribed 'Girly.' Chucking my coat, not caring as it lands on the floor in a heap, I stomp back through the kitchen and out the back door into the garden. I open the grate, burning my hand and throw the doll and note into the flames. I kick it closed with my foot and let out a scream, placing my singed fingers into my mouth.

21

'The room looks bigger now,' Ian states.

'I know, that tree was a bit too wide.' I think of our last minute dash for a real Christmas tree. Thank God it's all over. A fresh new year.

'Luke loves his train set.'

'He was so excited,' I say as I pack away the wooden track.

'I'm sorry it didn't work out, Char,' I look at Ian, my eyes narrowed, 'having a daughter. I really hoped we'd hear girl too.'

A lump rises in my throat. 'I wish we'd kept up with the incubating.'

'Oh, angel, it wasn't working. You didn't get pregnant.'

'But if we'd persevered or used more lime? Maybe my pH was too high?'

'Stop it, Char, it was all a load of crap.'

'Bella was still incubating when she got pregnant, so

you could conceive that way.'

Ian looks at me, pursing his lips.

'Don't start on me, please,' I add.

'I didn't say anything,' he snaps.

I finish packing away the trains and bridges feeling foolish for bringing Bella's pregnancy into the conversation. What was I thinking?

The next month creeps by slowly. I unlock the front door and switch on the lights. Heading to the main surgery, I power everything up and un-stack the autoclave, setting out the instruments for the first patient.

'You're early,' Chloe says, startling me.

'Hi, yes, you okay?'

'Fine, it's good to be back. Looks like Mr Watson is in first. I'll get his X-rays.' Chloe wanders over to the navy blue file in the far corner. Her slender figure has returned already.

'Does it feel strange coming in when you're still on maternity leave?' I call out.

'A bit, but I needed the money to be honest. Marie said she'll pay me cash to do a week on reception while Steph's away.'

'I bet she's sunning herself as we speak,' I say, thinking of our receptionist.

'More like burning herself seeing as she has auburn hair,' Chloe replies.

I chuckle.

Our boss, Marie, arrives. 'Hi girls,' she says out of breath after her short walk from the car. She sits herself on the stool, hands over her ample thighs. Breathing heavily, her white tunic fit to bursting, but she doesn't have the excuse of being pregnant.

'I'll make us all a coffee,' Chloe says.

We drink our beverages while waiting for Mr Watson, who is nearly fifteen minutes late. Marie tucks into some biscuits, saying she hadn't eaten breakfast. She licks the chocolate off her fingers. I think it's unlikely that other dentists eat sugary treats all throughout the day.

'You must find out what you're having soon, when's your twenty week scan?' Chloe asks.

'It's in two days actually.' I instinctively rub my protruding tummy, which is straining against my uniform.

'Wow you kept that quiet. I hope you have a little girl. She could play with Verity-May.'

Verity-May. I feel like a sharp pointed stick has speared me through the heart. The name I so longed to call my daughter. The name she stole from me. I move my hand away from my stomach. It shouldn't matter anymore, I'm never going to have a daughter now anyway! 'I don't think I'm going to ask what it is.'

'Really? I was so eager to know. You're so patient.'

'I didn't find out with Luke. I'm not sure, I'll decide at the time.' Oh God, please stop. I hate lying. I'm so transparent, everyone sees straight through me. I'm being irrational, people don't generally find out what they're having as early as I have.

At the sound of the surgery door, Chloe and her mass of thick dark hair disappear up the hallway.

'Mr Watson is here, he got held up in traffic, can you

still see him?' she asks.

'Yes, send him down,' Marie replies.

I feel I'm going to have to fend off Chloe regarding my scan. Perhaps it's best to keep it to myself, they can all find out once I've had him. That way I don't have to see the pity in their eyes. Once he's here, people congratulate you, they won't be saying things like oh well, maybe next time. Or another boy, you'll have your work cut out for you...

The next day I take Luke to toddler group. He was wonderful, playing with all the other children, and not clinging to me like he usually does. I feel proud as I put him down for his morning nap, stroking his hair until he dozes off.

Chloe is doing both surgery work and reception for the next two days, the days I don't work. Marie hinted for me to do some extra hours, but I can't. I don't like to inconvenience my mother too much, she's already having Luke for me tomorrow morning. I flick the kettle on and wait for Rose to arrive. I don't hear her as she quietly enters the house.

'Hi, I hope you don't mind me popping in. No riding lessons booked in for weeks. It's all this bad weather.'

'Dreadful isn't it!'

'I know, first snow, now flooding. I expect we'll have a drought in the summer.'

'Yes, another hosepipe ban,' I say rolling my eyes. We settle ourselves at the kitchen table with a hot mug of tea each.

'It's your scan tomorrow morning, isn't it?'

'Yes; ten o'clock. I hope the doctor in Kent got it wrong. I know he hasn't though.'

'You never know, he may have,' she takes a sip then cradles her hands around the cup in an attempt to warm them up.

'I've been looking it up online, it's quite rare. I'm trying not to get my hopes up.'

'No, best not. Do you still want me to come with you?'

'If you don't mind. Ian's working, unfortunately. If you're busy though, don't worry, Mum will come with me, it just means bringing Luke too though.'

'I'd love to come,' Rose says, reaching over and squeezing my arm.

'I didn't tell you, did I, Bella's going to America. She's having PGD.'

'What does it stand for again?'

'Pre-implantation genetic diagnosis,' I state, hoping I remembered it correctly.

'It's the same as IVF isn't it, but only the girls are implanted.'

'That's right,' I say, 'Bella has to have some appointments here, to prepare her body. She can't book her flight until the doctor gives her the go ahead.'

'What happens to the boy embryos?' Rose asks, fiddling with her watch. Maybe she has a view on this. They are discarded, I read that online. Destroyed.

'I'm not sure,' I say, guardedly.

'Maybe they go to couples who can't produce their own eggs?'

'Perhaps.'

'I bet it's costing them an arm and a leg!'

'Bella's quite well off. I think it's over twenty grand including travelling. I hope it happens for them first time. Lots of couples have to have it done a few times before it takes.'

Rose doesn't say anything for a bit. I get the impression she's not keen on my friendship with Bella, just like Ian. She hesitates, twice. I wait for her to finally say her piece.

'Bella's husband, he must obviously know about the America thing. He's going along with it then?'

'Yes. He has to go to one of the appointments abroad, she couldn't do it without him.'

'He's happy to do that then, spend all that money, and more if it doesn't work first time.'

'I don't think he knows quite how much it's costing,' I confess. I'm feeling a bit defensive, where is this going?

'Does he know she got rid of his son?' My stomach knots.

'Actually, yes he does. Now.' I take a deep breath, trying to keep my voice level. Rose is questioning Bella, not me. I think I'm defensive because I feel guilty for looking up abortions. I have to remind myself that she's not having a go at me, is she?

'He's probably doing it so she doesn't do what she did last time.'

'Maybe.' I pick the polish off my fingernails.

'Will Ian do the P.G whatsit?'

I look up at Rose and wipe the nail varnish flakes off

the table. 'We discussed it, it's too expensive. Plus travelling, who would have Luke and the new baby? What if it didn't work? I so wish it could be done in London, or anywhere in England, but it can't, not unless there are genetic reasons.'

'You're going to try for a third then?' Rose sounds surprised.

'I'm not sure, maybe.' I try to make my words sound light hearted. 'I have to have this baby first though.' Yes I do have to have this baby first, one step at a time. 'So Daisy's no longer lame. That's good news.' I say to change the subject, I can't delve there at the moment, I'm still a little fragile.

The next day I meet Rose in the hospital car park. After fifteen minutes in the waiting area, we follow the nurse into the scanning room. I take off my coat and sit in the reclining hospital chair, handing over my notes to the sonographer. Rose sits herself in the seat opposite. The nurse turns out the light and begins the procedure I am so used to now, having had so many scans during this pregnancy. Please let her say girl. Doctor Thompson may have only got the odd prediction wrong, all of them male when he'd predicted female, but please let this be his first. What if she says girl? Which professional would I believe? I couldn't cope if she said that and got it wrong. What if that happens, I could think I'm having a girl and out pops a boy?

'Your dates?'

I'm brought back to the moment, feeling confused,

'Sorry, what was that?'

'Just checking your dates. Twenty point two.'

'Oh yes.' I peer in the dark room, Rose is looking at me strangely? Did I just miss a whole conversation?

After all the measurements are completed, the nurse confirms what I've been dreading to hear again. It's a boy. She switches the lights on and I avoid Rose's glance. Smiling as convincingly as I can at the nurse, fooling no one but myself, I take my notes, thanking her I pay the three pounds for a scan picture and I drive home, crying all the way. But I make a decision. This will be the last time I shed a tear about my baby's gender. I will pull myself together.

Throughout the final stages of my pregnancy I am true to my word both in public and private.

22

'Theo Sebastian Jackson. He's lovely,' my mother says, holding her arms out to take him.

It is sweltering hot here in the hospital. I'm not allowed the fan on because of the babies, but this is the hottest July I've known. Theo is two hours old. His birth went really smoothly, and quickly, just like Luke's. Luke has been to see his new brother. I don't think he knew what to make of him, or fully understands that his life will change now. All our lives will.

I'm being discharged later today. I've packed up my belongings. Theo is asleep in the perspex box they call a cot in here. He has perfect features, and lots of dark brown hair. I look down at him, sleeping soundly. I love him, I do. I just can't help wishing one thing. That he was a girl. I mentally shake my thoughts away. I'm not going back there again. I can't.

Ian drives us home. Walking up my front path, lugging

bags, while Ian carries Theo, I can see blue balloons in my lounge window. Blue. Entering the front door, Luke throws himself at me. I drop my bags and scoop him up.

'Welcome home,' my mother says, picking up my discarded luggage.

'Well done,' I hear Dad say from the kitchen. 'Tea?'

'Please,' I reply. 'So how are you Lukey? Excited to see your new brother?'

'Yes.' He looks doubtful. I study Luke, then Theo, who is still in his daddy's arms.

'Once he's older, Luke will find him more interesting,' my mother says reassuringly. I know she's right, but I feel low. I expect it's just hormones, it'll pass. I hope.

Six months slope by, another Christmas been and gone. I have started to feel an overwhelming surge of love for my new baby. It took slightly longer than it did with Luke, but he's here now. I wouldn't be without him. His cheeky little chuckle is delightful and he is such a good baby in a superb routine, which helps. Lack of sleep is never good for anyone's state of mind. However, while up at night feeding Theo, I sometimes think to myself, I'm going through the motions, doing everything I should do, but it's not what I had planned. I'll never have a daughter now, and I always thought I would. I walk into Theo's bedroom. In the dark I visualise a pink room with yellow butterflies stuck to the back wall. I feel like I can actually see it. Where the yellow butterflies came from, I don't know? I've never seen any in the nursery books I've looked through. It must be something my imagination has created, out of nowhere. In actual fact, the room is blue, with brown giraffe and elephant transfers. It is decorated beautifully, I did most of it myself. It felt like salt was being rubbed into my wounds at the time. It just feels final now. I peek in at the sleeping baby in the cot. My sleeping baby boy. All children look cute when they're asleep and Theo is no exception. Tiptoeing out onto the landing, and into Luke's bedroom, I see his mat of blonde curls poking out of his bedclothes. He's in a big boys bed now. I look down at his cherub face, gently snoring and sucking his thumb. I quietly close his bedroom door and head back upstairs. Ian is already in bed, reading his surfing book.

'Everything okay?' he asks.

'Yes. It really is you know. I'm still upset that I'll never have a daughter, but I love both my boys to bits.'

'I'm glad. The boys are terrific, and they will be great for each other too. I loved having brothers.' Ian kisses me goodnight and switches out the light. As I lie still, waiting for sleep to take me, Ian whispers. 'You never know, we may still have a daughter yet.' Did I hear him correctly, or did I imagine it?

I sit bolt upright. Does he mean what I think he means? I can't have my fragile feelings messed with. 'PGD?' I whisper.

'No, angel, I didn't mean that. I know that's what Bella's doing, but we really can't afford it.' There's a long pause as I stare into the darkness. 'Sorry,' Ian mutters.

'What did you mean then?' I bite back, feeling my temper rise.

'I mean, just naturally. You say you love your two boys. Well it's fifty fifty. Worst-case scenario, you could love a third boy too. Couldn't you?' Worst-case scenario. You say you love your two boys, is he doubting me? I know I've been a little down at times, depressed even, but I'm fine now. It was just the baby blues. Blue being the operative word.

'I guess I could,' I stutter. 'I'm just not sure I want a third child. I'll have to think about that one. You got my hopes up about PGD though.'

'Sorry, I didn't mean to.'

'Don't do that again, it's too painful for me.'

'You're seeing Bella tomorrow aren't you?'

'Yes.' Great, I know what's coming next.

'Don't let her fill your head with crap.' As I start to protest Ian cuts me dead. 'I know she's your friend and all that, but she's a bad influence. If you hadn't met her, our lives would be so much easier.'

'Well that's where we'll have to agree to disagree,' I say, lying back down and wrapping the covers over me.

'Come on, Char, you know what I mean.' I'm not listening. I've closed him out. He rolls over, noisily huffing and puffing. Separate sides of the bed. I'm so irritated that he said we should try naturally for a third. Although I'm happier now, there will always be something missing in my life. Something that only a daughter can fill.

'How are you?' Bella asks as she sits herself down at my kitchen table. Ian has taken Luke and Theo to the park for a couple of hours. I'm not sure where Bella's boys are, with Joe I guess?

'Yes, I'm fine.'

'Really?' Bella sees straight through me. I didn't sleep well, my mind whirling with possibilities.

'Well, I was fine, but then Ian dropped a bombshell last night. He said we could try for a third.'

'That's good, isn't it?'

'He means naturally though. I got the wrong end of the stick and thought he meant like you.'

'Oh.' Bella looks down at her glass of water. Perhaps she's not allowed tea or coffee with the different drugs she's taking?

'Yes, and regardless of that,' I continue, 'I'd just started getting my head around never having a daughter, and now he's got me thinking.'

'Well PGD's not all it's cracked up to be, so far, that is.'

'Really? How's it going then?'

'Crap. I'm so pissed off.'

'Why?' I ask taken aback.

'The doctors aren't helpful. The UK ones, anyway.'

'Even with all the money you're paying them?'

'They only do what they have to, no more. They keep pleading ignorance, and being difficult. It is legal here, but they don't do it. They will only do the preparation, the rest of it has to be done abroad. I feel like banging my head against a brick wall. It's so stressful.' Bella's eyes are shining, about to brim over. I cross the table to her and put my arms around her shoulders. 'They didn't even give me the correct size needles.' Bella rubs her eyes. 'Luckily I realised, I've got to start injecting myself with them soon.'

'That's dreadful. You should complain.'

'I don't want to piss them off. I need them too much. I can't do this without them, I've got no choice.'

'What are you going to do about the needles, how did you know?' Anger surges through me. How can they get away with treating her like this?

'I posted something about them online. A girl told me they were wrong, so I Googled it and she was right. I've ordered some of the correct sized ones on eBay. Hopefully they'll come in time for next week.'

'God, the doctors sound horrendous,' I say. Bella has got herself into quite a state now. I squeeze her shoulder to try and calm her.

'That's one way to put it,' she says in a high-pitched voice, holding her face in her hands. I comfort her as best as I can while the hormonal roller-coaster steams on. After her rant about the UK clinic subsides her face emerges, eyes small and puffy from crying. 'I bet my eyes look like piss holes in the snow,' Bella says half laughing, and sniffs.

'Yes, just like that,' I say, giving her a weak smile. 'So that's next then, you have to inject yourself?'

'Yes. Well first I go back on the pill, as of tomorrow.'

'Why's that?'

'To align my cycle with when they can fit me in. As soon as I'm ovulating, I'll book our flights. Then they extract my eggs. I've spoken on the telephone to the doctor in California. They seem really on the ball there.

It's the ones here that are crap. It's like the blind leading the blind. They don't want to get too involved, so I have to look up everything, and prompt them.'

'Where do you go? London?'

'No. Birmingham. And I don't recommend them! I have to go back up there next week to start my second course of drugs. I'm going to ask them to show me how to inject myself while I'm there. I'm dreading it. I hate needles.'

'But once it's all over, and you have a daughter, it will seem like nothing. I'm so jealous. I wish Ian would consider it, but we just can't afford it.'

'Get a loan.'

'He's worried it won't work first time. Then we'd have to borrow more, and possibly more.'

'That's true. I just can't think like that. I'll cross that bridge when I get to it. I'm just hoping and praying it works first time. All the lies about travelling and holidays that aren't actually holidays. My sisters question me all the time. They think we are so selfish, going abroad without the children. But I don't want to tell them the truth, they'd be funny about that too. You can't win.'

'They don't know then? I thought you were open with them, and your mum?'

'No one knows. We had a bit of a bust up.'

'Oh?'

'I don't want to talk about it.' She looks sternly at me so I drop it. When we first emailed each other she painted a picture of being proud to be doing all she could to get what she wants, not caring who knew. She mentioned being close to her sisters and their children. Has this all changed since she had the termination? I've never met them, surely I would have bumped into at least one of them if they were all as close as she'd suggested? I'm being silly. Stop it!

'It's such a shame it can't be done over here.' I say to fill the silence, 'I think Ian would go for it then.' It is more than a shame. It's not fair. Everyone should have the chance to balance their family if they wish to. It's not like years ago, when women used to have six or more kids, you'd likely get a mix then. Nowadays women have to go to work, to contribute to the mortgage. You can't keep having baby after baby. This makes me think of Bex, the girl online with six boys. Maybe some people can only have one gender? I immediately stop my train of thought, I don't want my hopes dashed further. That's if I do try again.

23

Walking into our conservatory I hear the rhythmic sound of wax being rubbed onto a surfboard. My lips purse as I see that the board is laid on my burgundy Marks and Spencer's wicker sofa. Ian looks up. Immediately the irritating friction sound ceases.

'Don't worry there's none on the cushions.'

I look at the sofa. I'm not sure that's true. I don't say anything.

Ian's been going out surfing more and more recently. Leaving me with the boys. He told me that Tammy meets him there. When I anxiously questioned him he assured me he's just teaching her – she has a boyfriend. I'm not sure that makes any difference. He's my husband, I have to trust him, otherwise what's left?

I'm looking forward to a day off tomorrow, horse riding with Rose. It's very rare that I get to do anything for myself anymore. That's what happens when you become a mother. My life is so different to Rose's. She has no children. But I wouldn't swap with her for the world. Ian's life has changed too, but not as much as mine. He still expects time to himself regularly. Very regularly. I don't expect it for myself, but relish it on the few occasions it happens. Bella seems to always have time without children. I guess Joe doesn't have a hobby like Ian does? Maybe he just really enjoys his boys?

'About the other night.' I walk closer to the surfboard.

'I'm sorry, angel, I know you want a daughter. But maybe two is enough for us?'

My stomach knots, is he going back on what he said? He can't do this to me. 'But you said... last night.'

'I shouldn't have. I don't think you would cope if we had another boy.'

'It's beyond my control. Everything is.' I feel my temperature rising, the heat creeping up my neck.

'Life's not fair,' he simply states.

'No, mine isn't. You can't do this to me!'

'Do what?'

'Move the goal posts.'

Ian picks up the wax and starts rubbing it on his board again. A lump forms in my throat, 'So that's it then? We can't try again?' Put the damn wax down!'

'Char-'

'Let's do PGD. I've looked into-'

'Like you look into everything,' he interrupts.

I sigh. I'm not going to win this. Holding back the tears, I walk over to the window, counting in my head to calm myself.

217

'I'm sorry,' Ian says, following behind me.

'Not as sorry as I am,' I shift away. I can't be near him. I wanted to tell him that my parents would lend us the money. We wouldn't need to pay interest or get into debt. Desperately I walk back to him. 'You can have it done in Europe.'

'For fuck's sake, will you just drop it! Bella's obviously got money to burn, we haven't.'

'Don't speak to me like that.'

'I've had it up to here,' Ian holds his hand above his head to drum in the extent to which I've driven him. I need to shut my mouth now. I know I do, but I can't.

'Well maybe Joe loves Bella more than you love me.' I sound like a petulant teenager, as soon as I've said it, I wish I hadn't. I've said it before in a similar argument. Ian's response is usually for me not to be so silly. Not this time.

'Well maybe he does,' he says storming past.

Hurt and frustrated I sit down on my wicker chair – the sofa is still occupied by the flipping surfboard. I hold my head in my hands. After a moment I look up at the beautiful black and white photo held in a silver frame on the mantelpiece. My two boys. Luke, grinning down at his brother, Theo. The tears erupt. It's not that I don't love them. I feel so guilty for the feelings I have. What's wrong with me? Why can't I feel complete?

'It's really therapeutic,' I say to Rose, as I tiptoe to glance at her over her horse, Jolly's back.

'It is, isn't it?'

I brush Jolly with a firm hand. His hair floats out, covering my fleece with thick reddish brown short hairs, clumps from the brush drift around and stick to me. I'm plastered in it. Jolly has become my favourite. He spooks easily, dancing around over the slightest thing, but he's got a lovely nature.

Bending down, I brush the dried mud off his legs. I change to a comb for his feathers – the long hair around his hooves, pulling it through the knotted clumps and untangling the hair. He doesn't seem to mind. It feels rough to me. Horse's aren't as sensitive as humans. Last of all I plait his tail. A French plait, the type you would do on a little girl's head, but not so roughly.

'Bella should be in California by now,' I say. 'Joe too. They left this morning.'

'Scary,' Rose says, applying oil onto one of Jolly's hooves with a pastry brush. They are dark and shiny now. The strong smell fills the air. 'How long are they out there for?'

'Joe, only a week. Bella, just over two.'

Rose smirks, 'I guess Joe only has to do one bit.'
I can't help it, I laugh. It's just the thought of poor Joe doing his sample. It's not funny though. Poor Joe. Poor Ian. Why do some people just get what they want, or be happy with their lot, naturally? Why wasn't I one of these people?

'Can I ask you something? Rose sounds nervous.

'Fire away.' Oh God, is she about to tell me something about Tammy?

'Why is it that you want a daughter so much? I know it

would be a different experience to your sons and that you would like a mother-daughter relationship, but there must be something else, something deeper?'

I stop and think for a moment, feeling relieved. Why is it? It's difficult to explain, even to myself. 'Because if I don't have one I'll always feel that I've missed out,' I state and continue grooming the horse.

'Night night,' I say tucking Luke in. I kiss him on the head. Ian enters the room. He gives him a peck on the cheek saying good night, then comes over and kisses me.

'Sorry,' he whispers as we walk out of the bedroom. We tiptoe into Theo's nursery. He is sound asleep. We stand there watching him for a while. His tiny body in his sleeping bag. The cotton padded bag lifts up and down gently with his breathing. Ian hugs onto me from behind.

'I'll have another one, but not PGD.'

'Thanks. Let me think it over. I need to know I'll be okay with another boy first.' I surprise myself, I should have agreed, why am I unsure?

'Good idea.' Ian kisses me again. I feel strange, is it happy, or apprehensive? Excited, or scared? All of these feelings flood through me. Can I do this again?

After a couple of days thought, I send Bex, the girl with six boys, a private message on Facebook, asking how she is and if she is going to try again. I can see she is online. Shortly after she replies.

Bex

Hi Charlotte, nice to hear from you. I'm fine. All the boys are doing well. I love them to bits. Having Noah made me realise that it doesn't matter what you have, boy or girl. I'd love to have another baby, I just love children, and I really don't think I would mind either way what I had, but I can't have anymore. My husband has had a vasectomy. So no more children for me. What about you?

I reply through instant messenger –

Charlotte
Glad to hear you're okay. Noah is such a sweetie, I love the photo you posted. All your boys look handsome in it, very proud of their new brother! I thought I'd found peace. I was getting used to the idea of never having a daughter, then my husband said he'd have a third child. That has made me really question myself. Will I be happy with another boy? And I think the answer is yes. Last time I went into it expecting to have a girl. I really thought it would work. I'm more grounded now. The only way for it to be one hundred percent is through PGD, which my friend is doing, but I can't. We can't afford it. I've not decided for sure yet whether to have a third or not. But if I do have another, I have to know that I will be okay either way. Also I never imagined I'd have more than two, so it's a lot to think about. Sorry to hear you can't have any more, when you would like another. Take care and keep in touch. x

As I log off the computer, I let out a long sigh, I don't think I've been particularly truthful. Did I ever find peace? My message makes it sound as if I would be okay with having another boy, I guess I would have to be. I hope Ian doesn't have a vasectomy. He wouldn't do that would he? No. Never. Bex seems fine with having six boys, she even thinks she would be fine with a seventh. I can't imagine feeling that way. I love Theo and Luke to bits, and wouldn't be without them now. But do I want three children? Although I haven't got one of each, both my boys are amazing. Luke is so gentle, not a stereotypical boisterous boy. And Theo's chuckle makes my day. Perhaps we could attempt the Australian website swaying kit, but keep in mind that it could still be another boy?

'Cup of tea?' Ian asks as I walk into the kitchen after tucking the boys in for the night.

'Please.' I sit down on the lounge sofa, kick my slippers off and curl my legs up on the cushion, blindly flicking through the television channels to take my mind off the question that is burning inside me. How will he react?

'You okay, angel?' He passes me my drink.

'Fine,' I take the cup and apprehensively smile.

'What is it, Char?'

'It's nothing, really. Just... well you know you said about having another baby?'

'Yes,' he replies slowly.

I switch the telly to mute and continue. 'Well the American sway didn't work. I briefly looked up that other sway, the Australian one.' Ian closes his eyes and rubs his temple. He exhales loudly. 'Oh don't worry,' I switch the volume back on.

Ian grabs the remote out of my hand, switching it off. 'I can't believe you want to do all that shit again. It's a load of crap, it doesn't work, surely you realise that now!'

'I'm okay with having another boy, really I am. But I

just feel I need to do something. Just to try and sway the odds slightly. At least then, I won't always think that I should have tried harder.'

'Char, no one could have tried harder than you did last time. You can't have forgotten what you went through, what we both went through. That diet was impossible. I can't do that again.'

'It's a different diet. And it's natural methods. No incubator.'

'It was ridiculous. Looking through the microscope, as if that cheap thing could magnify enough to tell them apart.'

'Fine. Forget it.'

'If you want to starve yourself again, you can,' Ian says gruffly. 'But I'm not. Not this time.'

Why is he being so difficult? He was the one who suggested we try again! 'I wasn't starving!'

'You were seven stone!'

'I was fine.'

Ian rubs his eyes then re-adjusts the sunglasses on top of his head.

'Will you attempt on the dates I say?' I push.

He sighs, 'I don't know, maybe.'

He'll come round. I switch the telly back on and move over to Ian's side of the sofa. Taking his arms I wrap them around myself. He tightens the grip. Everything will be okay. I'm kidding myself that I'll be happy with another boy, but I'd get over it. Initially I'd be gutted again, but I believe I'd love him just the same as my others. I honestly know in my heart that I wouldn't love a daughter more than my boys. They'd all be equal, but I desperately want to experience both genders. I can't wait to tell Bella. I wonder how she is getting on in California? I won't say my thoughts out loud. I don't want to ruin the rest of the evening. Not now Ian has agreed to swaying again. Well, kind of agreed.

24

'I am now officially in the two week wait.' Bella looks both excited and scared as she declares this to me. She has a lovely tan, her elfin-style hair has been cut even shorter, with golden tones added to her platinum blonde colour, making her face look softer. I notice her nails have been manicured, more than manicured, they're extensions, with pink sparkly tips.

'Fingers crossed,' I say. 'When can you test?'

'In twelve days. Although I'm testing every day with some cheap ones I got off eBay.'

'So it just shows negative at the moment?' Why would she test this early? I look down at my polka dot tablecloth as we sit around the table in the breakfast-room.

'Yes, I can't help it. Stupid I know, but it's what I've always done.'

'So where are the boys?' Bella looks flustered. I'm imagining it?

'With Joe,' she says, and changes the subject back to her trip. It turns out she did get to have a holiday. After Joe left she went to all the big shopping centres and bought a wardrobe full of baby girl outfits. I'm not sure that was a good idea, but I don't say so. She's on such a high. I don't want to burst her bubble with my negative thoughts.

After an hour of chat, Bella gets up to go. She says her goodbyes to Luke and Theo, who are playing beautifully together with their train set in the adjoining conservatory. Just as she reaches the hall her mobile starts blaring out its usual song. I hear her husband, Joe, on the other end of the phone, screaming. I can't make it out word for word, but the gist of it is that she's come round here, to me, leaving her boys home alone. That can't be right? Would she do that?

'I'm on my way,' she says, 'I've only been gone for five minutes.' What? That's not true. 'I had to get something from the chemist. I've been five minutes, ten max.' Bella raises her voice to a shout. She's lying. She's been round here for over an hour, and it was just chitchat, catch up. She could have brought her children with her. They could have played with my boys. I can't believe she's left them, they're older than mine, but surely too young to leave?

Bella doesn't look at me, she grabs her bag and dashes out to her car. I'm left standing at my front door, looking at my friend rev her flashy red convertible and screech off, narrowly missing my neighbour's cat. My stomach is in my mouth. Why would she do that? What if one of them switched the oven on, or the fire. They could have had a terrible accident, or got taken by someone. It doesn't bear thinking about. Perhaps Ian was right not to trust Bella? How could anyone leave their kids unattended?

Later that evening, after lots of cuddles and kisses with my boys, then tucking them in for the night, I fire up the computer and look up the Australian swaying site. I've not told Ian that you have to pay for their service and he hasn't exactly agreed to anything, but the most expensive package, the platinum one looks good. They claim to plan the dates, method and diet for you and give you online support. I hastily enter my credit card details and download the forms. It can take a few weeks for them to produce your personal plan, so I make a start on answering the various questions straight away. What's three hundred pounds in the scheme of things? Bella has paid much more, but hers is guaranteed. God, Ian will go nuts if he finds out! And will I even be able to persuade him to attempt when I need him to? It all sounds very precise and exact. What have I just done?

'You still on that computer?' Ian says as he enters our bedroom.

'Just shutting down.' Oh my God, I've spent money on a stranger giving me some magic dates? I'm such an idiot!

Lying in bed, I cuddle up to Ian as he gently snores. He is good to me. No he won't go to America, but he's willing to try again. This will be my last attempt. He rolls over and wraps his arms around me. He'd love a daughter, a daddy's girl. She will complete our family. It has to work this time. I find myself thinking about Bella.

Did she really leave her boys home alone? Restless and agitated I twist and turn, disturbed through the night. Eventually sleep embraces me.

Having never actually met Bella's husband, Joe, apart from the brief glance through the window the morning I hurried out a few days after Bella's abortion, I am surprised to answer the door to him. His jet-black hair looks ruffled and he has dark circles under his eyes. I can tell that he is very attractive, and this is not his usual style.

'Have you seen Bella?' he asks hoarsely, after a brief introduction.

'No. I've not seen her for a few days. Is everything okay?' I open the door wide and gesture for him to come inside. We stand in the hallway, should I ask him in further?

'I don't know. The IVF failed. She was in a bit of a state earlier. We argued.' He repeatedly runs his fingers over the stubble on his chin.

'I'm sure she's fine.' God I hope she is. I wish I'd contacted her, I knew she was testing too early.

'I shouldn't have spoken to her like I did, she drives me insane sometimes.'

'She'll come back, she's probably just out doing something or other, not realising you're worried.'

Joe nods.

I wish I believed what I was saying, I've not heard from her since she left her children on their own. She didn't leave my house in the right frame of mind. I should have contacted her. 'Is there anything I can do?

Look after the boys for you?'

'Thanks, but my neighbour has them. You don't have any idea where she could have gone, do you? I've tried everywhere I can think of. I've not seen her since last night.'

'I'm not sure? You've tried all the family? Her sisters?'

'Everyone,' he says.

Exhaling a long breath, my mind whirls, where could she have gone?

'Can I leave you my mobile number, if you hear anything, text or call me. I'm so worried. I shouldn't have shouted at her.'

'I hope it wasn't too serious, your argument, that is?' I think about their telephone call I'd overheard. He was shouting at her. But he had good reason to!

'She wants to try again, with the IVF. I've said no. It costs too much, we've had to re-mortgage our house for the last attempt. We couldn't afford to pay the credit card bills. We should never have attempted, we're in debt up to our eyeballs. It's so crazy. I can't cope with it anymore. Sorry, I shouldn't be dumping all this on you.'

Re-mortgaging the house, credit cards, debts... Bella's always given me the impression they're loaded. Joe works in stocks and shares she'd said, although rather vague in details, I assumed he commuted to London to work? 'That's okay,' I say, accepting the piece of paper with Joe's number on it. 'If I think of anything, or if she gets in touch, I'll contact you. Let me know once she's back, won't you?'

Joe agrees and leaves. He looks drawn and dishevelled.

I hope Bella's okay.

'Have you seen Bella yet?' my mother asks a week later. She rocks Theo on her knee.

'No. Joe says she doesn't want to see anyone. I've tried texting her. Oh Mum, I'm so worried.' I glance over at Luke, who is merrily playing with his toy vacuum cleaner.

'I'm sure she'll be okay.'

'Joe found her at Alum Bay.'

'What, at the cliffs? How did he know to look for her there?'

'She texted him and told him where she was, said she loved him and the kids, that's what he told me anyway. I think it was a cry for help.'

Mum continues bouncing Theo on her knee, the boys are blissfully unaware of the conversation we are having. 'I wonder what she was doing there?'

'No idea. She's not replied to my text. Joe said she's just lying in bed, not showering or anything. He's had to take time off work, and their neighbour is helping with the school run. He's too scared to leave her.'

'Sounds like she needs to see a doctor.'

'I said that to him when he phoned. She's refused, apparently.'

Mum tuts and sets Theo down next to Luke, then moves him back a bit after Luke protests at Theo touching his hoover. I pass a fire engine to Theo, who now sits up really well on his own. We put some cushions behind him, just in case he falls back, but he rarely does. 'So what's next for you?' She places a toy laptop close to

Theo.

'What do you mean?'

'Are you trying for another? Wasn't it an Australian method, this time?'

I choose to ignore my mother's eye rolling gesture. 'Yes, I sent off my forms over a week ago.'

'Forms?'

'It was more of a questionnaire. They wanted to know about past conceptions. They wanted to know lots of funny things actually. If you do any sports, if you sweat, your cycle at the moment, who's the most dominant in the partnership.' I skip the sex drive bit, my mum doesn't need to hear or know that.

'Goodness.'

'If you're stressed out,' I continue, 'occupation, if you smoke or drink alcohol.' I take a quick breath, 'If your husband is bald or has a full head of hair.'

We both laugh. Luke starts clapping his hands, then Theo copies.

'He's clapping, isn't he Lukey. Do pat-a-cake.' After three rounds of nursery rhymes and actions with the children, I hear my phone bleep. It's a text from Bella, I read it aloud. – SORRY I'VE NOT BEEN IN CONTACT. I'M FINE NOW, JUST BEEN A BIT WOBBLY. JOE HAS SAID WE CAN DO PGD AGAIN SO ALL'S OKAY.

'She got her own way then,' Mum observes.

'I guess she did.' Joe had better work hard on selling stocks and shares this month... perhaps he's on commission, that's why they are short on money?

Later that evening I check my emails. My new diet schedule has been sent. I scan through it, planning to read it more thoroughly later. One thing catches my eye. No horse riding. What? I scroll down to the husband part, praying that I don't have to ask Ian to quit surfing. Phew, it says he can still surf. He would never give that up for me anyway. Also cycling is fine, but not jogging. No swimming in a pool or the sea for me, due to the salt and chlorine. I scan over the diet, I'm not looking forward to that again, but this one doesn't look as bad as the last. Timing – they want me to go back on the pill to align my cycle with the dates I'm to attempt on. That's interesting, maybe it's to do with biorhythms or lunar? Who knows? I don't plan on attempting for a few months, but I need to go on the diet three months prior, and Ian just six weeks before. He's not agreed to it so I'll just have to make his dinners and packed lunches with the 'allowed foods' and hope that's enough. I scribble down some ingredients on to my list, I'll get them next time I go shopping. Quinoa seems to feature a lot. I'll try the health food store in town for that.

'You okay?' Ian asks, coming up the stairs to our bedroom.

'Yes, fine.' I log off and stand to give him a hug. Leaning into his firm body I breathe him in. Sea, salt, and the funny damp, rubbery wetsuit smell that I'm so used to. He kisses me on the head.

'I'm just going to have a shower, then maybe we'll watch a film?'

'Okay,' I release myself from his embrace. 'Bella

texted.'

'Oh?'

'Joe's agreed to PGD again.'

'In America?'

'Yes. It was only a text, so I don't know much, but I assume it's at the same place they went before, California.'

Ian pulls a face, and starts undressing for his shower. I hesitate. 'She also asked if we could all meet up at the beach tomorrow?'

'I'll take my board,' Ian says then walks to the bathroom.

He seems happy enough to spend time with Bella and her husband. I was ready for an argument. Tammy. She'd better not be there!

My phone rings, making me jump. The boys are in bed so I dash downstairs to the landline in the hallway, before the noise wakes them.

'Hello,' I whisper.

'Hi, it's Rose. You okay?'

'Sorry, yes. Boys are asleep. I'll move into the conservatory.' I walk through our breakfast-room looking at all the mess I need to tidy up. I bet Rose's house is pristine.

'What are you up to tomorrow? Fancy riding, I'm going to take Daisy out now she's sound. It's supposed to be sunny.'

I've not told Rose yet that my horse riding days are numbered. 'I would have, but Bella invited us to the beach. I've not seen her since she went walkabouts.'

'That's okay. Is it just you two and the kids going?'

'No. All of us. She said husbands too. Ian's never met Joe before, well I hadn't either until recently.'

'Do you think they'll get on... Ian and Joe? Ian doesn't like Bella does he?'

'He's bringing his board so I expect it'll just be the three of us with the kids.' I hope he doesn't mention her leaving her boys. I should have kept that to myself.

I say my goodbyes to Rose and begin to dread the impending beach trip.

25

I instantly recognise Bella's red convertible BMW, already parked up at the Bay car park. She'll need a bigger one when she has another baby.

'You won't say anything funny, will you?' I quickly ask.

'Not this again. No. I'll keep my opinions to myself. Scouts honour,' Ian promises.

There are no spaces left so we park in the adjacent field.

'I'll come back for my board,' he says, lifting out all our many bags from the boot.

'What about Theo's pram? Will you manage to take it down the steps?'

'Yes, I'll take it first. Actually, you carry Theo and I'll pack up the pram with the bags and lift it all down. Luke will walk, won't he?'

'It's dangerous.'

Ian doesn't reply. He scans the parked cars. Is he

looking for Tammy's light blue Ford Ka? I follow his gaze, hers is the only car I've seen like that with a roof rack. I hope she's not here!

There are a number of wooden steps leading steeply down the cliff to the beach, it's quite an ordeal to get to if you have young children. Lovely once you're down there, then dreadful trying to lug it all back up again!

Ian pushes the pram laden with our bags full of swimwear, towels, spare clothes, buckets and spades, our packed lunches and all Theo's paraphernalia. I carry Theo, he hugs on to me. Luke holds my spare hand as we walk towards the cliff steps.

'Ice cream!' Luke points to the van selling lollies.

'Not now Lukey, on the way back.' He protests loudly. 'Look at the sea.' I say to distract him. It works.

Ian carries the pram over his head down the steps. His muscles show through his T-shirt as he struggles down. I hold back. People overtake me so I stand to one side on the veranda. I look down. It's so steep. I don't think I can manage without any free arms. It doesn't feel safe.

'Charlotte, hi. Let me take one of them.'

'Thanks, Joe.' I gratefully entrust Bella's husband with one of my most precious possessions, Luke. Thank goodness Joe came up to help, there's no way I would have managed alone. He carries Luke in his arms. His dark hair looks shiny, he's not the same stressed-out man who knocked on my door. He looks content. Happy. I'm glad. I've not asked Bella how she changed his mind about trying for a girl again. She scared him. I think he'll give into anything she asks. Ian kind of does with me, but not to that extent. I know we can't afford it, and I've learned through Bella's experiences that it's not pleasant, and doesn't necessarily have the outcome you hoped for.

Ian starts up the steps towards us.

'This is Joe,' I say, stopping for a moment.

'Hi, I'm Ian.'

'Hello,' Joe nods with Luke still in his arms. That felt awkward.

'Just getting my board and wetsuit,' Ian says passing us on the steps. I thought he was going to help by taking Theo from me. Frustrated and feeling abandoned, I carefully take one slow step at a time, using my free hand on the metal railing and holding Theo tightly in the other, I finally reach the bottom. Bella's to the right of the steps with towels and beach mats laid out.

Her two boys are loud and raucous. One of them is stamping on the other ones sandcastle.

'Adam. Stop it!' Joe shouts over my shoulder. He lets go of Luke's hand.

'Thanks,' I say holding out mine for Luke to take. Joe smiles then jogs over to the squabbling pair.

'Hi, Bella.' She pats the towel she's sitting on. I put Theo down next to her.

'How are you?'

'Fine, thanks. You?'

'I'm good.' I start unpacking my bags that Ian discarded near Bella's beach mats. I unfold our blanket and lay it out, having to pull each corner in place afterwards, it never lies flat whenever I do this!

'Here's your bucket and spade, Luke.' He takes it and

starts flicking sand about.

Joe seems to have calmed his boys and is digging a moat all the way down to the sea, I pull out a sun hat from Theo's bag, his beaker of water, and a couple of plastic toys and put in front of him.

'How's it all going?' I gently ask while placing the hat on Theo's head. He swiftly pulls it off and throws it. I pick it up and place it back on, covering his fine dark hair.

'I'm okay. Doctor Spencer came out to see me.'

I exhale, realising I was holding my breath I try to act natural and hide my relief from her. I'm so glad Joe listened to what I'd said. I was worried that I was speaking out of line.

'She's put me on anti-depressants. But I think I might stop taking them.'

'Oh? Why's that?' I say repeating the process of putting Theo's hat back on. He flings it again.

'Joe's agreed to PGD. I'm fine now.'

'Are you sure? I don't think you're meant to suddenly stop taking them.' I glance around, Ian's still up at the car and Joe's out of earshot. 'Why were you at Alum Bay? We were all worried,' I whisper.

Bella picks up Theo's hat for me and places it on his head. 'I wasn't going to jump, if that's what you think?'

'Of course not.' Why would she say that?

She doesn't make eye contact. Pausing, she looks up and opens her mouth to speak. Ian comes down the steps in his wetsuit with his board under his arm. My heart sinks.

Just as Bella forms a word, he cuts in. 'I got changed in

the car. All right, Bella?'

'Hi,' she says. The conversation is over.

'I'm just going to catch a couple of waves, you're okay, aren't you?'

'Yes, go ahead.' I say, although I do find it slightly irritating. Joe is running up and down in and out the sea with his boys. I hear the sound of their happy screams, enjoying their father's attention.

Ian skips off with his board, then he's gone. Gone to the sea. His limbs moving fast and strong through the breakers. Arms for paddles.

I re-apply sun-cream to a protesting Theo, then walk over to Luke and do the same. He's content digging.

'When do you go back to America?' I query.

'Next year. May.'

'Oh, that's a while away? A whole year.'

'Yes, it's a combination of things, and when they can fit us in.'

'Are you going to add to the mortgage again?' Shit I forgot Joe told me this, not Bella.

'We're fine. Joe is taking care of it.'

I look down at the sand, not sure what to say next. Theo picks up his beaker and dribbles water down his cheeks.

Bella helps Luke to pat out his sandcastle. 'Wow, look at that. It came out lovely. Can you find some pretty shells to decorate it with?' she asks him.

'Yeah,' he says and heads off.

'Not too far Lukey,' I call out.

'I'm having a party for Theo next week. Just a small

affair, would you like to come, with Adam and Si, Joe too?'

'God, one already! That year's flown by. Yes we'll all come, that would be lovely.'

'Great. It's on Saturday, two till four, so that he has his nap first. I won't be eating though.'

'Are you attempting already? The new diet plan, wasn't it?'

'Yes the Australian one. And no, not trying for three months. But I have to start the diet now. They sent me through my dates. My first attempt is six a.m. Wednesday fifth of August.'

'That's precise. So I guess Ian won't be eating either?'

'He's not dieting.' Bella raises her eyebrows. 'He doesn't have to start it until six weeks before.' I won't mention that he's refused to participate this time round.

'I couldn't sway naturally again. PGD is the only way to go,' she says, even though her first shot failed.

'Ian won't budge. I have no other choice. I tip milk formula from the dispenser I filled earlier, into a bottle of cooled boiled water. 'If it's a boy, I'd be disappointed to start with, but not because he's a boy, because my dreams of having a daughter will be gone.' I shake the bottle vigorously and pull a bib over Theo's head, replacing his hat again.

'I know, it's like grief isn't it. You have to mourn the loss of the daughter you never had. If only you could choose.'

Agreeing, I pick Theo up and give him his bottle, he sucks enthusiastically, holding it himself. Bella moves towards Joe and her boys to help with the sandcastle construction.

It's such a lovely day for early May, arms and legs bared, the sun penetrates my white skin. It's not warm enough to go swimming, unless you're wearing a thick winter wetsuit, like Ian. Scanning the beach, I search for Tammy. My stomach flips. Is that her? No. Relief floods through me. I shake my head, feeling foolish. Ian swerves in and out of the rolling waves. I watch him as he stands on his board riding one, then falls into the huge white horses.

'How's the stock market going?' I call out to Joe as he walks towards the laid out towels.

'What?'

'The stock market?'

'No idea?' he looks at me blankly.

'I thought that's what you did for a living?' I glance over at Bella as she pats a spade on the upturned bucket of sand, out of earshot.

'I work at the hospital. I'm a porter up at St Mary's.'

'Oh, sorry, I must be thinking of someone else.' I pause, confused, 'How long have you worked there?'

'About twelve years. It's not a great job but it pays the bills, just about.'

I smile. Why did Bella lie about his occupation? And how does she manage to pay for her lifestyle? It can't all be loans? Maybe her flashy car is on credit? I know she's got a mortgage because she's re-mortgaged for the procedure. Why doesn't she work too? Apart from her one hour a week cleaning for Mrs Whicherly, her elderly neighbour across the road from her, she doesn't seem to do much else? The boys are both at school – if they're not overly well off, unlike I've been led to believe, she could help by contributing. Bella looks over at me. I manage a weak smile. Something strange is going on here and I can't work it out.

26

Theo's birthday party is over. Everyone has left now, apart from my mum. Dad's gone down the allotment.

'The bath's ready,' Mum calls out to Ian.

While Ian baths the boys, my mum and I tidy away all the mess.

'It went well didn't it?'

'Yes,' Mum replies. 'Bella's boys managed to behave themselves.'

'They did. Joe's brilliant with them, isn't he?'

'Bella's really lucky, she needs to try and keep hold of that one. She couldn't manage without him. Did you notice that he did everything?'

'I know,' I sigh. Mum passes me another plate to wash up. The dishwasher's full already. 'He doesn't work in London.'

'Oh, on the Island then? A stockbroker, isn't he?'

'Bella told me he was, but the other day on the beach I

asked him. He's a hospital porter.'

'Oh, my word,' my mother laughs.

'At St Marys,' I snigger. 'I'm not laughing about the job. Nothing wrong in that, but it's a bit different to stocks and shares.'

'Well I never. How did Bella explain that one?'

'She doesn't know I know, and I pretended to Joe that I'd confused him with someone else. God only knows where she gets all her money from.'

'The plot thickens.' Mum hands me another plate.

'It certainly does.'

'Did you eat anything?' she questions me, changing the subject.

'I'm on the new diet. Remember?'

'Oh, Char. I'd hoped you'd see sense. It didn't work before. It won't this time either.'

'I just have to try, Mum. One last go.'

'Is it easier than the last?' She sounds resigned.

'I thought it was, but now I'm not so sure,' I falter, feeling her reluctance.

'Oh?' she wipes the washing up bubbles from her hands with a tea-towel and turns to look at me.

'There are a wider variety of foods, but really small quantities. It's so difficult without salt. You have to make everything from scratch.'

'You can buy reduced salt foods though, can't you?'

'Not really. I was looking at mayonnaise jars at the supermarket the other day, the reduced fat ones have more salt in them than the full fat ones!'

'So what are you eating then?'

'Hold on, I'll just check what they're up to,' I walk into the bathroom. 'All okay?'

Ian stops reading the waterproof bath book and looks up. 'Yes, we're fine aren't we boys.'

Luke cheers wanting the story to continue. I smile and head back into the kitchen, leaving them to it.

'Yesterday I had scrambled eggs on toast,' I say.

'You can eat bread?'

'Homemade. I baked it in my bread machine. Online there was a salt free recipe.'

'You can have lots of toast throughout the day, that's okay then?'

'No, I'm only allowed to eat one slice.'

'That's ridiculous. So what else can you have?'

'A handful of nuts, literally about twenty, but not peanuts. Yoghurt, cucumber, apples and pears, rice crackers.'

'So that's lunch, what about dinner?' I hear her mind ticking away, calculating my calorie intake.

'I can have two small potatoes twice a week, peppers, rice and quite a few different veg, but only twice a week for each type. Chicken, I can have chicken. I don't know how I'm going to manage it. Especially where Ian needs to eat similar foods.' My eyes well up. I put the tea-towel down and rub them.

Mum hugs me, 'Oh, Char, don't be upset.'

'I can't help it. It's so hard, already! Plus Ian hasn't agreed that he'll do it, I was just going to cook things up for tea and lunch and not tell him. But I don't know what to make!' I whisper, not wanting Ian to overhear.

'You can eat unsalted butter, and flour?'

'Yes,' I snivel, running my fingers under my eyes to wipe off the mascara that has more than likely smudged over my face.

'I can't cope with you starving yourself again. I'll make you some chicken and vegetable pies, like mini pasties, but with a plain white sauce. We could make a batch up and freeze them – that would make dinners easier, wouldn't it?' I smile and nod as the tears roll down my cheeks. My mother is truly wonderful. 'I'll make a selection tonight and bring them down tomorrow. Twice a week you can have them with potatoes, the rest of the time with rice or pasta.'

'Thanks, Mum, you're a life saver.' I look at the left over bowl of party crisps. Mum follows my gaze, but doesn't comment.

'What are you eating tonight?' she looks concerned.

'All sorted. Grilled peppers with plain couscous.'

'Yum.' Mum playfully licks her lips and we both laugh. 'How are these boys doing?' she says walking into the bathroom. Theo is sat in his yellow bath seat. Luke is giggling as Ian rubs soap between his hands then carefully parts them, blowing a huge bubble. Theo chuckles too. My boys are gorgeous!

Mum leaves, after reading the children their bedtime story. Ian and I sit in the conservatory. I burn my lavender oil and switch my water feature on for the negative ions.

'A year or so and Theo will be in pre-school,' Ian says taking a sip of tea.

I'm on cranberry juice, I can't even have peppermint tea on this new diet. 'I know, all grown up. Luke will be at school in September.'

'Are you sure you want to do it all again, Char? It seems a shame to start over.'

'I hope you're not changing your mind? I've started the diet now – everything's planned.' I panic.

'No, no. it's up to you, just saying it's a shame to go back to the baby stage, that's all,' he adds quickly.

I stare at him, dismayed. Picking up my packet of contraception pills I pierce a tablet through the plastic and pop it in my mouth.

'What's that?'

'I've got to go back on the pill, only for twenty days. It's to align my cycle.'

'Oh.' He places his mug down.

'I need to ovulate on the week we're attempting. We are still doing this, aren't we?'

'Yes, yes, sorry I said anything.'

A week after the party and I've finally found places to store Theo's new toys. He's asleep for his afternoon nap so it's an ideal time to give Luke some one-to-one attention.

'God there are some evil people out there.'

'What?' I say looking up at Ian. His brow is furrowed, sitting on the sofa, anger emanating from his body.

Luke eagerly claps his hands, he's waiting for me to roll the ball back to him. I uncross my legs and kneel up slightly, looking at Ian quizzically.

Luke cries out impatiently, the ball is still in my hand, I roll it back and he grins.

Ian folds up the newspaper roughly and slams it down on the table.

Startled at the noise, Luke bowls his ball in the wrong direction. Getting up on his feet, he hurries over to me, dropping himself quickly into my lap. He snuggles close, sucking his thumb.

'What's up?' I ask Ian, cross that he's upset our son.

'Sorry.' He looks over at Luke, 'I just read about this evil couple. They tortured their three year old daughter. Killed her,' he whispers, trying to shield the information.

'No,' I say, cuddling Luke even closer to me and covering his ears, although he's too young to understand.

'She was only a year younger than Luke. Disgusting. They should be hung for that,' he says.

Later that evening, when the boys are fast asleep, I break down in tears. 'I'd do anything for a daughter,' I complain to Ian, 'anything at all. And those - those animals killed theirs.'

'I know, angel, it's awful.'

I cling onto him, 'it's a terrible thing to happen to any child, regardless of whether they're a boy or a girl. I just can't help feeling envious.'

'I know,' he says.

'I'm so selfish, this dreadful thing has happened and I'm thinking like this. I just want a daughter, that's all. It's only natural, I'm sure all women want one.' Am I trying to convince Ian, or myself?

He doesn't say anything as he releases me from his

arms.

'I don't think people with daughters understand, especially if they had a girl first time round. It's only mothers of sons who can sympathise, that's if they dare admit their own feelings. That's what I think anyway.' I pace around the room. 'What woman wouldn't want a daughter? What's wrong with wanting one? I'm so annoyed that in this day and age it's still a taboo subject. You have to be grateful for what you get, and only hope for a healthy one. Surely that goes without saying,' I pause, taking a breath.

Ian picks up his surfing magazine. I continue my rant, 'I know I'm lucky and all that, but if I'd had a daughter first time round, or second, I wouldn't be feeling this way now. Perhaps I'd be one of the smug mothers of daughters, never knowing or bothering to understand how someone else could be feeling.' I've said too much, I'm a horrible person, I should just forget it all and be happy with my boys.

'When are we doing it then?' Ian asks, resigned, noisily turning a page.

'You're still willing?' I should have just jumped at his question, taken it as an agreement, but I need reassurance.

'You know I'll do it, Char.'

'Day after Luke's birthday.' I reply, my heart soaring.

That's it, we're all set to go.

The months trudge by. I get thinner – not as bony as last time, but I'm on my way to getting there. Luke is turning four in a few weeks, the summer drawing to a close as autumn rears its colourful head.

Ian wraps his arms around me. 'Come on let's go upstairs.'

Oh shit. How am I going to get out of this? 'I can't. Wrong time of the month.'

He sighs. I can't pretend I'm on my period until after Luke's birthday. But I'll have to try. My first attempt is six in the morning the day after the party – how on earth am I going to make this go to plan?

Luke's party goes well. Evening comes. I prepare everything I need for tomorrow morning and settle myself in bed. Sleep consumes me, I feel like my eyes are flickering, then it is blackness. Hollow and empty. I'm standing in a room with my children. I think they're my children, anyway. Five of them. I don't recognise their features, they don't look like mine? The four older ones are boys, they're squabbling. I look into the cot. My daughter. I know she's mine, she's beautiful with golden locks. She opens her mouth. She has teeth. Black teeth. I scream but no sound emerges. I run to the mirror and look at my reflection. I smile, mine are black too. Rushing back to the cot, I see that the baby's face has turned pale green. She smiles at me and her teeth have changed shape, like fangs. Her green face wrinkles and her hair transforms into dark matted, coarse fur, like a rat's. My throat is closing. My breathing constricts. She's cackling, the baby is laughing at me. Her eyes flicker and roll in her head, spinning and spinning until they also turn black. I run. It's dark again. I'm falling. Help me.

I jump at the sound of my alarm bleeping.

'God, what time is it?' Ian asks as I press the stop button. It's five, but I don't answer. I hurry out to the ensuite bathroom and pee on an ovulation prediction strip. I feel strange. My mind is whirling, did I have a dream last night? Or a nightmare? I can't remember. I need to concentrate. A slight line appears. Great we're on target. I jump back into bed, I think Ian has drifted off, I nudge my way over to him. 'It's too early. I'm still asleep.'

'Oh come on,' I protest, rolling myself on top of him. I kiss him while wriggling out of my pyjamas. After not much coaxing he gives in. Thank the lord, it's all going to plan. It feels so good after weeks of holding off. But I must try not to enjoy it too much. I rein myself in and think of something un-stimulating. Shopping. I need to add plain flour to the list – I've almost run out of Mum's ready-made pies...

After the deed is over I excuse myself to go to the bathroom. Unbeknown to Ian, I insert a lime douche to keep my pH low. Well that was the first date carried out. Only once today, but tomorrow I need Ian to cooperate in the morning and the evening. I hope it all runs as smoothly as it has today. Stress is the last thing I need but I don't see how I'm going to keep Ian from catching on that this is not just another diet. I'm embarking on another swaying mission.

27

Like Groundhog Day my alarm bleeps early in the morning. After peeing on an ovulation prediction strip and checking the light blue line to see if I'm still on target I jump back into bed and roll onto Ian.

'Can we leave the baby making until tonight, angel?' His voice thick with sleep.

'No. We'll do both.'

'Oh really?' he kisses me roughly, tugging at my pyjamas. His hands caress me. It feels like old times, before my obsession. Shocked by his sudden urge, I feel competitive as I shake away the fears of Tammy. He sucks my earlobe, my trigger. Going in for the kill he flips me over onto my back, forcing my legs apart with his knee. It's exciting, but I mustn't orgasm. I can't. He brings me to the edge. I try to stop myself from letting go. Ripples surge through me. After no pleasure for weeks, other than yesterday when I somehow managed to distance it, I feel like I'm going to explode. I need to stop myself. He nibbles my earlobe again. My nerve endings pulsate as I climax.

Heavy breathing, sweaty and clammy I lie back in a daze. I can't believe I let that happen. All the planning. The money I have spent, and now I've completely ruined my sway.

'I'm so cross with myself,' I tell Rose the next day, 'the only saving grace is that it was missionary position. But I wish I hadn't. Orgasms are for swaying to have a boy.'

'I'm sure it'll be okay, you've still got more dates to attempt on this week though, haven't you?'

'Yes, but I'm not going to bother.'

'Really? You've only done it once.'

'Twice,' I correct her, 'thankfully I did a lime douche to lower my pH. Hopefully that will have helped the situation!'

'Just carry on as planned. You have to so you can come off that diet and put the weight back on.' She sounds concerned. Not this again.

'Because I was in a spin about it all, I didn't push Ian to do it again in the evening.'

'So?'

'So he won't have released. It all makes a difference you know.'

'If you say so,' she laughs, tickling Theo's toes.

'Time for your nap, little man.' I scoop him up and carry him into his nursery. Let's hope I'm not pregnant. I really want a good shot at this. I kiss Theo and place him in his cot. Drawing his curtains closed, I pause to look at him as he sucks his thumb and turns onto his side. I close the door gently and head back into the conservatory.

'What time do you pick Luke up?' Rose asks.

'Three. He goes to pre-school all day on a Wednesday and Friday.'

'You'll have your work cut out for you, three children under five. I don't envy you.'

'I'm not pregnant yet.'

'You might be?'

'Let's catch some rays while Theo's asleep. I'll bring his monitor out with me.'

We set up the reclining garden chairs and lay outside in the September sun. I roll up my navy linen trousers and relax, sunglasses in place. Theo's wails ring out on the monitor. Sighing, I get up and walk inside to see him.

'Poopy nappy,' I inform Rose when I return.

'Gross. Another thing I don't envy you about.'

I laugh. Settling back down, I brace myself for having to get up to him again. After ten minutes I relax into my chair.

Should I ask Rose about her sister? I don't know how to bring it up. I can't it's not fair to put her in the middle. Awkwardly I remove my sunglasses and prop myself up. I have to ask. I feel as if it's burning in my chest.

'Tammy still surfs then?' I reach down and pick a blade of grass. The lawn needs cutting.

'I think so. You probably know more than me.' Rose lifts her shades and looks through me. 'Oh, Char, you don't still think there's something going on with Ian and my sister, do you?'

I look down at my hands and peel the piece of grass in half along its seam.

She exhales. 'You're mad. He adores you. Honestly I'm sure you're worrying for nothing.'

'You're right,' I say, 'I'm being paranoid. Ignore me.' I flick the grass away.

'Tammy's got a boyfriend, you know.'

'I know. I know. Forget it. I'm ridiculous, it's just that he talks about her a lot, and sees her too.'

'Surfing,' Rose cuts in, 'nothing else.'

'I'm jealous. They can both share a sport.'

'You could go with him.'

'No I couldn't. Someone's got to look after the children. We can't both have a hobby, or not the same one at least.'

'I suppose. Stop worrying. Tammy and Max are really happy. Don't tell anyone but I get the feeling he's going to pop the question.'

'Really?' my heart soars with relief. Stupid, as it doesn't mean that nothing is going on with her and my husband. Or perhaps there was something between them, and now it's over. Could I forgive him? How can I be questioning Ian's feelings for me after the way he made love to me yesterday morning? I smile at the memory, although it shouldn't have happened, it might help to bring us back together again. I recline my chair, basking in the warmth.

Two weeks later I pace up and down the conservatory. I'm due on today but I've had no bleeding at all. Shall I take a test? No, it wouldn't have worked first time, would it? Especially with all the lime I used afterwards. I rub my sensitive breasts through my jumper. They are tingly, which could mean either I'm pregnant or I'm about to come on. I've got my plan sorted out for this month. We have five attempts pencilled in, depending on my ovulation date. After messing up last month's baby making with an orgasm, putting myself dangerously in boy territory, I was relying on the fact that I had another chance. Now I'm not so sure I have.

Jogging upstairs, I locate my pack of pregnancy tests and pee on the stick then wait the agonising three minutes. If I'm pregnant then I can eat something nice. But if I'm not, at least I can concentrate on getting my sway perfect next time. I squeeze my eyes shut. Please don't let me be pregnant. I didn't do it right. I turn the test over, my heart thumps loudly. Two blue lines. Positive. Oh my God. I'm pregnant again!

28

The scent of frying steak fills the room. I flip the meat over with a spatula.

'Smells lovely, angel,' Ian cuddles me from behind. 'Hang on a minute. What's going on? Steak? It's usually one of those bland pies with plain pasta on the menu.'

I smile, my cheeks bursting.

'You're not?'

'I am.'

Ian runs his hands through his hair. It could do with a trim, it's past his shoulders now!

'What's up?' Suddenly I don't feel hungry anymore.

'Nothing. I just wasn't expecting it yet, that's all.'

'Neither was I. You're okay with it, aren't you?'

'I guess so. I'm just not looking forward to what's coming next.'

'The baby stage?' I enquire, confused.

'No. All the bloody madness. Trips to Cambridge and

Kent. You being upset all the time.'

I turn the heat off the hob and start to plate up our food. 'Can you go and get the boys while I set the table please.' I feel hurt. The Cambridge trip didn't work out. That wasn't my fault. Well I guess it was because my bowel was in the way so they couldn't carry out the procedure, but the trip to Kent went smoothly, unless you count the fact that my poor mum had to look after Luke while she had a sickness bug, and the snow and ice. Plus the fact that the doctor confirmed from the nub shot scan that I was having another boy, but other than that...

'I've phoned Doctor Thompson's surgery and booked my nub gender scan. It's in two months,' I say while rummaging through the box of coloured threads resting on Rose's mahogany coffee table.

'In December?' she asks.

'End of November. Twenty ninth, I think. I'll be twelve weeks exactly then. I've not told Ian though.'

'He'll go again, won't he?'

'Yes, I'm sure he will. I'll tell him nearer the time.'

Rose nods, stroking her cat, the one with the white patch. I sit back on her leather sofa and pick up my cross-stitch, threading through a sage coloured silk. The cat jumps off her lap and swipes at it. 'No, Pickles, stop it,' Rose says, playfully pulling the cat's tail.

'I think I've got the wrong shade of green anyway,' I say, 'I'm not sure I'm doing it very well either. It's all bumpy, not like yours.'

'I've been embroidering for years. Look, you need to

unpick that bit.' She takes the white sheet of fabric and its botched up threads from me.

'Look at the back,' I say, 'it's a knotted mess.'

'I think you've chosen a really difficult design for your first attempt. Why don't you start smaller? A bookmark or something?'

I smile, 'I really wanted a family tree. I thought I'd frame it and put it up in the hall.'

'But you've not completed your family. You've still got one cooking,' Rose laughs.

'I've got eight months left. I figured it would take me longer than that, and I'd do the last baby name and date of birth after I've had her.'

'Her?'

'Or him,' I quickly correct myself as I stare at the log burning stove and its surrounding stonewall.

'You will be okay, won't you,' Rose says unpicking nearly all of my efforts.

'What do you mean?'

'You know what I mean. If you have another boy.'

'Of course I will,' I say with a conviction I don't actually feel. Rose looks at me, then continues unpicking my threading, with the help of the cat.

'Thanks,' I say, taking the wooden hoop, which holds the fabric in place from her. I re-thread my needle and start to follow the pattern again while Rose struggles to hold Pickles back.

After an hour of achieving nothing, I say my goodbyes.

'How did it go?' Ian asks when I return home.

'Okay. I don't think I'm going to carry on though. It's

too fiddly. Boys behave?'

'Fast asleep, I didn't hear a peep out of them.'

'That's good.'

'You know I'm surfing first light.'

'Oh. When will you be home?'

'After lunch.' My heart sinks. I had hoped tomorrow would be a family day seeing as it's Sunday. Ian had to go into work today and he's already worked late four evenings this week, then been surfing the other two. I expect Tammy will be there at the bay...

I struggle to contain myself over the next two months. Avoiding but bursting to tell Ian that I've booked an appointment. Now it's close I'll have to tell him. He's been so distant and distracted. Surfing more and more and working overtime at the garage, leaving me and the boys alone. Why haven't I told him I've booked a slot with Doctor Thompson? I'm worried. My stomach churns, I've never felt doubt like this before. Ian and I have always been so solid.

'Ian?'

'What?' he replies zipping up his wetsuit.

I'm just going to have to blurt it out. 'We've got an appointment with that doctor in Kent.'

'What!' he cuts in.

'This Saturday. It's the nub shot one,' I stammer.

'I know what it is! I was there last time, remember?' I swallow hard, pleading with my eyes. 'It's not happening, Char, not this time.'

'But-'

'No buts.' He turns to leave.

'Ian. Wait.'

'It's a no, Charlotte. That's final.'

'But...' I stand still, open mouthed.

'We can't go again anyway, we were only there a year ago. We'd look even more conspicuous than we did last time!'

'It was two years ago and I thought of that so I booked it under my maiden name. You could wear your hair tied back and I could wear lots of make-up.'

'Go in disguise?' he sneers. 'I said no, Charlotte. That's final. I'm sure Bella will accompany you.' He storms over to the key-rack and extracts the bunch for his van.

'What time will you be back?'

'Late,' he says, slamming the door closed behind him. Thank God the glass panels stayed in place, unlike the disaster last time he stormed off in a huff a couple of years back. He's not going to change his mind, I can tell that, and he called me Charlotte, twice. My full name. Has he called me angel since I told him I was pregnant?

With shaking hands I reach for my mobile.

ANY CHANCE YOU CAN COME WITH ME TO KENT NEXT SATURDAY? I hit send and cross my fingers. Within moments I have a reply from Bella.

SORRY I CAN'T. ME AND JOE ARE IN BIRMINGHAM. Shit I'd forgotten about her appointment on Friday, they must be staying overnight? Desperately I send the same message to Rose. Hopefully she'll come? There's no one else I can try. The only other person who knows about it all is my mum, and she'll be having the boys for me. I can't believe Ian is being like this. I stand and impatiently wait, twisting my hair round and round my fingers. Stop it. I scrunch it in my hands and roughly pull it making myself wince.

After reading my reply from Rose, saying she can't make it either, my stomach really does churn and I vomit violently down the toilet.

That's it. I'll have to cancel. I can't go on my own. I'm too sick. There's no way the morning sickness will clear up before the scan date. Everything is going wrong. I messed up my sway so it's bound to be another boy and now my husband is so fed up with my obsessive behaviour he has cleared off surfing. Or worse.

After my tears have dried up I take a deep breath and telephone the surgery, cancelling the appointment I'd so longed to go to. I will never forgive Ian for this. Never.

29

Sunday 30th November. The day after what would have been my scan date. I should know what I'm having by now. The little nub would have either have been pointing upwards like last time or parallel to the spine if it's a girl. But I didn't go to the gender scan, thanks to Ian. I feel so disappointed and bitter that the date has passed and I couldn't persuade him to reconsider. Things have changed, we barely speak, and now Christmas is around the corner. Again.

Strapping Theo into his baby seat and Luke into his booster, I drive to my local DIY store. This year I'm going to be prepared for the festive season.

Theo rides in the trolley making chugging noises as Luke helps me to push in a game of trains. An elderly lady smiles at us as we chug past her. Bringing the play to an end, I pick up a box containing a five-foot artificial Christmas tree. Stuff getting a real one, I'm going to do things the easy way this year, like Bella, especially seeing as Ian doesn't seem to be in the mood to participate. He's out surfing again, on a family day. The last thing I'm going to do is ask for his help.

I drive home to see Ian's van parked outside our house. Back already? Carrying Theo and holding Luke's hand, I negotiate my way inside and find him with a holdall slung over his shoulder. It must be his surfing gear. He looks tearfully down at Luke and rubs his head. I feel like I'm going to be sick. This can't be happening.

'I've bought a tree. A fake one,' I say. He doesn't reply. 'It's in the boot.' I look up at him. He won't meet my eye.

'I'm sorry.' He bends down and kisses the boys heads.

'What do you mean?' Oh my God.

'I'm going to stay in Phil's flat for a bit. His tenant has left. I'm going to rent it off him.'

'What?' My world crumbles. 'You can't leave me, I'm pregnant.'

'I'm sorry.'

'I can't be a single mother to three children.' Theo wriggles to get down. I set him on the floor. 'Luke, take your brother into the lounge to play, please.' He takes Theo's hand and leads him away.

'Just a trial separation,' Ian says.

'It's nearly Christmas. You can't do this to me and the kids. It's her, isn't it? You're seeing Tammy, aren't you?'

Silence.

'Aren't you,' I repeat, my mind working in overdrive. Convenient that his brother's tenant has moved out. Has he been setting this up for a while?

'No. We're just friends. Nothing's going on. I just need some space.'

'Space!' I shout. 'Space! You could have thought about that before you got me pregnant again!'

'I didn't think you'd fall straight away. You didn't last time. I'd changed my mind not long after, but it was too late.'

'You'd changed your mind?'

'Stop shouting, Char, you'll scare the kids.'

'Don't pretend you're thinking about the children. Just get out!'

'I'll call you.' He picks up the holdall.

'Don't bother,' I hiss clenching my teeth. When the door closes my legs turn to jelly. I slump to the floor in the hallway too numb to cry.

A few lonely days pass. I keep thinking about the last time we made love, when this baby was conceived. He was really into it, was he thinking of her? Was it a goodbye, one last parting shot? I still can't bring myself to tell anyone that he's gone. That would make it real. It doesn't feel real, so it can't be. My husband, nearly five years of marriage, and ten years together, has left me. Trial separation? Poppycock as my mother would say. Space. Where's my space, not everyone can walk out and start a new life, not the woman anyway. And I wouldn't want to. I couldn't leave my lovely boys. There's definitely more to this than he's letting on. Despite my fears, would Tammy really dump her fiancé Max, for my husband? Why would she want the baggage? And this isn't the Ian I know and love. It must be something else. To leave his children. He loves them. He loves me, doesn't he? I'll phone Rose, maybe she knows. But not now. I can't process things properly yet. I can't think clearly and the morning sickness is still raging on.

The weekend arrives, I dress the children in matching outfits – brown cord trousers, a long sleeved navy T-shirt, with a light blue knitted tank top over it. I smile with pride at my smart boys, one with curly golden locks, the other with fine brown spikes.

There is a knock at the door. Why doesn't he let himself in? He still has his key. I open the door, positioning myself against the overflowing coat-rack. Ian gives me a curt nod then stands awkwardly in the hall.

'They're in the lounge,' I say, feeling nervous. He's my husband but he is acting like a stranger. I'm dying to ask him about the flat and how he's getting on on his own, but I stop myself. Not in front of the children. It could end up getting nasty again.

'Daddy,' Luke calls out.

'Come to Daddy.' He envelopes them into his arms. 'What time do you want them back?'

'After tea?' I suggest. I suppose they need to spend some quality time with their dad, they've missed him. I've missed him. My heart feels hollow. The pain of having to hand my children over for the first time feels like some sort of punishment. I guess it gets easier with time. I won't find out though, this is just a temporary arrangement.

'About six?'

'Yes, that's fine.' I hand him a bag packed full of all the essentials and kiss my sons goodbye.

Now what do I do? I wander through the silent house, it seems so cavernous and empty. Now that I've actually got some time to myself, what on earth am I going to do with it? I pick up a picture of four smiling faces – me, Ian, Luke and Theo. One big happy family, or so I thought? A picture tells a thousand lies. What went wrong? Everything got out of control when we were trying to conceive Theo, but this time round was easier? I rub my belly. Ian didn't even ask how I was or how the pregnancy is going? He knows how sick I've been. I return the silver framed picture back to its place and grab my handbag and car keys. I can't stay here on my own.

Pulling up in Rose's yard, I kill the engine and flip the boot open. Exchanging my shoes for wellies, I stride across the muddy farm in search of her.

'Char, hi,' she says emerging from the barn. I hope I'm not interrupting something. I should have phoned first.

'I just thought I'd pop by. Are you busy?'

'No, not at all. Steve's just left.'

'Oh,' I say.

'We're taking it slowly, seeing how it goes,' she giggles. 'The horses needed shoeing anyway.'

'Really?'

'Yes, really.' My stomach knots with jealousy. She looks so happy and radiant. 'Who's got the boys, your mum?'

'No. Ian.'

'Not surfing then?'

'Not today.' How am I going to say this without

breaking down? I don't want to cry again. I'm done with crying.

'You okay, Char? You look a bit peaky.'

'It's just-'

'Ah, the morning sickness,' she cuts in, 'good sign though ay?' Apple the appaloosa neighs loudly. 'They're hungry, I'm just about to give them their breakfast.'

'I'll help.' I follow her into the storeroom.

Rose unstacks seven buckets and adds a shovel of horse mix to each.

'Shall I cut the carrots?'

'Please.' She hands me a knife. I pull open the bag and cut them lengthwise and then into half.

'One each?' I enquire.

'Yes, that'll do.'

The smell of the horse food fills the storeroom. I inhale the country aromas as I drop carrots into each feed bowl.

'What's up? You're ever so quiet?'

My stomach lurches. 'Ian's left me.' I admit as I stifle a sob.

'Oh my God! Really?' she hugs me, 'When?'

I wipe away my tears and lean into her. When? Why ask when? 'A week ago.'

'A whole week. You didn't tell me? I texted you a couple of days back, you didn't say?'

'It's all my fault, Rose, I've been so preoccupied with trying for a girl. I never gave him enough attention, not really.'

'Don't be silly. He's a grown man, not a child. I can't

believe he left you in your condition.'

'He said he'd changed his mind about trying for a third, but it was too late because I was already pregnant.'

'The little shit,' she says, venomously. Taken aback by her tone, I wonder if she too has suspicions about him and her sister. Rose looks away. 'Sorry, I'm just so mad that he's left you. And his kids too. What the hell's the matter with him?'

'You're right, he is a shit, more than a shit, a twat.'

'That's right, let all the anger out.'

'Bastard,' I spit.

After a torrent of cursing, the impatient horses bang their hooves against the stable doors. I help Rose to put the buckets of mix into each stall. With the smell of food enticing them, they are annoyed at having to wait while we swear and holler, trying to think up vile words to describe my husband, acting like school kids on a mission.

'Have you told your mum?'

'Not yet.'

'So you've been dealing with this on your own? Oh, Char, you really should have told me. I don't like to think of you upset and alone.'

'I'm not alone, I have Luke and Theo.'

'It's not the same,' Rose says, as she fills a bucket with water from the yard tap. I take the handle and lift it up, spilling drops against my wellies as I rock side to side walking it to the first stable. 'You shouldn't be carrying that. It's too heavy.'

'I'm pregnant, not incapacitated.' I struggle on.

Rose shakes her head.

Entering the stable, I rub my favourite boy's long brown nose. Since Daisy became lame, I now ride Jolly the most often, well, until my recent swaying journey, that is. He snorts and dips his muzzle into the bucket of water, then comes up, disappointed it's not more food. 'You greedy thing,' I say as I bolt his door.

'You're not lifting any more buckets. Okay?'

'Okay.' I wander over to the barn and perch on a hay bale. Should I ask Rose about her sister? Last I'd heard, Max had proposed. I'm being stupid, they're just friends. Rose joins me. We sit in uncomfortable silence for a while. I get the feeling she knows I have questions that will put her in an awkward position. Even if she does know something, would she tell me? We may have been best friends since primary school but blood is thicker than water, so they say.

'I know I've mentioned this before,' I start, 'but I have to ask. Do you think anything's going on?'

'Between Ian and Tammy, you mean?'

'Yes.'

'To be honest, I don't know. She and Max seem to be going through a rough patch at the moment.'

I don't want to hear this. 'I thought they'd just got engaged?'

'So did I. It seems it's off now.' A sickly feeling lurches through me. 'But they're still together,' she quickly adds, 'just.'

'What do you mean, just?'

'They've postponed it, I believe. I've not spoken to

Tam, but Mum says she thinks there's something amiss. I'm sure she's wrong though. You know what my mum's like. She reads anything into the smallest of things.'

I force a smile. It is true, Mrs Hutton is a gossip. She exaggerates beyond belief, but I feel there's an element of truth in what she's saying. I hate Tammy for monopolising Ian's time in a way that I couldn't. I can't compete with someone with no ties. How can I possibly be carefree and enjoy a hobby with him when I have children to look after. His children, for that matter! Maybe she's innocent? But I still hate her.

A rogue sheep enters the barn. One of the old, tame, hand reared ewes. She puts her head into the bag of carrots and starts to munch.

'Oi!' Rose shouts shooing the matted sheep out. She leaves with a long bleat, which starts a chorus from the other ewes. Not long after, the horses join in the cacophony.

'Come on, let's get some lunch,' Rose says, 'treat ourselves at the pub.'

'Good idea. I am separated now after all,' I say with a forced smile. Single and pregnant is the last thing I imagined for myself.

30

Christmas day. I wake up early and alone. Last night it felt miserable setting out the mince pie and glass of milk for Santa without Ian. I hid my feelings from my sons and made it as fun as possible. Luke has stopped questioning why his daddy isn't living with us anymore. And Theo's too young to understand. I placed their stockings at the bottom of their beds, filled with gifts from Father Christmas. All their other presents are under the tree. All except for Ian's.

'Mummy, he's been. Mummy,' I hear the excited shouts from the boys bedroom. They share a room now, and they love it. I felt guilty turfing Theo out of his nursery, and apprehensive about the change in sleeping arrangements, but they settled in together beautifully, as if they had never been apart.

I rush down the stairs, wiping tears from my eyes, and begin the joy of Christmas. After the whirlwind of present opening, wrapping paper strewn all around the room and toys discarded, I dress the boys, and then myself with the clothing I chose last night. Having searched through my maternity garments to no avail, then my usual wardrobe, I looked to my summer outfits in desperation and came up with a berry coloured sleeveless smock-dress. Teamed up with my black long sleeved stretchy top underneath and leggings, it's made a perfect combination, accentuating my neat bump.

I set the Christmas pudding on the hob to steam, then increase the temperature on the oven and consult my checklist. Everything is ready. Now to prepare myself, before Ian arrives. The boys are happily playing with their new battery operated trains. I sit in the lounge on the sofa and start to paint my face. In-expertly smearing matte beige liquid colouring. I check my image in the mirror. I look like I've been Tangoed. What am I doing? I never wear foundation. Ian won't know what to think. But that's what I want. I want him to look at me differently when he arrives. I need him to see that I'm coping independently, but at the same time I want to spark his attraction. We can sort this out. He can't be happy being apart from his family at Christmas? I rub the excess colour off with some toilet tissue then start on my eyebrows. When did I last pluck them? They look like furry caterpillars. I tweeze them into neat arches, then apply smoky grey eye-shadow, blusher and mascara. I finish off with a light pink lip-gloss. I look at my reflection. Pathetic and desperate. Completely unattractive. Wiping the gloss from my lips, I hear the bell ring. I hastily ruffle my hair as I race to the door. My heart leaps.

'Daddy's here,' I call out to the boys, as I let Ian into his former home.

'Hello dumplings,' he says to the children as they rush to him, almost knocking him over. He smiles at me. I rub my tummy, a gesture which I hope will remind him that he is going to be a father again. 'Merry Christmas,' he says.

'You too.'

'Father Christmas dropped off some more presents to me, and they have your names on them.'

The boys cheer.

'Come on, let's take them into the sitting room,' I say, ushering everyone out of the hallway. I watch from the side-line as Ian helps the boys to open the gifts. I note that there is nothing for me. What did I expect? He's gone overboard for the children, they've got way too much and we've doubled up on the battery operated trains, I did tell him I was getting them! I watch the boys open Lego, bricks, play-doh and huge stuffed teddy bears. He's making up for being a part-time dad I guess? Well hopefully that'll change and we can all be as one again.

'Glass of eggnog,' I offer.

Ian looks at me awkwardly. 'I can't stay long.'

'But it's Christmas. I thought you'd want to spend time with us?'

'I'm having the kids tomorrow though, aren't I? We discussed it. You said I could.' He stands up, vacating the sofa. Uncomfortable.

'Yes. That's still fine,' I bite back my tears. Spotting the metallic green wrapping on the gift I bought him, I edge closer to it and gently kick it further under the tree. Unnoticed, I hope.

'My parents are looking forward to having them for tea. I was going to ask you actually, would it be okay if they stay the night too? Mum's got a travel cot, and I'm going to stay over. My flat's too small.'

'Oh. I don't know?' I look at my hands. What's happening? His flat. This isn't sounding as temporary as he'd initially suggested.

'They're my kids too.'

I stand up, needing to be the same height as him. 'They've never slept out before. I don't want to be apart from them. Not at Christmas.' I say as confidently as I can, unmasking my unease by twisting my wedding ring round and round. He can't be asking this. Not now.

'Oh come on, Char, be fair.'

'Fair, you're the one who walked out on us.'

'I walked out on you. Not them. I want them to stay over.'

Tears form in my eyes. I hear a hissing sound. I rush into the kitchen. Shit, the pudding water has evaporated. I switch the gas off the hob and boil the kettle. Hopefully I'll be able to salvage the Christmas pudding, but it's looking extremely unlikely I can salvage my marriage.

I manage to survive the rest of the day. My parents arrived not long after Ian left, which relieved the pressure slightly and gave me some adult company. My mother kept tight-lipped about her opinion of Ian and we made the day as special as we could for the children. I declined my brother's invitation of a Boxing Day dinner. I'm going to stay in bed and while the day away.

Bella texted, wishing me happy Christmas. I replied miserably, informing her that I've been hoodwinked into letting the kids stay over at my mother-in-laws. I decide not to tell Rose, she's spending the holiday weekend with Steve, I don't want to ruin her first Christmas with her hunky blacksmith boyfriend.

The next day, resigned, I pack the boys overnight bags. Why did I agree to this? Did I agree to it? I'm not sure that I did? Travel cot indeed, where did that come from? I visualise Viv excitedly dashing out to purchase it. Now they can all play happy families, without me.

'Have a lovely time, won't you. Mummy will miss you both,' I kiss my children goodbye.

'Thanks,' Ian says awkwardly shifting on his feet. I stand still, feeling numb and betrayed. I can't speak to him. I'm fuming inside. 'I'll bring them back tomorrow afternoon.'

'Morning. I want them back early.'

'Okay. Have a nice day.'

I wave at the boys and close the door. Nice day. Was he being sarcastic? Walking into the lounge I stand and stare at Luke's slippers discarded on the copper coloured rug. I pick them up and weep, hugging them to my tummy. I can't stay here, perhaps I will go to my brother's after all? No. I don't want to spend time with him and his children, when mine won't be there to play with their cousins, and I couldn't bear to witness pity from him or my sister-in-law. I boil the kettle and resign myself to boredom and loneliness.

My phone rings. It's Bella. With blurry eyes, I stare at her number flashing on the screen. It goes to answering machine. I quickly pick it up.

'Hi,' I grumble.

'You can't be on your own on Boxing Day. Come to ours.' She sounds merry.

'I don't want to encroach on your Christmas.'

'Don't be silly. Joe won't mind. He can play with the boys while we catch up, have a few drinks and let our hair down.'

'I'm pregnant.'

'Okay, you can have orange juice.'

I wander into the boys bedroom with the phone, mulling it over. It will be strange celebrating with someone else's family.

'Come on. I'll see you in half an hour.' The phone-line dies before I have the chance to protest. I pick up one of Luke's bedtime toys from his pillow. Not his favourite - I packed that in his overnight bag. It was heart wrenching saying goodbye to them. I hug the toy gibbon close, inhaling the smell, then place it neatly back. I then lower the cot bars and rearrange Theo's toys and blankets. His favourite rabbit has gone with him to Ian's parents too.

That's it, snap out of it. Grabbing my bag and keys and locking the door behind me, I get in my car and drive the short journey to Bella's house.

'Come on in. Make yourself at home.' Joe says warmly

accepting my jacket.

'Thanks.' I follow him through the large, modern, open-planned kitchen, which is still as gleaming as ever, to the sitting room.

'Char, I'm so glad you came,' Bella beams, already looking three sheets to the wind. Joe takes her wine glass from her as she staggers towards me. Abruptly she stops in her tracks and slumps on the dark leather settee. 'Spoil sport,' she hisses at him as he places the glass on the coffee table.

'Hi Adam, Si,' I say feeling as if I'm intruding. They grunt and continue playing on their handheld computers.

'I'll put the kettle on,' Joe says and walks off, shaking his head.

I rub my cold hands together, the flames in the gas fire, designed to look like a wood burning stove flicker gold and blue. The mantelpiece is impeccably dressed with an artificial garland. Roasted orange slices and tied bundles of cinnamon sticks decorate it beautifully. Although I can tell they are shop bought as they are all exactly the same circular shape and have no scent. It is completed with a tartan stocking hung either side. The tree tastefully matches with red and gold baubles. Not like my homely one with its mismatch of colours and trinkets that Luke and Theo made.

'I've got an idea,' Bella whispers, too close for comfort, her breath reeking of booze. She stands, using the couch arm to steady herself and wobbles off into the other room.

I wish I'd stayed home.

Joe comes back with my drink. 'Thank you,' I say accepting it as he sits next to me.

'Sorry about Bella, I don't know what's got into her.'

I smile at him.

Bella reappears with her iPad and plonks herself between me and Joe. She taps away surprisingly fast for someone who is intoxicated.

'Babybind,' she says.

'What's that?' I ask.

Joe exhales loudly.

'Oh shut up.'

I shift uncomfortably. Joe doesn't respond.

'Look it says at sixteen weeks they do a gender scan. It is actually called that,' she turns and waves her finger in my face, 'because-that-is-what-it-is-for,' she says slowly emphasising each word and ending with a hiccup.

I look at the screen. 'It's in Southampton.'

'Exactly,' she passes it to me.

I scroll down. 'Eighty pounds and ninety-eight percent accurate. Open Saturdays,' I read.

'You could get rid of it,' she whispers loudly. I look over at her children. Simon glances at me, then looks down at his computer. Adam, however, stands up and leaves the room.

'Ad,' Joe calls out. He shoots Bella a look of despair and chases after his son. Simon follows after them.

'Your kids,' I say.

'I was only saying, that's all. You can abort up to twenty-four weeks, you know.'

I look at the iPad. 'Twenty-four. That's terrible, people

give birth more prematurely than that and the baby lives.' Bella reaches for her glass and takes a gulp of wine. 'I'm not terminating whatever the outcome, but I think I might do this, seeing as it's local. Don't you want to see your kids?'

She gets up in search of her family. I watch her hug Adam and Simon in turn. They dubiously return her gesture. Her home is perfectly in order, designed exactly how she wants it. But her children break the mould. They are pieces that don't fit in her puzzle. Is this what I'm like?

Joe sets out a board game and we spend most of the afternoon playing Monopoly, eating the delicious meal he prepared in between, then returning to our places. The boys seem to be happy again, basking in their father's love, the stupid drunken words of their mother unmentioned as the game recommences. Bella states that she's bored and wanders off so Joe shares her few houses and hotels between the children. Adam gives up and starts up his computer game again, but he did really well for his age, so we declare Simon the winner and pack it away. 'Thanks for that,' Joe says.

'What?'

'You're brilliant with the boys, they've really taken to you.' He places his hand on my shoulder. Looking into his hazel eyes, I feel strange. He smiles, showing his charmingly crooked teeth. How had I not noticed them before? I'm a dental nurse, teeth are my thing. He removes his hand and scratches his head, looking away. Awkwardly I twist my hair around my fingers.

'What the fuck,' Bella shouts. I jump. 'It's got two lines. Two fucking lines.'

Pregnancy test in one hand, wine glass in the other, she takes a noisy slurp and thrusts the white stick at me.

I look at it, two lines, pale, but there all the same. 'You're pregnant?'

'Well I'm not keeping it.'

'Hang on,' Joe says looking dazed. 'Of course we're keeping it. You're not doing what you did last time!' he implores.

'But the PGD?' she whines.

'It's out of our hands.'

Bella snatches the test from me and throws it at him. She gulps what's left of her wine then slams the glass on the coffee table.

'Calm down. And stop drinking.'

Bella slumps to her knees and hollers, her hands covering her face. I tensely rub her back. 'You could be carrying a girl, you never know.' She looks up, her cheeks flushed and mascara smudged around her eyes.

'And I meant what I said.' Joe says, 'I'm not having a repeat of last time. Especially not with what you said earlier. No private scans!'

I help Bella to her feet. 'I need to go to sleep,' she says.

I fetch my coat and handbag while Joe settles a distraught Bella into bed.

'You don't have to go,' he says when he reaches the bottom of the stairs.

'I think it's best, I'm tired too.'

Joe's eyes gaze intensely into mine.

'Congratulations,' I say. And leave.

31

Feeling apprehensive, I force myself to eat some breakfast.

'Here you go, boys,' I place their plates with jam on toast in front of them at the kitchen table. Theo picks his quarter slice up and licks the strawberry spread off. Most of it is glued to his forehead in a sticky mess. I can't be caring about that now. I hear my door open. Hopefully it's Mum. That way the boys can go with her before Rose arrives. I'm in such a state, I need to be on my own for a bit.

'Hi darling,' my mother kisses me on the cheek. 'How are my beautiful grandsons?'

Theo drops his toast. It slides down his dungarees, smearing ruby colours on his leg and it lands face down on the floor. I stare at the mess, dismayed. The tension and anxiety is too much, a tear leaks out, rolling down my cheek.

'No point crying over spilt toast.' Mum picks it up and disposes of it in my food caddy.

'I'm not crying about the toast.'

'I know. I know.' Worry lines are etched on her face. What am I doing to her?

'I'm scared. I don't want to dare to hope. I've got so much riding on this.'

'What do you mean?'

I lower my voice, 'If it's a girl, maybe Ian will come back.'

My mother shakes her head, loosening a few strands of ash blonde hair from the grip securing it back.

'What?' I ask.

'That man has got a lot to answer for. If I see him.'

'Mum!'

'Sorry, darling, it just makes me so mad when I think of how he left you and the kids. I've a good mind to pay him a visit myself.' She roughly rearranges her hair, clipping it back tighter than before.

'Please don't.' Luke gets down from his chair and runs over to us. He hugs my knees.

'Hello, Lukey,' my mother says picking him up and visibly relaxing.

'I want out,' Theo calls.

I unfasten his reins and lift him out of the highchair. Mum rubs his head and smiles. Kissing him I set him down with his brother.

'Does Ian know about your scan today?'

'No. I'm not-'

'Hello,' Rose calls out, emerging from the hallway. 'Oh

hi, Jan.'

'I didn't hear you come in,' I say.

'Hello, Rose. How are you?' my mother asks.

While the pleasantries are exchanged, I check my handbag, making sure I've packed the address of the clinic.

'Now you girls, listen up, after the scan, go and buy something, anything. Treat yourselves.' She hands me some folded notes.

'Mum, you shouldn't have. I can't take this.'

'Take it. But promise me, no matter what it is, boy or girl, you'll come back with something.' She smiles at me.

'Thanks, Mum. See you later boys. Be good for grandma.' I kiss them both.

'Bye, Jan,' Rose says as we leave for the short walk to the high-speed passenger ferry.

The ride on the Red Jet is bumpy. My tummy is turning and flipping in more ways than one. A combination of kicks from the baby, nerves about the gender scan and motion sickness is not a pleasant mix. Rose and I make small talk. I'm dying to ask her about Tammy. Is she still with Max? What does she know? She doesn't mention Ian, which I find strange in itself. I'm being paranoid. I expect she doesn't want to open the wound and upset me before I find out if I'm getting what I've always wanted. Was it worth it? I'll think about that when I know the results.

'There should be taxis waiting at the other end. Have you got the address?'

I search through the bottomless pit of my handbag and

eventually find the printed page from the website that Bella showed me. 'Yep,' I say as the boat docks. Will Joe give in and allow her to have this scan? I doubt it, he can't trust her...

Rose was right. There are six taxis waiting in a row. We walk up to the first and get in.

'Where to?' the olive-skinned man barks at us in his foreign accent.

I hand him the paper.

'I take this,' he says, rubbing his dark beard.

'Yes. Fine.'

He nods and sets his meter reading.

'How long will it take?'

'Huh?'

'Is it far?'

'Twenty.'

We share a glance, 'is that twenty minutes or twenty pounds?' I whisper to Rose. She shrugs her shoulders.

We are driven through the busy city, past a vast park and are then seemingly lost. He circles around a residential street then stops in front of a huge red-brick house in what appears to be a poorer area of outer Southampton.

'Are you sure this is it?' Rose asks.

'Huh,' he says, pointing at the address on the paperwork.

'Thanks,' I say, taking the proffered page back.

My stomach knots. It's going to be a boy, I know it.

He presses the tariff meter and the figure almost doubles. I hand him a note and wait for my change. I'm not giving him a tip especially seeing as I'm dubious about whether we're actually at the correct destination.

He glares at me and drops the change into my hand.

'Thanks,' I say and struggle out of the cab.

After wandering up the street and around the corner, we finally arrive. A large white sign outside says 'Babybind' in navy-blue italic lettering. I take a deep breath, feeling butterflies fluttering in my insides.

Turning the brass knob, we let ourselves in through the old fashioned wooden door. A receptionist takes my name and ushers us to some modern lilac sofas seated around a glass coffee table with a selection of glossy magazines laid out. She offers us a hot drink, which we both decline. It is a relief to be in a clean, clinical environment. A huge contrast to the scenery outside. I nervously flick through some fashion pages while Rose gets us some water from the dispenser. Which way will this go? I'd know already if Ian had cooperated at twelve weeks. Just four weeks ago, I had what I thought was a good marriage and was excited about having a nub scan in Kent, again. Now I'm on my own, sixteen weeks gone and have been studying scans, alone in the evenings. I wish my sway had gone better, it's a boy. I think I'm going to be sick. No, I must think about something else. It's done now, I can't change anything. All will be revealed shortly.

Bella texted yesterday, apologising for her behaviour on Boxing Day, and asked me to keep her unplanned pregnancy a secret. I agreed. I wasn't going to tell anyone anyway, she doesn't know how far gone she is yet, having completely messed up her cycle taking different pills to align her period and other drugs ready for the procedure, it is impossible for her to tell. I hope she's okay. The surprise condition means she will have to cancel the California trip, I understand why she's disappointed. I hope she doesn't turn strange again and go walkabouts like last time...

'Mrs Jackson,' a nurse calls out. She has a huge smile on her face, making me feel even more nervous.

Rose sets our drinks down.

'Come with me?' I ask.

We follow the smiling lady through to the scanning room.

'Take a seat,' she gestures to me. Rose sits opposite. There is an enormous flat screen television mounted to the wall. 'If you'd like to come closer,' she says to Rose, 'that way you'll be able to see the screen. I'm April.'

'Hi,' I say as Rose takes a seat next to me.

The gel is applied and we look up to see my baby. Is that something? No. It's the cord, isn't it?

After all the necessary well-being checks are carried out, we get to the point at hand and study the gender, this is a gender scan after all, that is how it is advertised on their website, as Bella, drunkenly, had pointed out to me.

'What are you hoping for?' April asks.

The palms of my hands feel sweaty. I hadn't expected such a direct question. 'A girl.' God did I just admit that?

'Let's take a look for you,' she smiles. 'Do you have any other children?'

Feeling at ease with her I decide on honesty, 'Two

boys.'

'Ah. Fingers crossed we see three lines.'

'Three lines,' Rose repeats.

'That's what we look out for in a girl at this stage. It's called a potty shot.' I nod, having read up on their methods already, 'A boy will be glaringly obvious, usually that is.' She zooms in, changes to 3D, goes back to 2D and re-focuses again. A while later she repeats the process. I look at the clock, we've been here nearly an hour. How much time will she spend on me before she gives up? Another ten minutes pass. I feel dejected.

'Come on baby, don't be so difficult,' April says with a grimace rather than her usual smile.

I bite my lip and nervously look over to Rose.

'That's a good sign though, isn't it?' Rose asks.

'It might be,' April agrees. 'I certainly can't see anything, but it could be hiding.' My breath catches. 'Until I see those illusive three lines, I can't tell you what you want to hear.'

Tears form in my eyes. Please God, let it be a girl.

'You're from the Isle of Wight, I see.'

'Yes.'

'So it's not ideal for you to come back another day, free of charge?'

My stomach drops. 'Not really.' Oh no, I want to know today! I can't go through the night wondering and hoping.

'I tell you what, go for a walk. Drink a fizzy drink, jump around and come back in half an hour. I'll squeeze you in between patients.'

'Thank you so much.' I wipe off the gel and place my top back over my protruding tummy.

Rose and I walk vigorously through the streets, literally having to step into the road to avoid bin-bags, which are spilling out their smelly contents. We cross the road due to a dirty old mattress blocking our way. The tatty yellow-brick terraced houses look menacingly at us, their greying net curtains hanging disgracefully.

'I don't like it here. Let's turn back,' I say after we pass a group of youths smoking something distinctly herbal. We hurry through the residential estate and join back on to the street where the Babybind clinic resides.

'The way some people live,' Rose exclaims, 'terrifying.'

'Let's stick to the top roads,' I suggest, feeling apprehensive. That could have become a nasty situation. Maybe I'm being over sensitive, but I certainly feel unsafe to say the least. We find a newsagents and buy a can of cola. I down it as fast as I can.

'I couldn't do that,' Rose says.

'It's a case of having to. I never drink this stuff, dreadful for your teeth.' An image of Joe's crooked incisors come to mind. I smile.

'If your boss could see you now, dental nurse, guzzling back the Coca-Cola.'

I laugh, firing cola spittle over my sky blue elasticated skirt. I wipe it, smearing in the brown coloured stain. 'Oh well, this is my last baby, I won't be needing these clothes again.'

'What if it's a boy? Will you still stick to that?'

'I won't have any other choice. Plus Ian and I aren't really, you know, together.' I say as breezily as I can. It hasn't fully dawned on me yet how I will cope with the grief of never having a daughter. I suppress the feeling, like I said, I'll have no choice, unless Ian comes back, or I move on. No. Ian will come home. He will.

An awkward silence. What does Rose know? Tammy is her sister after all. I can't ask, it's a difficult situation for both of us.

'Come on, it's been half an hour, let's go in.'

I take a deep breath, my nerves bubbling into a crescendo.

We let ourselves into the large building. Thankfully April pops her head out of her surgery before we get to the reception desk. Immediately we are ushered into the ultrasound room. I seat myself in the reclined medical chair and look up to the huge mounted television. I can hear my heart pounding.

'Come on baby, don't be awkward,' April says, pushing the probe firmly on my tummy. I desperately need to pee, the pressure is immense. With the baby kicking, I'm being prodded inside and out. Rose squints up at the screen. I follow her gaze. I feel queasy as the cola threatens to re-surface.

The black and white picture comes into focus, the area of interest to the fore. I gasp.

32

'It's a girl,' April says cheerfully.

I don't say anything. I stare at the black and white footage on the screen in front of me. Three white stripes outlined in black, surrounded by what I figure is the thighbones, stand out. My shaking hands cover my mouth.

'Char, congratulations,' Rose beams.

I sniff and look up at April who also has tears in her eyes. Perhaps she's had similar hopes herself at some point and can relate to mine? 'Thank you so much,' I say.

'You're welcome.' She types: 'It's a girl,' on the scan picture along with an arrow pointing at the potty shot, and prints off some glossy photos, handing them to me in a smart cardboard frame. I thank her again then Rose and I leave the surgery.

'Right, pink shopping here we come,' Rose states.

'Hold on, I'll quickly text my mum and Bella.'

'Ian too?' she queries as I tap away on my phone.

'No. I'm going to surprise him in person when we get back.' I smile, linking arms with my best friend and we walk down the hill in search of a taxi.

We are dropped off at West Quay Shopping Centre.

'Keep the change,' I say to the driver, feeling overjoyed.

'John Lewis?' Rose suggests.

We excitedly rush in, heading straight for the newborn section. Rifling through the rails, nothing grabs me. 'How about this?' Rose holds up a pale pink jacket.

'It's all winter stuff, it'll be summer when she's here.' I find myself drawn to the boys clothing. Strange because whenever I've been shopping for boy stuff in the past I see mountains of girls clothing jumping out at me. Now I actually want to buy something, nothing stands out.

'What about this?' Rose shows me a denim dress with strawberries embroidered on the pockets. 'What are you doing?' she asks, as I hold up a pair of jeans.

'For Luke, I'm trying to find Theo a matching pair.' I struggle through the racks, eventually finding his size and pop it in my basket.

'Nothing else you want then?'

'No I'm a bit disappointed actually.'

I pay for the boys' skinny leg jeans and we decide to have some lunch. My mobile rings.

'Mum?' I hear a strange sound on the other end of the phone. 'You okay?'

'I can't stop crying, I'm so pleased for you.'

'Where are you?'

'At the supermarket. Dad's got the boys.'

I laugh. 'Get home quick before anyone sees you.'

'It's marvellous, isn't it?' she croaks.

'I'm over the moon. It's not sunk in yet.'

'Just absolutely marvellous.'

'I'll see you later then, Mum.'

Rose and I chuckle about my mum's show of joy and relief in a public place.

'I'm not going home until you've bought a pink dress, or at least a cardi, anything so long as it's girly.'

We finish our jacket potatoes and leave in search of pink. After a further four shops, in desperation we go back to John Lewis.

I march to the children's section and rifle through the racks of clothing. 'This is nice.'

'It's not pink, but come on, let's just buy it,' Rose says, exasperated.

I take the turquoise and purple dress to the counter. She'll be able to wear this with tights if it's cold. She'll, she. Is this even real? Rose passes me a pack of vests, tights and a cardigan, all in various shades - cherry, magenta and salmon. She raises her eyebrows.

'The baby will look like a flamingo in that,' I say holding up the tutu. I pass the extra items to the shop assistant who packs them all together and hands me the card reader for my payment.

'Bella hasn't texted you back?' Rose observes as we leave the undercover multi-storey complex.

I take my phone out of my handbag to check. 'I have a message. I didn't hear it beep.' I press the picture of the envelope. 'CONGRATULATIONS, SO PLEASED FOR YOU. I HAD A SCAN TODAY TO CHECK MY DATES. SEVENTEEN WEEKS. IT GETS WORSE. IT'S TWINS!' I read aloud, then instantly regret it.

'Twins,' Rose yelps, 'gosh! You didn't tell me she was even pregnant.'

'Sorry she asked me not to tell anyone. She didn't know she was that far gone. She doesn't sound happy. Seventeen weeks. Hadn't she realised? Strange. She's a week ahead of me.'

'Déjà vu. You were due around the same time before, with Theo.'

Silence hangs in the air as I think about last time. She didn't have her baby. Now she's having two.

We board the high-speed passenger ferry, and cross the choppy sea back to the Island. I text Bella congratulations. At least she now has two chances at a girl. The boat docks and we walk back to my house. Rose says goodbye and drives off, waving to my mum who has rushed out to hug me.

'Well done, darling!'

'Where are the boys?'

'Inside with Dad, they're watching Jungle Book.'

'Would you mind having them a little bit longer? I want to tell Ian the news.'

'Off you go. Best not disturb them. If they know you're back you won't be able to get away.'

'Thanks, Mum.'

I jump in my car, slinging my shopping bags in the back seat and drive the short two-mile distance.

Excitement bubbles away in the pit of my stomach. I rub my belly and smile to myself. I'm going to have a daughter. I park the car outside, skip up the steps to Ian's flat and give the door a knock. No answer. I know he's home. His van's outside. I try the handle. It's unlocked. Should I let myself in? It feels strange. He is my husband and I've got some important news. Of course I should let myself in. I'm here now, I don't want to delay telling him, I'm bursting.

Walking through the landing, I see his jeans discarded on the floor. I shake my head. How untidy and lazy. I refrain from picking them up and walk through the kitchen-diner to more mess. I kick his top closer to the washing machine and continue. A red and white lacy bra tossed in the far corner by the two-seater sofa stops me in my tracks. A sound escapes from my throat. I steady myself against the refrigerator. The door to the bedroom, across the way, is closed. I stand stock still, my heart pounding. I feel like I'm going to vomit. I cross the lounge and stand next to the door. Hot sweat prickles the surface of my skin. I can't hear anything. My hand trembles on the doorknob. I hesitate. Taking a deep breath, I fling the door open with unexpected force. My eyes sweep over the scene as my brain kicks into gear and registers the naked bodies before me.

'Fuck,' Tammy says, pushing Ian to one side and covering herself with the duvet.

'Char! It's not what you think.' He jumps out of the bed and fumbles trying to locate something to cover himself with.

'Really? Well it looks bloody obvious to me,' I say as he pulls his pants up.

Tammy looks down, unable to meet my glare.

'How could you do this to me? Both of you!'

Tammy doesn't say anything but has the grace not to look at me. My anger rises. I want to punch her, drag her by the hair and kick her senseless. He's my husband and now she's tainted him.

'We need to talk,' Ian says.

My heart is pounding. Without thinking about the consequences, I raise my arm and slap Ian across the face with all the strength I can muster. The sound reverberates around the small bedroom.

Tammy gasps. I scowl in her direction. She looks away, ashamed, her cheeks a shade of crimson, which I'm sure my face matches.

'Char, I'm sorry. It was a mistake. A one off.'

'I don't believe you. I bet you were fucking that slut at the same time as getting me pregnant.'

Neither of them responds, which to me, is confirmation in itself. With my head held high, I walk out of the bedroom, slamming the door behind me. I run through his flat to the front door.

Ian chases me on the landing and grabs my arm.

'Get away from me,' I shout. I miss a step and stumble, trying to grip the handrail. I hear Ian shout my name as I fall down the four concrete steps and land on my side, sprawled on the floor.

The baby. My little girl. I hold my tummy and lie still.

'Char!' Ian rushes to me. He helps me to my feet. 'I'll

call an ambulance.'

'I think you've done enough.' I stand up unsteadily and hold on to the handrail. Then I take a couple of deep breaths and leave.

'Char, come back.'

Ignoring him, I make my way to my car and burst into tears. Shocked and numb. I'm bleeding. I can feel the warm sticky blood oozing in my underwear. I've lost her. I know I have.

33

I stagger inside holding my stomach, feeling fraught.

'Charlotte, what's up?' my dad says.

'I fell.'

'Fell!' Mum rushes over to me.

'Let's get you to the hospital. Jan, you stay here with the kids.' Dad ushers me out of the house, taking control. He drives my car at speed. 'A&E?' he says, as he abandons my beaten up old Renault Clio in a disabled bay.

'No.' I steer us away from the main entrance and up the short hill, 'the maternity department.' We push through the automatic doors and rush over to the lady at the desk. We are calmly told to sit and wait for a doctor to call us. Dad looks panicked. I thought he was going to explode at the woman for not acting as if my fall was a major priority. Worry lines run deep, resembling tracks on his forehead. I notice his once short dark hair is now speckled with grey flecks, like salt and pepper. When did he become so old?

'How did you fall?' he asks.

'I don't know. I just tripped.' I can't admit to myself what happened, let alone anyone else. He narrows his eyes. I'm no good at lying, unlike some people.

I check my phone. Five missed calls, all from Ian. I switch it off and drop it back into my bag. My dad is silently observing. I excuse myself and go to the toilet. Blood, just as I thought, but not as much as I'd expected. As I leave the bathroom, a petite Asian lady calls me into her room and introduces herself as Doctor Patel. I lie back on a reclining chair and she covers my belly with fabric straps, hooking me up to a heartbeat monitor. Please let her be okay. Please.

Vertical squiggly lines appear on the small, attached screen. The noise of the heart sounds out in rattling waves.

'You were lucky,' she says.

'Really? But I'm bleeding?'

'The heart sounds strong. I'll do an ultrasound scan too and check you internally, to give you peace of mind.' She smiles.

The internal examination is painful, but I am reassured by Doctor Patel once more. It's not until I see my baby on the screen that I relax slightly.

'You need to take it easy, Charlotte. Lots of bed rest. Get your husband to do everything for you and your children.'

My husband. That stung. My heart lurches, the vision

of them together resurfacing. No. I need to concentrate on my baby. Not him. Mum will help me. I don't need Ian.

Mum hugs me and cries, while the boys cling to my legs. Dad hovers, relieved. I break down. Heavy sobs convulse through me. My eyes are sore and blurred.

'Char, it's okay. The baby's fine, isn't she?'

Dad takes the boys into another room. I feel ashamed that I've lost control in front of them.

'Ian was in bed with Rose's sister,' I blurt out.

'What?'

'I caught them, just before I fell.'

My mother embraces me while I hysterically sob. 'The bastard,' she mutters. I've never heard her swear before. I laugh through my tears.

My parents stay to help with the children's bath while I try and relax like the doctor ordered.

'I'll stay the night,' Mum suggests after she's tucked the boys into bed.

'I'm fine. Honestly. I just need some sleep.'

'Okay, darling. But I'll come back in the morning. About eight.'

'Thanks.' I knew I could count on her.

My parents leave, concern carved on their faces. Dad kisses me on the way out, the events of the day ageing him further.

I need to sit still, but I can't. I slowly pace around the conservatory, fiddling with the pendant on the silver necklace my boss gave for my ten years of service, before

I was even pregnant with Theo. So much has changed since then, I now have a third on the way and my joy of having a daughter has been marred by my husband's infidelity. I should text him, let him know that the baby's all right. No. After what he's done to me, he can suffer like I am. Thank God she's alive. After that fall I felt sure I'd lost her. I couldn't bear that. To come so close then for it all to be taken away from me.

I have to tell him. I can't punish him in this way. It's childish. I trudge through to the lounge in search of my phone.

BABY'S FINE, I type. No kiss on the end. No niceties, just a statement. It rings, a picture of Ian's face flashes up. I press end and think about throwing my mobile across the room, but instead I place it back on my mantelpiece with shaky hands. I'm not ready to speak to him.

Straightening the sofa cushions with tears in my eyes, I decide to call Rose. Has Tammy told her what I walked in to? After filling her in on my shocking discovery and the end result with me tumbling down the stairs, Rose is stunned into silence. I wonder how Tammy's version of events will differ?

'But you're okay? The baby?'

'We're fine. I just need to slow down. Rest and relax. But it's hard. I've got so much on my mind.'

'You were bleeding? I'm so sorry, Char. My damn sister. I never took your suspicions seriously.'

I walk over to the bay window in the lounge and start to draw the curtains closed. I think I catch a glimpse of

Ian standing outside?

'You were right all along,' Rose says.

My breath catches and I hurriedly draw them tight then quickly nip to the door and pull the bolt across.

'Char, are you there?'

'Yes, sorry.' I wipe the tears from my eyes. 'It's not your fault. Ian's to blame. And me. I drove him to her.' I sit down on the sofa and rub my tummy.

'Don't be silly. He went along with it. Led you to believe he was on board. Then pulling the rug from under your feet.'

'It just hurts so much. How will I cope with three kids on my own?'

'You'll be fine. You're a strong independent woman.'

I laugh.

'I'm serious, Char. Who needs a man anyway?'

Rose's attempt at cheering me up doesn't work. She means well, I agree and make my voice sound calm to reassure her. We say our goodbyes. I don't really want to cause a family rift for Rose, it wouldn't be fair.

I take my wedding and engagement rings off and place them by my phone. Then I go to bed to cry some more.

The bleeding stopped the following day. Although I don't think I will rest until I've had her. I try my best to relax, but it is difficult with Ian constantly telephoning. My mum is wonderful. She has been taking Luke to pre-school and looking after Theo on the days he's not at nursery. I couldn't have managed without her. My washing has been done, dinners cooked and my house cleaned. If she's worn out she certainly doesn't show it.

I contact Bella, but she doesn't want to meet up, even after I tell her about Ian and Tammy and nearly losing the baby. I feel upset that she won't make time for me. I know she's apprehensive about having twins, but I could help her. We could support and comfort each other. But she won't budge. I'm worried she's depressed again.

Ian texts to arrange his Saturday stint with the children. I agree but inform him he's strictly not having them overnight.

Mum tensely hands my children over to him, while I rest in bed upstairs, more like hide! I hope Ian feels awkward and ashamed in front of her!

The days roll into one and I'm sick of being bedridden, but at the same time I'm scared to move around too much in case the baby gets hurt. Marie, my boss is overly sympathetic, having had a cheating husband leave her too. Her sons were older than mine, and she didn't have a third on the way, but her wound still seems to be very raw and open by the way she venomously speaks about her ex-husbands betrayal. Lucky for her she didn't catch them in the act. Although the images will never leave my mind, I'm glad I caught them like that. Otherwise he could lie, say it was just a kiss. At least I know the truth, and any gaps I fill in for myself when I'm awake at night. I've told her I'll be at work next week but she refuses to have me back yet. She's such a kind boss.

Back to bed I go. The red and white lacy bra discarded on the sofa comes to mind. How did this all happen? Why?

34

Nearly a month after my fall and I have so far managed to avoid Ian. Mum has been dealing with the handover of children on a Saturday for me. But Bella still hasn't come to see me? I'm back at work now, but frustratingly confined to the reception desk on my boss's orders. Probably sensible though. I still feel apprehensive. Until my baby is in my arms, I won't feel that she is safe.

Tuesday morning, my day off. There is a knock at the door. Please don't let it be Ian again. No, he'll be at work.

'Bella,' I say, surprised. She looks drawn and pale. 'Come on in. I've been worried about you.'

'Sorry. I've been really rough. The morning sickness, it lasts all day.'

'Good girly sign,' I say, noticing her dark roots which create a stripe in the centre of her platinum blonde hair.

'Twin sign more like. I can't stop long.'

'That's okay. So long as you're all right?'

'I'm starting to get my head around it,' she says, munching away at a chocolate biscuit. At least she's eating.

I fill her in on my woes, and she listens without much comment or input.

'I nearly lost her. How awful would that have been! Bloody Tammy. I hate her.'

'A daughter. You're so lucky. I'd trade places,' she says.

'You might be having one of your own. Two even? And you wouldn't want to walk into what I did. I'll never get over it.'

'I'd sacrifice anything for a girl,' she looks down at her nails. No longer manicured, just tatty stubs.

'You're right. I won't let Ian and Tammy ruin it. A girl at last. Unbelievable.'

Bella stands up. 'I've got to go.'

'Already?'

'Yes. I've got things to do.'

Then she leaves. She looked broken. Desperate. I should learn when to keep my trap shut. How insensitive of me, rubbing it in that I'm having a daughter, when she is desperately hoping for one too. But she'll have one. I'm sure of it. She didn't look right though. I don't know what to do? I grab my phone and text Joe. Perhaps I shouldn't have, he may not appreciate me interfering? Too late now, it's sent. Moments later he replies saying he's worried too and has made a doctor's appointment for her. He ends his message with a kiss. Was that appropriate? I'm reading too much into it. Hopefully the doctor will put Bella on antidepressants again. Or perhaps suggest counselling. Something needs to be done.

Another Saturday rolls by. Ian collects the children and this time Mum's not here to do it for me. He tries to say sorry again but I cut him dead. I don't want to hear it. After he and the boys leave, I sit down and cover my head with my hands. Seeing Ian was harder than I thought it would be. He wants to put it all right. It would be so easy to take him back. Be a proper family again. It's the right thing to do for my children. But Tammy, of all people. No. I can't forgive him.

My phone rings making my heart somersault. It's Joe. What's wrong with me?

'Have you seen Bella? She's missing again.'

'I've not seen her since Tuesday. Where are you?' I can hear birds squawking in the background.

'Alum Bay.' Alum Bay? That was her last haunt when she disappeared. 'I'm really worried,' he says.

'What's happened?'

'The twins. They're boys.'

'She didn't tell me she was having a scan?'

'Didn't she?'

'I should have asked her when she was round. She's a week ahead of me so it stands to reason it would be about now.' Oh God. I went on and on about nearly losing my daughter.

'She's been very secretive,' Joe says.

'I've been so wrapped up in my own problems. I'm so selfish. Twin boys, Bella would have been devastated.'

'It gets worse.'

'Worse? Is there something wrong with them?' Oh no.

'No, nothing like that. All fine there. No it's Mrs Whicherly.'

'Who?'

'Our neighbour, the one Bella cleans for.' I stare out of the window focusing on an overgrown shrub in my front garden. Ian used to do the pruning and tidying. Twin boys...

'Is she okay?' I ask.

'Mrs Whicherly? No. she's accused Bella of stealing.'

'What? She must be going senile. Perhaps she's got Alzheimer's or something? She's pretty old, isn't she?'

'Old but not daft, unlike me!'

'What do you mean?' I ask, taken aback. It can't be true, of course it's some sort of mistake. How can he be doubting her?

'If she has been taking her money, it would explain some things. And the way Bella reacted. I just don't know? Anyway, if she gets in touch with you, call me.'

'Will do. I hope you find her. Keep me in the loop.'

He hangs up. Mrs Whicherly is a retired school teacher. Bella told me she didn't have any children. No one to help her. Bella's been cleaning for her for years. Since Adam was born. Sometimes she does her grocery shopping. I thought she was being kind and neighbourly. Now I don't know what I think!

I can't stay at home. I have to do something. But what? Joe's out searching at Alum Bay. I can't just sit on my hands. I grab my mobile and scroll down the addresses for Bella's number. It rings and rings, eventually going to answering machine. I leave a message asking her to call me back as soon as she can. I pace around the kitchen, feeling frantic and useless. What's going on? Stealing, surely not? There must be an explanation. It's a mistake?

I take my car keys off the hook in the hallway and sling my mobile in my bag, waddling out, I lock the front door behind me. I hesitate. I need to be careful. I shouldn't put my baby in danger. It's just a drive. I'll be fine.

I travel towards the west, to Alum Bay, my heart pounding. When I eventually arrive, I park up in the Needles attraction car park. No sign of Joe's car. Now what? How stupid and reckless of me. I look at my phone. A missed call from Bella. Shit. I hit redial. No answer. Please pick up. I should have stayed home! I try again. Still no answer. I phone Joe.

'Have you heard from her?' I question without any preamble.

'No.'

'I missed her call. I was driving, I didn't hear my phone.'

'Oh, shit.'

'I'm sorry. I'm at the Needles. Where are you?'

'Newport. I've just been into the police station. Nothing they can do until she's been missing for forty-eight hours. They've advised me to go home and wait for her to return.'

I look out to the vast expanse of turquoise sea. The water looks choppy, waves crash against the white chalk cliffs. 'Best keep your line clear in case she tries to call you again,' he says.

We say our goodbyes. Why had I been so rash? What

did I think I could possibly achieve by coming out here? And now I've missed her call. I'm so mad with myself. I place my phone in my lap and carefully drive home along the coastal line. I pass Compton Bay, Ian's favourite surfing venue. Tammy's too. Oh Bella, Bella! Twin boys are a blow, but she can get over this, can't she? She'll have to, there's no other option. She did once tell me you could have an abortion up to twenty-four weeks. If she is having one, at this late stage she'd have to give birth to the twins. Plus two doctors would have had to agree to the termination, so it's doubtful. What reason would she have given to persuade them? What if she's having it done illegally?

I arrive home, dialling Joe as I unlock my door. 'Heard anything?'

'No. You?'

'Do you think she's having an abortion again?'

'She wouldn't do that?'

'I think she would.' I sit down and rub my tummy.

'I'll call the clinic. Bournemouth wasn't it?'

'Yes.'

He hangs up.

I feel numb. I take a deep breath and get up and boil the kettle to give myself something to do. My mobile rings.

'Joe.'

'They wouldn't tell me anything. Patient confidentiality.'

'Wouldn't they even confirm that she wasn't there?'

'No.'

'It was probably a stupid suggestion anyway.' I run my hands through my hair, not knowing what else to say.

'Thanks, Char.'

'What for? If I hadn't have missed that damn call.'

'Don't beat yourself up. It's not your fault. I better get off the phone.'

'Of course.'

'I'll call you later.' He hangs up.

This stress is too much for me. I need to sit down, but I can't.

Throughout the rest of the day I intermittently try Bella's number to no avail.

Ian returns with the children. I find myself filling him in about Bella being missing. But I omit the stealing from Mrs Whicherly part. This is the most we have spoken in a month. It feels good to offload on him. He was my soulmate for a long time. Annoyingly he seemed to relish in it. Pleased that I was involving him.

Tucking Luke and Theo in for the night I think about Bella's boys, Adam and Si. How must they be feeling? I expect Joe's shielded them from it? Anyway, she'll be back, like last time.

I text Joe before bed, he responds having no further news. No kiss either. I fall into a restless sleep, tossing and turning all night.

In the morning I check my phone for messages. I then log onto the computer to check my emails, long shot but worth a try. Nothing.

Breakfast with the boys followed by a DVD on this grey, rainy Sunday morning.

My mobile rings. Where did I put it? My heart is in my throat as I dash to my handbag trying frantically to locate it. I violently toss the contents of my bag on to the work surface in my urgency and quickly answer. Ian. My heart drops.

'You're home. I'm on my way round,' he says.

'What? No.'

'Five minutes.' The phone goes dead. I really don't need this now. I wish I hadn't spoken so openly to him yesterday.

Ten minutes later, Ian bursts through the door. 'Charlotte, sit down. I need to tell you something.'

I do as he asks. What the hell is he going to say? It had better not be about that slut, Tammy. I hope she's not pregnant!

'I found Bella. I'm so sorry.'

'What?'

'I was about to go surfing at Compton,' he pauses.

'And?' I say impatiently, trying not to visualise his and Tammy's surf session together.

'She's dead.'

I cup my hands to my mouth. My eyes blur as I struggle to contain my breakfast.

'Char.'

'What? She fell down the steps?' I'm confused. The steps at Compton are steep and dangerous but I doubt they'd kill you. Break some bones. Her neck?

'No. She was washed up there. The coastguard said she probably jumped from Afton Down. You know the large white chalk cliffs that meet the dark –.'

'Yes,' I cut in.

'It's where all the people go who want to jump, because it's the tallest and most accessible from the road. That's what the coastguard told me. Char, I'm so sorry.'

My mind whirls as I try to picture where he is describing. I was looking at the cliffs yesterday. Neither of us checked at Afton. I don't know where he means exactly.

I need some fresh air. I can't breathe. I stand, then drop to the floor covering my face with my hands. Loud sobs emerge from my chest. She was depressed. Desperate. I should have kept a closer eye on her. I've let her down. If only I'd heard my phone. I'll never forgive myself.

Ian kneels down beside me, wrapping his arms around my shoulders. I collapse into him, howling uncontrollably.

'Angel, I'm so sorry,' he says, kissing the top of my head and gently rocking me. 'Ssh, it's all right. I'm here now.' He cradles me, I feel safe for the first time in ages. For a split second everything else is forgotten.

'Joe! Does he know?'

'I gave the police his name and address. I don't have his number.'

'I need to go to him,' I say struggling away from Ian.

35

I stand in the breakfast-room with my mother-in-law feeling self-conscious and waiting for the inevitable.

'Sorry to hear about your friend. You were close weren't you?'

'Yes.' I break down. Viv stiffly puts her arms around me. It feels awkward. After a moment's hesitation, she releases me from her embrace.

'Coffee?' she asks.

I nod as she fills the cups. We seat ourselves in the conservatory. She's not here to console me about Bella's death. She's here about her son. I wait with anticipation, sipping my drink. I feel too weak to bother trying to fill the silence. I don't care.

'Why did Ian leave?'

'He hasn't told you? He's been gone for months.'

'I want your version. Why would he leave his pregnant wife? I just don't understand?' she says. Her tone is harsh.

'He was cheating on me,' I throw back at her.

'So you kicked him out?'

What the hell has he told her? 'No. He left. I didn't find out about the affair until I walked in on them. Look, I haven't got the energy for this, Viv.' I stand up.

'Sorry. Please,' she looks me in the eyes, begging me to sit. I do. 'You can get through this. His dad once cheated on me. You get over it. Make it work, for the sake of the kids.' This is news to me. Like father like son obviously.

'For all I know, he may still be with her?'

'If he is, you don't need to worry, I'll sort it out.'

Finding it difficult to rein my anger in, I take a deep breath. 'No. Please don't do anything. I'm not sure I want him back now!'

'But the kids?'

'He's the one who should have thought of that.' My chest is flushed. With shaky hands I finish my coffee.

'Look, Charlotte, he's spoilt. It's my fault. The youngest of my three, he was always the baby of the family. He still acts like a child. He's just gone off the rails. He'll get himself together. You mark my words.' Her family loyalty to her sons, although annoying, can't fail to impress. It's so deep, like molars in the back of the mouth, difficult to extract, mostly unseen, but with the deepest roots imaginable.

'Viv. He's in his thirties. It's not your fault.'

'I wanted a girl too you know.'

My stomach drops.

'What's he said?' I can hear my heart pounding. I'll never forgive him if he's divulged our personal lives to his mother.

'Nothing. Just that it's a girl and you're really pleased. He said you fell. Nearly lost her.'

'No thanks to him.' I hope that really is all he's confessed to her.

'Oh?' she enquires.

'That's when I walked in on them. In bed!' What a bitch, coming round here, defending her son when I'm grieving for Bella!

Viv looks away. She doesn't want to hear me running her son down. She doesn't want to feel ashamed that her baby could hurt someone so deeply.

'I'm sorry it happened to you. I forgave my Derek.'

'That was your decision. Where's Ian? At yours?'

'Yes. He and Derek have taken the boys to the park.'

'Does he know you're here?' I ask as it finally dawns on me.

'Yes.'

'Unbelievable.'

'You won't speak to him. What else could he do?'

'Sorry to rush you, Viv,' I say, standing up, 'but I have to go out.'

She reluctantly vacates the sofa, rubbing down her trousers. Looking forlorn, she flicks her dark shoulder length hair. I'm not sure why. It doesn't move. Even a tornado wouldn't displace her highly lacquered mane.

'Be gentle on him. It's his first offence.' First? How many does she expect him to have? How many has her husband had? I want to scream. I want to physically force her out of my house, the interfering busy-body. I stop myself. Maybe one day I'll be in her position. One of my sons, or my daughter may hurt their partner and call upon me, their mother, to try and salvage the situation...

She air kisses both my cheeks and leaves.

Fancy Ian sending his mother round to do his dirty work for him. Is he still with Tammy or was it a one-off like he says? Do I even care?

After she leaves I start preparing a lasagne for Joe and his boys. I doubt they're eating properly. I feel so angry after my unwelcome visitor. I bet Viv knows how much I wanted a girl. Ian wouldn't have told her how she was conceived, would he? The incubator and test tubes come to mind, although that was Theo's conception. It's all part of the same thing, the mad swaying diets and techniques were carried out for both of them. No, he'd be too embarrassed to tell his mother that. I hope!

As I fry the mince and onion I decide to put to rest my fears of what Ian may have said, there's nothing I can do about it. I can't change it.

Oh Bella! Why did she jump? What was she thinking as she walked to the edge and looked down at the rocks below? Did she dive or just step off? Eyes open or closed? If only I'd heard my phone, maybe I could have prevented it all? I add the chopped tomatoes and stir them in. The bright red mixes with the brown mince. Blood. Hysteria washes over me and I can't stop crying. The onions sting my eyes and make my nose run. I blow it with some kitchen roll and resolve to pull myself together. I continue with the recipe, making the white sauce, which I then add to the dish in layers with the pasta sheets. Finally grating the cheese on top, I cover it in cling film and leave the house, securely locking the door behind me. Ian still has his key. If he turns up with his mother I'll be so cross! No. He wouldn't? I head to the car feeling uncertain.

Arriving at Joes, I notice the curtains are drawn. I knock the door. No answer. I should have phoned him first. Walking down the gravel side path, I push open the door a crack, feeling unsure and a little strange, I let myself in. What a mess. I wouldn't know where to start. Everything appears to be out of place. Books piled up next to the sink, their edges curling upwards. Clothes stacked up on the chairs, but not in a neat orderly fashion. What day does the cleaner come? Feeling stupid, I take a deep breath. Of course there's no cleaner. Bella always used that excuse about her untidy house. It was a lie and I was gullible enough to believe it. Why on earth would Bella do Mrs Whicherly's cleaning, yet have someone come in to do her own? But she was being neighbourly, assisting an elderly woman who needed help. I guess doing Mrs Whicherly's house had its perks with the extra cash that Bella so desperately needed for her trips abroad. I shake my head and set the dish down on the crumb covered island counter in the middle of the kitchen.

'Joe,' I call out.

He emerges from the lounge, swollen puffy eyes and messy hair.

'She left a note.' He hands it to me.

Unfolding the lined pages, I read Bella's messy scrawl.

Not like her usual neatly formed writing.

Dear Joe, Adam and Simon,

I can't go on living like this. I love you all dearly, and I know I'm being selfish, but you're better off without me. I can't cope with four boys. I only ever wanted a daughter. Why couldn't I just have one like Char!

My stomach flips and a cold sensation travels through me making me feel heavy and numb.

Please tell Mrs Whicherly that I'm sorry, she trusted me and I didn't deserve her trust. I feel so low and unstable. Anti-depressants or counselling will not work, I know that. Therefore, I feel it is best for me to disappear. Adam and Simon – I love you both with all my heart, all the daughters in the world could not replace either of you. I'm sure you'll never understand my longing, but please find it in your hearts to forgive me one day.

I'm sorry.

Mummy (Bella) xxx

My hands are shaking. 'Where did she leave it?' I give the note back to him.

'It was on the counter. I hadn't noticed it before, I thought it was a shopping list or something. There was a life insurance policy inside the envelope too.'

'When was the policy set up?' I ask as the thought occurs.

'Just over two years ago.'

'It should cover suicide then. I thought you were going

to say it was when she found out about the twins.' I wince and lean against the counter. 'How are the kids holding up?'

'Numb. They don't want to talk about it, to me anyway. It's lucky they have each other. Why did she do it, Char? The twins. She could have had them first. Given them the chance of life. I'll never forgive her for being so selfish.'

'She was desperate.' I put my arm around his shoulder and comfort him as he cries.

'Her parents are coming round tomorrow night to make arrangements for the funeral. Will you help me pick a song, for when they... you know.' He breaks down again, burying his head in my shoulder. When his face emerges, he stares intently into my eyes. I feel hot. My heart races. I think he's going to kiss me.

I pull away. I'm imagining it. He's emotional. People act weirdly when they're grieving. 'I've made a lasagne for you and the boys. You must keep your strength up.'

He nods. 'Thanks.'

'I'll think of a song, something special.' I pick up my car keys.

'Stay. Please.'

Reluctantly I take off my coat. I can't leave him. Not like this.

I sit on the sofa waiting while Joe opens a bottle of wine in the kitchen. I don't like to decline, although I wouldn't choose to drink alcohol whilst pregnant. I'll just have a sip.

'Bella's sisters have been looking after Adam and Si.

They get on well with their aunties.' He walks though the lounge and takes a seat on the sofa next to me.

'That's good,' I accept the tall stemmed glass and take a small mouthful. The last time I sat in this room with Joe, Bella was drunk. Boxing Day. That was the night she found out she was pregnant. Completely unaware that there were two babies and that they would both turn out to be boys. Her instinct was to have a termination. She was disappointed that she couldn't do PGD again. Why did it have to work out this way? Why couldn't at least one of them have been a girl? We could have been so excited together. Buying pretty clothes and discussing girl's names.

'You okay? You're miles away,' Joe says bringing me back to the present.

'Sorry. I just feel so angry. Why couldn't we both be having daughters? Everything could have been so different.'

'Why couldn't she just be happy with sons?'

His words sting. But I know he's right. I'm looking at it all the wrong way. We were both lucky all along. We just didn't appreciate what we already had.

36

I stand in the third row of pews on the left hand side at St Mary's Church, watching the polished beech-wood coffin being carried down the aisle. The same aisle I walked down when I married Ian.

The grey stone church has white lilies in pink vases on the windowsills of the brightly coloured stained-glass windows. The large building is far from full.

Classical music fills the vestry, the song Joe and I had chosen, Annie's song, was rebuked by Bella's mother.

Joe walks behind the coffin, he nods as he passes me, then takes a seat at the front with her parents. Bella's mother decided that the boys were too young to attend. She is probably right. Joe told me his sister, Sarah, has come over from Devon to stay and look after Adam and Simon. Joe's mother died of cancer a few years ago. His father has dementia and Sarah and her husband look after him in an annex adjoining their home. I'm pleased Joe has his sister to offer him support for a few days. It will take the pressure off of me, although I do enjoy spending time with him.

On the afternoon that I took round a lasagne and reluctantly stayed, we spoke about our childhoods, our schooling and our first loves. He reminisced about his early years with his sister and how much he missed his hometown. We have a lot in common, he too enjoys reading and used to have riding lessons as a young boy. That afternoon I also admitted to myself how lucky both Bella and I had been with our families and our sons. Our blindness at wanting a daughter meant we didn't appreciate what we already had. Why couldn't we realise that?

I look at the order of service. A beautiful black and white picture of Bella beams up at me. I've never seen her smile like that before. She looks young and carefree. Why-oh-why did this happen?

We sing the first hymn, "All Things Bright and Beautiful," followed by a eulogy by her crumpled father. He speaks about his daughter's affection for animals, her love for her sons and her passion for ballet and sailing, then rejoins his wife who immediately embraces him in a show of affection. It feels as if they are putting on an act. I'm being unkind. I didn't know she could sail, or that she particularly liked animals. She had no pets of her own.

Joe stands slightly apart. Alone. No one comforts him. I want to reach out and hold him, tell him it will all be okay. But it won't be. Never again will it be okay.

I feel conspicuous standing here, being so obviously

pregnant. I'm alive with a daughter inside me and Bella's dead. Why was I the one who got what I wanted? I feel guilty enough about that and to top it off I'm now fraternising with her husband. Ashamed. That's how I feel.

I look behind me. Mrs Whicherly is standing a few pews back on the other side of the aisle. She mops her eyes with a tissue and glances my way. I don't expect she would recognise me, we've only met briefly once. Kind of her to come after what Bella did, but Joe has paid her money back. She can't grumble any longer.

With sombre faces, Joe along with Bella's parents, walk over to the flower-covered coffin and touch it, lingering there for a few minutes. I can't believe she's inside that wooden box with its shiny handles. Oh God, why? Her poor children haven't got a mother anymore. I imagine my boys if I were gone. Their lives would be so different. They would live with Ian and my mum's life would change too. She would probably try to be a mother figure to them, taking them to school and collecting them while Ian was at work. Eventually they would have a step-mother, perhaps it would be Tammy? It doesn't bear thinking about.

Joe and her parents huddle together as the curtains close around the coffin. She is going to be buried in the surrounding graveyard. Tears fall freely down my cheeks as the organ starts up. Joe leads the procession up the aisle, closely followed by her parents. At the church doors, everyone kisses the three of them, offering their condolences as they line up. I copy this. Her parents don't know me. Her mother stares as I kiss Joe on the cheek. He holds my hand firmly, circling his thumb over my knuckles, then finally releases it. I move on. Numb.

The wake is held at the local golf club. Canapés, along with wine or juice are offered. I accept a soft drink, but refuse the food. I can't stomach it. I mill around among the fifty or so people, all of whom I don't know. I recognise Bella's two sisters because they look just like her, but I don't introduce myself, they appear stand-offish. Self-consciously I pat down my black maternity dress and wander through to the buffet. I am saved by Joe.

'Shame about the music. She would have hated it,' he says.

'It kept her mum happy though.'

'Bella didn't much like her either,' he spits.

'Sorry for your loss,' a large, balding man cuts in, giving Joe a bear hug. He smiles at me, quizzically.

'This is Charlotte, Bella's friend. Char, this is Bella's uncle, Richard.'

We shake hands. 'How did you know her?' he asks, taking a chicken vol-au-vent from the table beside me.

I can't tell him we met online, both desperate for a daughter. 'Toddler group,' I say.

Joe smiles at me.

Richard talks affectionately about his niece. I like him. Her parent's however, seem cold and uninviting. They have just lost their daughter though, and two unborn grandsons, I can't blame them for being miserable.

Feeling tired, I tell Joe I'm going to leave.

'Please stay. Tell me about your scan. Didn't you have your twenty week yesterday.'

'It went well.'

'Still a girl?'

What a strange question? I feel uncomfortable talking about this at my friend's wake. Especially in light of the reason she took her life. 'They couldn't tell. Baby was being uncooperative. I'm glad I had my private scan, so I know though.'

'That's girls for you, stubborn.'

I smile, having heard the same thing about Theo when I had his scan. Boy or girl, they're all the same really. 'I'm sorry, Joe, I have to leave. Mum's bringing the boys back in half an hour.'

It's a lie. They're not back for at least two, but I don't like it here. I feel unwelcome, like an intruder. Other than Uncle Richard, Joe has barely been spoken to. If I leave, maybe he'll do his rounds, thank everyone properly, and speak about his wife's short life. He needs to say that she will be sorely missed. He's not done that yet. Everyone knows she was pregnant. It's a touchy subject, which is being brushed over.

March and April roll by, followed by a sunny, warm May. The daffodils have been and gone. A brown withered flower head lies upon the grass. I fling it in my compost bin. My tummy is bulging fit to burst as I bend over, tending to the weeds in my overgrown jungle of a garden. Six weeks before my daughter is due.

Joe telephones me most days. Ian too. I feel as if I'm in

some sort of triangle. Perhaps it's a square if you include Tammy.

My mobile rings.

'Hi Rose,' I say.

'Hi, look I don't know how to say this so I'm just going to launch into it.'

My stomach churns. This doesn't sound good.

'I just thought you should know, Tammy's asked Ian if she can move in with him. Max has kicked her out.'

Bile rises in my throat. This isn't happening.

'I've got to go, bye.' I hear her say my name as I press end. I feel bad, but I don't want to hear any more.

How could they? Anger fills me as I text Ian with trembling hands.

I HEAR YOU HAVE A NEW HOUSEGUEST. HOW COSY.

My phone rings. Seeing Ian's face flash up, I wish I hadn't texted him. 'What?' I answer.

'I said she can't. I don't want her. I want you. I'm sorry. Her parents will have to take her in. Nothing's going on you know. I've told you, it was a mistake, a one-off.'

I don't want to listen to his lies so I press the red end button, again. Now I've cut off the two people who I am closest to in my life in the space of seconds. This isn't me.

I feel bad for Mrs Hutton, Rose's mother. Surely Tammy has a friend to call on. If nothing is going on, there would be no way she would be asking to move in with Ian.

My phone bleeps. One word. SORRY.

IT'S OVER, I hastily reply, COLLECT THE REST OF YOUR STUFF ASAP. I hit send, then break down. What did I expect? A happy reunion? No, but not this.

A sudden pain jolts me, followed by frantic kicking from within my stomach. I lurch forward, my heart beating a million beats per second. It's too early. She can't be coming yet.

I quickly dial Rose.

'Sorry, but I felt I had to tell you,' she says. 'I couldn't keep it to myself. Tammy begged me not to say.'

A primitive moan escapes me.

'Char, what's going on?'

'I think the baby's coming,' I manage to exclaim.

'Are you on your own?'

My eyes mist over. The pain unbearable. 'Yes. Be quick.'

'I'm on my way. Have you called an ambulance?'

I drop the phone to the ground and fall on all fours. Crippled. This isn't good. I'm not due until July.

37

Rose helps me into the hospital building and flags down a nurse. She finds a wheelchair and rushes me through the bright corridor. The pain is intense. I squeeze my eyes shut and endure the agony as I travel to the ward at breakneck speed.

'Charlotte, can you hear me?' someone says.

'She's floppy.'

I feel myself being lifted under the arms and knees onto a bed. This doesn't feel right. It's different.

'Aaargh!' A stabbing pain jolts through me.

'She's responsive.'

'Char, it's me, Rose.' I feel her grip my hand. Opening my eyes I see a blur of faces. There must be at least ten people crowding in the small room. Someone is examining my tummy, pushing it down. It hurts.

'The anaesthetist is on his way. Then we'll give you an epidural.'

'What?' No.

'Your baby has moved. She's back to back. It's best we get a line in, in case we have to do a caesarean section.'

'Caesarean? I don't want one. The boys came out fine.'

'It's just a precaution.'

Rose grips my hand and says something to the nurse. I'm hardly conscious. Tearing, burning sensations. I scream out.

The nurse doesn't speak as she checks my pulse and hooks me up to a heartbeat monitor. It bleeps continuously.

I let out a sharp cry of pain again.

'Take the gas,' she says handing me the tube. She presses a buzzer while I gasp and pant.

'Suck it,' Rose says, fear in her eyes.

I do as she says, breathing it in. It has very little affect on the searing heat, other than making me feel nauseous. I inhale it again, deeper this time as the contractions assault me.

A man and a woman dressed in white rush through the door. The nurse talks to them in hushed tones with their backs to me.

Another man dressed in green scrubs charges in. 'I'm Mike the anaesthetist. Let's get started. We need you sitting with your legs off the bed.'

I do as I'm asked with the help of two women.

'Why isn't she in a gown?'

'I'll help you,' Rose says.

'Aaargh,' I shout out as I am prodded and poked, pulled and stretched into a rigid backless tunic.

A cold wet feeling on my spine. I think a cloth is being wiped on the area. Someone is speaking to me, probably explaining what is happening. I can't hear the words or process them. Petrified. I'm going to die. Or lose her. My boys, I can't leave them. A sharp piercing feeling courses through me. I scream.

'Stay still, Charlotte.' The raised voice of one of the men is urgent. The nurse pulls me forward so my head is resting on her shoulder. My back is arched. Overwhelmed, everything spiralling out of control, the tears start to fall. I feel a cold sensation on my lower back then a sharp scratch shortly followed by warm tingles spreading down my legs. They feel heavy. I am manhandled back onto the bed and onto my back.

'The baby's heart rate is too high.'

Rose is looking at my thighs, horrified, I follow her gaze and see bright red blood seeping on the crisp white linen.

I hear Rose shout for the nurse. My daughter. I'm losing her. My brain is detaching. I can't focus.

'General anaesthetic. Now!' a woman shouts. 'Call Mr Foster. Let's get her into theatre.' I feel dizzy, strange. Faint.

Everything stands still. Slow motion. Like miming. It's a play I'm watching and I'm part of the show. I look up to the far corner of the room. Bella is floating near the ceiling. She hovers over to me.

'Bella.'

'Relax, Char.' Her elfin blonde hair is perfect. She is wearing a black vest top and coral skirt, I always liked that combination. She smiles at me. Light surrounds her.

'I miss you,' I say.

'I miss you too. I'm so sorry, Char. You have to try and survive this. Don't give up.'

'I won't.'

'I'm so selfish. I shouldn't have done it. I was desperate.'

'I'm sorry, Bella. I let you down.'

'No. You didn't. Calm down. You'll have your little girl soon. And it doesn't matter what you have. I learnt that the hard way.'

I nod. 'I know.'

'Look after Joe and my boys for me. They're suffering.'

'I will. I promise.'

A nurse's face comes into focus. She's saying my name. Bella is gone. The nurse is holding up some fingers. Three, I think.

'My baby.'

'Charlotte, I'm going to countdown from ten. Ready?'

I can't answer.

'Ten, nine,'

My eyes close.

'Eight, seven.'

A vast black expanse.

Bella where are you? I'm scared.

'Six.'

Gone.

Heavy eyelids flicker. Someone is here. I feel so sleepy. I can't come round. I think my belly hurts? I'm not sure. It feels tight but raw. Cut across the nerves. Numb but not.

'Charlotte. It's time to wake up now.' A woman's face with her hair tightly gelled back to her head comes into focus. 'Your husband is here. You've been out for the count for eight hours.'

'Ian?' My lips feel dry and cracked. There's a dull ache in my abdomen. I'm confused and groggy. Where am I? The baby?

'Where is she?' I panic.

'It's okay, angel, she's fine.'

'What?' I struggle to get up then collapse back down.

'You need to rest, Charlotte,' the nurse says after checking the monitor attached to me. 'I'll leave you to it for a bit.'

'She's so beautiful. You won't believe it. Only four pounds though so she's in the neonatal unit. You had us worried, Char.'

I sit myself up with the help of Ian. He holds a glass of water to my lips. It's the most refreshing thing I've ever tasted.

'You lost so much blood. They had to give you a transfusion as they were getting her out. The blood was draining out of you as fast as they were putting it back in. You haemorrhaged.'

Ian looks older, he's aged in this short space of time.

'I arrived as they were whizzing you down to theatre,' he continues taking a breath. 'You looked so frail and vulnerable. I thought I'd lost you.'

'Oh my God,' I glance over at the four bouquets of flowers on the table opposite. Ian follows my gaze at the brightly coloured arrays. I've lost so much time.

'My mum bought the yellow bunch, Rose the pink and your parents got the multi coloured ones. Oh and the lilies are from Joe.'

'From Joe?'

'Everyone has been beside themselves. Your mum only left half an hour ago.'

'The boys?'

'They're fine. I've moved back home.'

'What?' I can't take this in.

'To look after them. If you'll have me back I'd love to make it a permanent thing.' His hand hovers as if he's going to touch my face, he must think better of it because instead he tucks his tangled hair behind his ears.

This is too much.

'I want to see my daughter,' I say.

'I'll go and ask.'

Has everyone else already met her? A vision of Ian's mother, Viv, holding a pink bundle comes to mind. What if I don't bond with her?

After some persuasion, the nurse agrees. Still hooked up to a machine, I'm wheeled to the neonatal ward. I look through the window at the tiny babies in cots. Is one of them mine? Ian follows behind as we pass them. I am pushed into a second room, full of newborns. My eyes dart around wildly. Which one is mine? We stop by one of the incubators.

'Here she is,' Ian says.

'I'll leave you to it.'

I smile as the nurse walks away then look down at my

baby. Minute and wrapped up like a parcel in white. My daughter. She too has a line in her wrist, and she also has a tube taped to her face, which disappears up her nostril. Where's the sudden rush of love? But it didn't come instantly with the boys either. How do I even know that she is mine? I could have been taken to any one of these babies and told she was my daughter.

'Isn't she beautiful' Ian gushes, 'what shall we call her, Verity?' He rests his hands on my shoulder.

'I don't remember having her,' I sob.

'I know, angel. It was a shock to us all. Six weeks premature.' He massages my neck. 'Mum says she looks like me.'

'Your mum's been in?' Jealousy and anger flood through me.

'Your parents and Rose too,' Ian adds.

'Everyone's met her. Held her. But not me.'

'We're not allowed to hold her yet. She's likely to be here until her due date.' He hesitates, 'They've decided to bottle feed until you're well enough to express.'

'I can't even feed her!?'

'You're too weak, angel. You nearly died. They're tube feeding her some formula stuff for now.'

'I'm a failure.'

'Don't be so silly. Our parents, and Rose could only look through the window. It's only us allowed in the room. In case of infection.'

Relief. I don't want anyone else having a special moment with my daughter before me.

'Do you like Isabella Rose? Verity doesn't feel right

anymore, since Chloe took the name.'

'After Bella?' Ian says.

'And Rose too.'

I lean over, wincing at the pain in my stomach. 'Can I touch her?'

'Sure.'

I put my hands through the holes in the incubator, and stroke her flaky fingers. She curls them around my index finger, gripping it tightly. She's so tiny and helpless. My eyes well up as the overwhelming love hits me.

'Izzy, for short. Not Bella,' Ian says.

38

I sign the hospital paperwork ready for me and Izzy to be discharged. Four weeks of hospital food, no home comforts and more importantly, I've missed my boys.

'I'll sleep on the sofa, if you'd prefer? But I want to stay.'

'Sofa it is then,' I say to Ian, but in an affectionate tone.

We've grown closer since Izzy was born, and I nearly died. I'm not ready to let him off the hook completely though.

Ian takes all my bags to the car while I say goodbye to the nurses who have been wonderful in showing me how to care for my tiny Tinkerbell. Her skin has changed from a scaly purple baby birds covered in blue veins, to a healthy natural colour. I strap her into her space-age buggy and slowly push her along, making my way to the exit to join Ian who should have moved the car to the loading bay by now. I look down at Izzy asleep with her thumb in her mouth, she is perfect, just like her brothers. It's such a relief to have her. I can finally put down my obsession with gender and move on from it.

'Sorry,' I say as I walk straight into someone coming the other way. I look up to see Joe's charmingly crooked smile. He is as handsome as ever in his porter uniform.

'You checking out?'

'Yes. Finally. I've not seen you in over two weeks. All okay?'

'I'm glad I caught you before you left, Char.'

He looks anxious, what is it? I look at him expectantly. Why has he not been to see me, or replied to my text. And why hasn't he answered my question? An uneasy dread creeps over me.

'I'm moving away, for a few months, maybe a year.'

'What? Where to?'

'Devon, with my sister and her husband. She's got the boys into a local school there. That way I can see more of my dad and help her out. It's difficult for her, what with his dementia.'

I don't know what to say. I'm shocked. He can't leave. I stare at him, unable to form a word. His dark hair looks freshly cut. Clean shaven and well presented.

'I've been thinking about it for a while actually. Devon's a nice place to bring up the children. Not that the Island isn't but, well, I think I need to move on.'

'You're not coming back, are you?' My eyes well up.

'You need to move on too. You've got your daughter now, and sons. Ian, he wants you back.'

I look down at my bare hand and rub the finger where

my rings used to be. Joe follows my gaze and smiles. He's right, it would never have worked between us. Not that it has ever been openly discussed. But memories of Bella are too raw. At times I'd imaged myself as step-mother to his children. Having promised Bella during my operation, even if it was a hallucination, it still felt real when I spoke to her and vowed I'd look after Joe and her boys. At fleeting moments I'd daydreamed about us all out together at a family picnic, five children - four boys and one girl.

'When do you leave?'

'Tomorrow.'

'What?' I feel sick. That soon?

'I've been putting off telling you. I'm going to miss you so much, Char.'

I surprise myself, throwing my arms around his shoulders in an embrace. His arms tighten around my waist. He rubs my back in a circular motion. I can feel my tears forming track marks down my cheeks. 'Stay in touch, won't you?' I murmur into his ear.

He turns his head, looking straight into my eyes. Time stands still. My heart beats fast as he leans in. Our lips meet. I close my eyes as we share our long awaited first kiss. After a moment I open my eyes, it doesn't feel right. There's no spark. My stomach isn't doing somersaults like it should be. I don't know what I expected. Fireworks maybe? It feels flat as I am standing in the corridor of the neonatal ward, kissing a man who isn't my husband, while my daughter sleeps in her pram next to us.

Ian. He'll be back in a minute. I pull away. Joe

scratches his head awkwardly.

'I'll miss you,' I say. And I mean it. I will miss his friendship, but nothing more.

Ian comes out of nowhere with a look of shock on his face. How much did he see?

'Joe just came to say goodbye. He's moving to Devon tomorrow,' I stammer.

'Good luck, mate,' Ian says. 'The car's loaded and ready.'

'Bye, Char, and thanks for all your support over the months since... you know.'

'You're welcome. Have a safe journey, and you will keep in touch, won't you?'

'Of course.'

Ian steers me away in a protective, possessive manor which astonishingly I don't find annoying. He takes over, pushing Izzy along and turns to look over his shoulder, at Joe.

'You've been seeing him, haven't you?' he accuses as soon as we reach the car.

'No.' How dare he question me.

'You looked very close.'

'He was saying goodbye. Who are you to preach to me? Trial separation wasn't it?'

'Will you ever forgive me?'

'She was my best friend's little sister. Why choose her of all people. Do you realise how humiliating that was?'

'I'm so sorry. If I could rewind time, change it all, I would. I only ask for one more chance, please.'

'I don't know.'

After he securely straps our daughter into the car, we start to drive home. Home to a house my husband has taken upon himself to move back into. After six or so months of living without him, he's back. I wonder what other changes have been made while I've been staying overnight in hospital? Not too much I guess, I have been home regularly to stock up on clothes, see the boys and generally have a change of scenery. But it's not the same.

It seems so long ago now when I fell to my knees in the garden, but it's only a month. Four short weeks and so much has changed. I now have three children, Joe's moving away and Ian seems intent on staying.

I look back at Izzy, with her thumb still in her mouth, then forward at the street lamps whizzing by. My stomach rumbles. The clock on the dashboard says five-thirty, they'd be dishing up my tea in a silver foil tray by now. Spinach and cheese cannelloni, that neither tasted nor resembled it, with a wilting side salad and a drying slice of bread. Followed by a yoghurt. Thank God we're both leaving. Back to normality.

My mind drifts to thoughts of Tammy.

'I remember once, when I was about twelve,' I say, my voice sounding scratchy, 'it was summertime, warm and dry, much like today. I'm not sure why I'm thinking of this particular moment. There were many of them. I went to Rose's house, I remember feeling really jealous. Her sisters, Tammy and Georgina were playing with their toy ponies.'

Ian takes a deep breath as he changes gear, guilt written all over his face at the mention of Tammy. 'Why were you jealous?' he asks, his voice soft and sympathetic.

'Rose had sisters. I think that was the first time it really hit home about Suzy. I could have had this closeness with my sister if she hadn't died. I never knew her. I was too young to remember. All I have are photographs imprinted in my mind. You know, the picture on Mum's mantelpiece in her lounge. Suzy was three when I was born.' I glance at Izzy. 'To lose a child must have been so tough, it tears you in half. You'd never be the same again. I realise now, boy or girl, it's all the same, but as a child, although I loved my little brother, I always thought how it could have been with a big sister too. I remember feeling so envious, wishing I could have what Rose had. Maybe I've been trying to recreate that somehow?'

Ian signals and turns down a residential street.

'Where are you going?'

'Please, Char, please forgive me. I love you so much, and my kids. I was so stupid. I never loved Tammy. She was a mistake.' He pulls up the handbrake and cuts the engine.

I wince. 'It still stabs me in the heart, when I think about that day. What I walked in to, you and her in bed together.'

'Hurting you is the biggest regret in my life. Losing you was a wakeup call. I'll never hurt you again as long as I live,' his eyes are watery, about to brim over.

Tears stream down my face. Can I forgive him? I want to, that's a good start. Perhaps kissing Joe and realising he's not Ian was what I needed?

'It was my fault too. I drove you to her,' I finally admit

out loud to both him and myself.

'No angel, don't be silly.'

'I did. I was so obsessed with having a girl. I was acting like a nutter at times.'

Ian laughs. 'So will you try to forgive me?' He wipes his eyes with the back of his hand.

I smile. 'Yes. But one step at a time.'

He leans over and gives me a peck on the cheek. My stomach flips. It feels good.

He starts the engine and continues home, parking the car outside my house. Our house.

'I can't wait to see my boys. Only seeing them for a couple of hours each day has been hard,' I whisper through tears.

'It was hard on them too, they missed their beautiful Mummy. It's time to be a proper family again.'

Closing the car door I look over to the bay window of my lounge which is covered in pink banners and balloons and below the decorations are the handsome tiny faces of my sons expectantly looking out for me. My heart pounds proudly, full of love. We leave the car, hand in hand, Izzy in her seat on Ian's other arm. I am greeted by Luke first, then Theo, both bursting with joy. I cuddle them as best I can with my scar still healing. Showering them with kisses.

'Welcome home, angel,' Ian says.

Lucinda Blanchard

ACKNOWLEDGMENTS

A great big thank you to my college teacher, Felicity Fair-Thompson, and to my beta readers – Heidi, Fran, Dominique, Anna, Hazel, Lynne, Paula, Vanessa, Karen, Andrea, Mary, Carol, Jane and my mum.

Equally, another deeply felt thank you to all at Wight Writers – they know who they are, for their perseverance in listening to my story each week and critiquing with their valuable feedback.

I would also like to thank the many people on the forums who answered my questions about the different methods of 'swaying.'

To my brother, Daniel Gustar, thank you for your time and patience with my cover – you'll be sick of pink and blue eggs by now, not to mention red arms and shades of green!

Many thanks to my mother and father, Lynda and Tim, for their support of my story idea, and my Gran, Margaret, for her weekly reading.

A huge thank you to my best friend Heidi for enduring listening to me read aloud to her every time I saw her, and to Fran for her photography skills with her mobile phone, and for proof reading the final draft, as well as many other drafts!

Finally, thank you to my husband Paul, for his encouragement, and to my children for being such good sleepers, enabling me to write in the evenings.

I could not have written this novel without them.

Lucinda Blanchard

ABOUT THE AUTHOR

Lucinda Blanchard was born and has always lived on the Isle of Wight - apart from a few months backpacking around Australia when she was in her 20s.

She is married with three young children.

Lucinda Blanchard

Made in the USA
Charleston, SC
12 October 2015